Crazy 8's:
Soldiers Still

James Karantonis

Black Rose Writing | Texas

ISBN: 978-1-68433-553-4
PUBLISHED BY BLACK ROSE WRITING
www.blackrosewriting.com

Printed in the United States of America
Suggested Retail Price (SRP) $18.95

Crazy 8's: Soldiers Still is printed in Calluna

*As a planet-friendly publisher, Black Rose Writing does its best to eliminate unnecessary waste to reduce paper usage and energy costs, while never compromising the reading experience. As a result, the final word count vs. page count may not meet common expectations.

Over a decade ago, I wrote a screenplay about soldiers on the psych wards during the Vietnam War. The screenplay was never produced. My agent, the late Lew Weitzman, told me to write the stories. So I showed up for a creative writing course at Howard Community College. And never left. Thank you to Lee Hartman, my first writing instructor, and Professors Ryna May and Tara Hart. And "thank you" Lew.

A special acknowledgement to Stephanie May, cover artist and book design consultant.

But even with all of this support there would be no novel without my muse, Mary Lou.

The names used in the novel are fictitious, all except one: Sergeant McCabe. He was the most honorable soldier I ever knew.

Several short stories in the novel previously appeared in *The Muse*, a literary publication of Howard Community College in Columbia, Maryland.

Dedication

The longer the war went on, the more soldiers came to the psych wards.
Sometimes it seemed that more came than went. In my storytelling I have
never, nor would I ever use the real names of the soldiers. And here is
another truth . . . I—do—not—remember—the—soldiers'—names.
But I remember them.

James Karantonis
Medic and Psych Tech
1966-1969
Crazy 8's: Soldiers Still
(partly truth and partly fiction.)

*Graduation from medic and psychiatric training
from Fort Sam Houston. 1966*

Crazy 8's: Soldiers Still

Contents

Bits and Pieces - Prologue

I was twenty-two years old, a medic and a psychiatric technician during the Vietnam War. I remember what I believed when I entered the Army—that the war was the sole cause for the physically and mentally wounded soldiers. On my first day at an Army hospital in the hills of Pennsylvania, I walked through the corridor past rooms filled with the physically wounded. Some soldiers in or next to their beds were connected by tubes to intravenous stands, with solutions drip, drip, dripping into the patient. One soldier was in a clear plastic tent and I could hear the rhythmic, swooshing sound of oxygen pumping in place of lungs. A burn patient was enclosed in a hammock while a medic turned a handle as if the soldier were on a barbecue spit. Another soldier had his neck wrapped in white gauze, except for the dime-sized metal opening below his Adam's apple. His chest rose as the hole sucked air inward and made pfffff sound as he exhaled.

I could see that bits and pieces of the soldiers were missing: gauze bandage over an eye or ear; an empty sleeve stapled to a shirt's shoulder; crutches for a missing foot or leg. Wheelchairs were everywhere. It seemed obvious to me. It was the war; the war was responsible for these wounded soldiers.

I exited the main hospital, crossed the narrow base road and followed a mulched pathway over a grassy knoll to a two-story, faded red brick building that hid secrets; the place where the Army kept the psychologically wounded. I saw young men watching me from the second floor through windows with thick wired grids.

On the psych ward I saw soldiers with every type of behavior and illness: Paranoid schizophrenia; manic-depressives; obsessive-compulsives; even catatonia; soldiers with delusions and hallucinations; drug and alcohol abuse; and antisocial personality disorders—a person who disregards and violates the rights of others. I had known guys like that in high school. Here on the psych wards, the damaged part of the soldier was on the inside. No bandage marked the entrance wound. The war had injured the mind.

During those years on the ward I caught glimpses of the soldiers' past: a visit from the fathers and mothers, wives, girlfriends, rabbis and priests; contributors to the healing process to repair the broken part caused by the war. But I also learned during that time there were soldiers who had psychological problems before the war; before the firefights; the battles; the explosions; the fire and smoke, the death. For some the illness had shown itself from the first day of basic training with the constant yelling, "Out of your bunks, Now! Now! Give me twenty. Now! Now! Crawl faster. Now! Now!" the marches, the physical exhaustion, the separation from home, the fear of the unknown.

Damage to a number of soldiers had been done years before by an abusive father, a smothering mother, having no friends, or bullied by classmates. Whatever defense mechanism that had kept their illness in check in civilian life had now failed; war was not the cause, but instead the catalyst. I learned that each of them, each of us, takes something from all of the visitors in our life, the good, the bad and the indifferent.

We are all bits and pieces, bits and pieces.

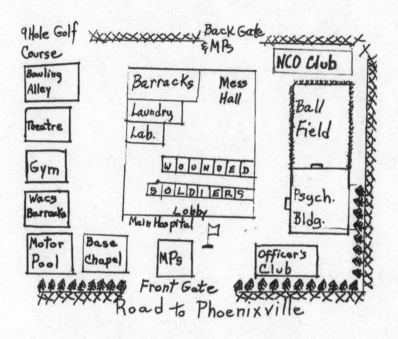

9 Hole Golf Course

Back Gate & MPs

NCO Club

Bowling Alley

Barracks

Mess Hall

Ball Field

Theatre

Laundry

Lab.

Gym

WOUNDED

Psych. Bldg.

Wacs Barracks

SOLDIERS

Lobby

Main Hospital

Motor Pool

Base Chapel

MPs

Officer's Club

Front Gate

Road to Phoenixville

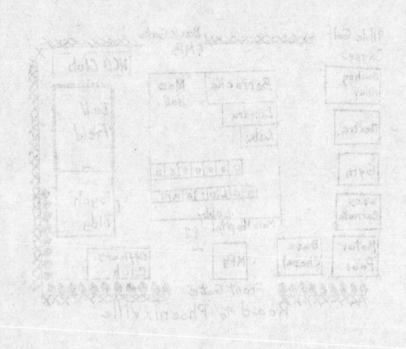

Play Ball

Abbott: "Well, let's see, we have Who's on first, What's on second, I Don't Know is on third ..."

Costello: "That's what I want to find out."

Abbott: "I said Who's on first, What's on second, I Don't Know's on third."

The psychiatric unit's ballfield was exclusive. To become a member, a soldier had to lose his mind, or at least have the Army believe he had. The ballfield was across the narrow base road from the main hospital and connected to the psych building. Two medics, officially psychiatric technicians, were enjoying the warmth of an autumn sun as they sat in the grass leaning back against the keep-them-in-here-and-do-not-let-them-out-there fifteen-foot high chain-link fence. The fence surrounded three quarters of the field and abutted the two-story psych building that defended the rest of the perimeter. A side door of the building opened directly to the ballfield. The building was last used during World War II, then Korea, but now reopened for the new war, Vietnam.

The two techs, Zack Tonakis and Robert Turner, were careful not to get grass stains on their white pants and white smocks that announced they were the caring side of the military. Buddies and bunkmates since both were inducted into the Army, and then months of training as medics and then more training as psychiatric techs, and now by luck of the draw here they were a year later at the same Army hospital, bunk mates. Bad times encouraged making friends quickly, even for the short term.

To impress women, the psych techs emphasized that they were "psychiatric techs" believing it made them sound more intelligent than the average medic. Zack thought it sounded as if they repaired TVs, as if the horizontal and the vertical holds of the soldiers were on the blink. And today the psych techs responsibility was to monitor these patients, soldiers still, as they enjoyed a game of softball.

Zack, older at twenty-two; Turner was twenty. There was one obvious difference between the two techs, information the Army considered necessary by including the question of "Race" on the first form. Tech Zack Tonakis checked "Caucasian." Tech Robert Turner, "Negro." Zack with his Greek ethnic background on display had olive skin, dark hair and thick eyebrows. Turner had tightly curled black hair and thin eyebrows almost invisible against his brown skin. For Zack, not only the current situation but his deep-seated rebelliousness may have served as an added incentive as to why he took to the "Negro" Turner so easily. For Turner it was the young man's faith in the goodness of people that made it easier to bond with Zack the "Caucasian."

Robert Turner preferred to be called by his last name, that's why the neighbors back home referred to him as, "Turner's boy." "Say hello to your dad, Turner." This may have sounded strange to strangers but seemed okay to him since he respected his father. That was unlike what Zack told Turner he felt about his own father. Robert Turner's father was somewhat of a leader in speaking out and organizing for better treatment in the community now that new laws had been passed, civil rights laws. Also, unlike Zack, Turner never had the college opportunity. He went to work straight from high school. He had two younger brothers and a younger sister, and it was expected by his parents that he, being the first-born, would work to help the others.

For the patients in the field, there were similarities in age and uniform. Most were nineteen or early twenties, with a few in their thirties, the Army lifers. They all wore dark blue cotton shirts and pants over thinner and lighter blue scrubs. Their dark blue outfit was referred to as patient blues. White plastic wristbands and nametags pinned to their shirts personally announced who they were. Almost all wore black shoes, polished or unpolished. A few wore white cotton open-back slippers, which made it difficult to run to catch fly balls even if they made the attempt. Ball games for the psych wards were reminiscent of pre-little league games, peewee leagues, where boredom overtakes a five or six-year-old and he sits down in the field, picks at the grass, plays with ants, or moseys over and talks to a friend. And similar to peewee ball, a psych ward game could have as many patients on a side as could walk out on the field and stand.

"Okay, two outs, two outs, get one more." Pacing the sideline was Tech Krupp, the self-appointed manager of ward 2A's team. Krupp always saw himself as a manager, director, boss, the top dog. It could have been overcompensation for all the early years when he was the shortest kid in class, and now, still was the shortest. As far back as elementary school, the boy Krupp was usually overlooked when the other boys chose sides for baseball, football or any of the sports. It wasn't until he watched an old film on late night TV of Edgar G. Robinson playing the famous hoodlum, Little Caesar, that the boy saw how intimidation of others didn't depend on how big you were. You had to act as if you were in charge and be tough about it. And Krupp got away with acting tough because so few boys were willing to challenge him, to fight about it knowing he was more than willing to fight, no matter how much bigger they were. Soon Krupp's demeanor and personality became one and the same, a bully.

On the ward Krupp was the senior tech, proof that not all those dressed in white cared about the patients. How he got to be a medic and tech in the first place is one of those 'Hey It's a war and it's the Army.' Every aspect of life for Tech Krupp was a game. But a game where there was one winner and all those others: the losers. Whatever got you the prize was justified. Even as a young boy when the neighborhood kids got together to play monopoly Krupp would stuff his pockets with play money from his own board game so he could slip in an extra hundred or a twenty when he needed it, anything for an edge. Anyone can do it was the boy's reasoning, so why not him?

"One more out, one more." Krupp barked instructions. "Be ready! Be ready!" He suddenly pointed emphatically to the first baseman and yelled, "Hey, First Base! Catch the damn ball if they throw it to you. Catch the damn ball!"

The first baseman was a patient that Zack and Turner and other techs referred to as Cherry Pie Stover. He was Private Stover when he came here, but rank was left behind when soldiers entered this building. And as for officers, the Army sent them elsewhere for treatment. Stover with his long arms and legs and well over six-foot frame belonged on a basketball court instead of a ball field. For softball games, the psych patients weren't issued ball gloves, but Stover didn't need one, not with hands the size of catchers' mitts. The soldier was tall enough to catch an errant throw before it reached the clouds. As for the cherry pie in front of Stover's name, Zack gave him that moniker after an incident at the mess hall where the soldier showed an exaggerated enthusiasm for a single subject. The Greek word is monomania. For Stover it was for cherry pies. But that wasn't why he was on the psych wards.

"Hey, Greek." Tech Turner nudged Tonakis. "Do you see the patient standing a little behind Cherry Pie Stover?"

Zack tried to focus on the guy who was partially hidden by Stover's large frame at first base.

"Name game!" Turner said.

"Damn." Zack was caught. "Okay, give me a minute." He searched for the name of the patient Turner had pointed out.

Previous psych techs had invented the name game and passed it on to newcomers who readily adopted it. The game was modeled after the comic duo Abbott and Costello's "Who's on first" routine. For the techs, it seemed more new patients came to the wards than old ones left, and unless the techs were standing next to the patients their nametags were of no help. To recall a patient's name, the techs used a crutch that tied the soldier to a behavior or an incident. The pet names weren't cute sounding in the same way Grumpy, Bashful and Sneezy were, but the names worked. The game was only played by the techs; they knew it wouldn't be a good thing if the patients' heard their nicknames.

Zack Tonakis was certainly used to nicknames. He was called Greek by almost every student throughout high school. "Hey Greek;" "How's it going, Greek;" "Where you going, Greek?" There was also an indirect benefit for Zack. When a friend called his home and asked, "Is Greek home?" it really pissed-off Zack's dad that they didn't use his son's first name. More than once Zack's father told him and told him loudly, "It's a lack of respect for me, not using the name I gave you, my name!" This lack of respect for the father was okay by Zack the son.

Zack also knew being called Greek was an uncomfortable reminder to his dad that he couldn't run away from his ethnic background. His father had shortened his original surname from Karantonakis so as not to sound so foreign. As if the name Tonakis didn't get Zack the question, "What are you, Greek or Italian?" It wouldn't have surprised Zack if his father had taken the last name "Jones" or "Smith" leaving no clue of Mediterranean roots. Zack figured his dad had issues with his own father in the same way Zack had issues with him.

Zack was proud of his ethnicity, even if he didn't know much about it. He knew from the history texts that Greeks started democracy, had a lot of Gods, and what gave Zack bragging rights, Greeks had started the Olympic Games. He knew that movies showed Greeks as loud and always dancing. He couldn't imagine his dad dancing but dad was loud, especially when he yelled at Zack. Very loud.

"Okay, Turner, here goes." Zack started the name game and hoped that by the time he identified the other patients on the ballfield the little guy's name would be there. "At first base, Cherry Pie Stover. At second, an easy one, Joker Berkowski."

Berkowski, a string bean of a patient, crouched next to second base, hands on knees, and eyes on the batter at the plate. "Swiiing batter, go on Swiiing batter," was Berkowski's patter. The Joker had what observers would say was a natural talent. A sharply struck ball to the left of the infield, Berkowski would scoop it cleanly, spin airborn and snap a throw back to first. It was as if his body was double-jointed, able to move in different directions at the same time.

Berkowski had earned the nickname, Joker, from the techs and the patients based on his antics the first few weeks he had been on the ward. He had gained an appreciative audience for routines that helped them pass the monotonous routine their lives had become. Berkowski's bald head and big ears complemented his fondness for playing the fool. His ears were a gift from dad.

•   •   •   •   •

"I said get over here. Get over here." Berkowski Senior pinched the top of his young son's ear and pulled the boy closer. To the customers in the store they made an odd sight as the father walked quickly through the aisles, holding onto the boy's ear as the youngster struggled to keep up.

Berkowski's baldness was his own doing. As a young boy on a trip to the circus he noticed how the clowns seemed to steal the show, especially after the slower, more tedious acts of horseback riding, slow moving elephants, and high wire walkers. The clowns lit up the arena, and many of them were bald with tufts of bright red or green hair standing out near their ears. The boy never forgot that. And on the day of high school graduation with students in black caps and gowns, when tassels were flipped on the caps, and caps were thrown into the air, Berkowski got the attention and appreciation of every classmate for a graduation memory. Bald.

Berkowski was voted high school's "Class Clown." Classmates thought he was a riot, but not so his teachers or principal. When Berkowski was drafted into the Army, his bunkmates in Fox Company thought he was a real comedian. But not the drill instructor or company commander.

•   •   •   •   •

It was near the end of basic training and not a soul in the barracks that night was qualified for guard duty due to exhaustion from the day's marches. The recruits were asleep except for Berkowski. Silently, slipping from his bunk to the floor, Berkowski, playing a soldier infiltrating enemy lines, low-crawled from locker to locker and bunk to bunk, exchanging fatigues and boots from one location to another. The next morning it was reveille and pandemonium.

"Hey, these can't be my boots. Too tight. Can't be . . ." "Hey, whose fucking pants are these?" "Where are my clothes?" Confusion, and then laughter. It was clear who had created the catastrophe when outside at formation Berkowski stood at attention, a grin on his face, the only soldier on time and dressed accordingly for morning inspection. Some of his antics were outrageous, some not so successful. Berkowski was transported to the psych wards.

•　　•　　•　　•　　•

"That's Lawyer Lucas behind second base, we can hear him from here." Zack identified the wiry patient who paced a few steps to the left, then the right, and back, then stopped, stared, then ranted to the patient who waited at the plate with bat in hand. Instead of "Swiiing Batter," Lucas shouted, "Hey batter, you don't have to swing. They can't make you," confusing an already confused batter. "Play Ball!" Lucas announced it, mimicking an umpire starting a game. Then he questioned himself, "What if I don't want to play ball? Don't I have rights? What about the Bill of Rights?" On and on he argued his case.

"Behind Lucas," Zack said, "just where we put him is Catatonic Cart." The patient, sphinxlike, faced the outfield. The techs had placed him there behind two other patients as insurance, trusting that the other players would intervene if a ball was hit his way. The techs also concurred it was probably better to be hit by a ball in the back of the head than between the eyes.

"And at shortstop," Zack continued, "the Puerto Ricans, Perez and Vasquez."

Just then Tech Krupp interjected his managerial instruction to 2A's multiethnic infield. "Hey Perez, taco brain, get your head out of your ass." On the field, Perez responded in Spanish to Krupp's motivational talk by using the word "cabròn" signifying "asshole" preceding Krupp's name.

Perez was from New York City, Vasquez, Puerto Rico. Ethnically the same but physically, Perez was in his early twenties with light brown skin, slender and much taller than his compadre. Vasquez was a toughened thirty-year-old with a face like a weathered football. He resembled an Army jeep, wide and durable. According to Vasquez's records when he enlisted into the Army his English was sufficient enough to meet the recruiter's monthly quota. The recruit, after three weeks in basic training, suddenly failed to understand a word of English. Instead of the Berlitz School of Languages, Vasquez was sent to the psych ward. Fortunately for Vasquez and for the ward, Perez was already there and could serve as translator.

"So who's on third?" Tech Turner got into the act.

"That's Pushups Tabor," Zack responded. Tabor had the sculpted physique of a Mr. America. First thing in the morning the soldier was on the floor knocking out one hundred pushups. "And behind him," Zack shook his head in resignation, "none other than Slob Shumacher." With his pants hanging on to his watermelon butt, Shumacher emptied a bag of salty nuts into his mouth that was opened wide enough to catch a softball if hit in his direction. Shumacher wiped the salt from his lips and cheeks with the back of a sleeve that registered foodstuffs from multiple feedings.

"Playing left field" Zack now spoke with a nasal pitch mimicking a play-by-play announcer, "the patient who constantly mutters what no one ever understands, Mumbling—"

"But," Turner interjected, "who has a decent throw to home plate."

"Right," Zack said, and returned to play-by-play announcing, "The fielder with the rocket arm, Mumbling Grier. And, backing him up, if he can stop fussing with his clothes, is Obsessive Godwin."

As the soldier Grier mumbled, "Shoulda done someim, shoulda, shoulda . . ." Obsessive Godwin, who could barely hear what Grier was saying let alone understand what he was mumbling about responded. "It's okay, buddy, let's play ball, it's gonna be all right." he said as he pinched the front seams of his pants and pressed his fingers downward to impart a semblance of a crease.

"Ward 2A's lone center fielder today—"

"As a matter of choice," Turner said.

"Riiiight, and a damn' smart decision," Zack said. "Let's hear it for Paranoid Firenza." Firenza didn't trust having a player stand behind him to back him up, or, for that matter, to stand nearby and make any sudden moves. And periodically he scanned outside the fence suspiciously.

"Shaky Metz and Bible Skinner are in right field," Zack quickly added.

Today, Metz's hands shook in time with his facial tics. He was a one-man-band: hands, head and right foot tapping. If and when a fly ball was hit to Metz, he would extend his shaking hands in preparation for the catch and then at the last second he'd let the ball fall to the grass. He'd retrieve it and throw the ball to the infield. Shaky Metz wouldn't catch a fly ball, only prepare to catch one.

Skinner was Metz's partner in right field. Skinner, as skinny as the name implied, not quite an albino but close, wore thick, black framed, Army issued glasses that hid his almost nonexistent eyebrows. He had the Good Book tucked into the waistband of his pants. Bible Skinner spent more time looking to the blue of the sky than toward home plate. "Oh, please, Lord, don't hit the ball to me. Please, don't hit the ball to me." Skinner hadn't learned that if you prayed for the ball not to be hit to you, then, for certain, here comes the ball.

Zack moved back to the infield, but still not to the player behind first base. Zack announced the next patient as if through a ballpark loudspeaker, "And catching today, ay, ay, ay . . . for Ward 2A, A, A, A, . . . Scarface Kelly, e, e, e, e." When Kelly first came on the ward, it took a while for the techs to adjust to the sight of Kelly's face. The right side, smooth, dark black skin, the left, melted furrows of hills and valleys that but for a minor miscalculation had left his eye unscathed.

"And pitching today, looking like he's enjoying the hell out of the game—"

"Even if he isn't," Turner said matter-of-factly.

"Is Smiiiiling Hardy."

A line drive to Hardy's head couldn't knock the smile off his face. From the morning till the evening, he smiled. Hardy's skin was cream-colored and with his tightly curled reddish hair the recruiter had questioned why Hardy had checked "Negro" on the induction form.

"Damn," Zack said, "I still can't recall the little guy behind Stover at first. He may as well be invisible."

"Don't ask me, I don't know it either," Turner confessed. "But you owe me a beer."

Just then a 3A patient placed the bat in the right position and hit a slow pitch by Smiling Hardy toward second base.

"I got l! I got it! All mine! Easy out! Coming to first." Berkowski effortlessly scooped up the rolling ball. At first base, Stover stretched his long legs and arm out to receive the throw. Berkowski drew his arm back and then brought his hand forward in a throwing motion. He snapped his wrist. The form and delivery were perfect, except his throwing hand wasn't holding the ball. He intentionally had dropped the ball behind him before following through with a bogus throw to first.

At first base Stover's look said, "Where's the ball?" He looked down and around and then to Berkowski. Berkowski spun around, snapped his fingers and pointed to the ball on the ground.

"Gotcha," Berkowski said and gave a gotcha grin.

The infield erupted with hoots and laughter, including Stover who especially appreciated being part of the joke. The Ward 3A patient who had hit the ground ball waved to his applauding teammates on the sideline as he walked to first. Catatonic Cart may have been the only patient not to respond. Joker Berkowski took a deep-from-the-waist bow, first to Stover, then to the catcher Kelly, then third base, and he continued to bow his way around the outfield.

"Berkowski! Get off the field!" Krupp shouted. "Off! Get the hell off the field. Off! Off!"

It galled Krupp that the patients enjoyed Berkowski's antics. Even more infuriating was being forced to be part of the audience. Laughter was against Krupp's treatment plan. Tech Krupp, the poster boy for schoolyard bullies, moved on to the field, fists clenched at his sides. Berkowski hastily retreated to the outfield as Tech Krupp started, then stopped, then started to chase him. Berkowski ran in circles in the outfield, flapping his hands, imitating wings on a bird. If a fool can feel foolish, Krupp felt just that, so he made a management decision and gave up the chase. He followed it with a ruling.

"You're banned, Berkowski, banned from the game! Banned!" Krupp emphatically pointed, first to Berkowski, then to the psych building, then to Berkowski, and the psych building.

Zack and Turner looked at each other in disbelief.

"Does Krupp actually expect Berkowski to head to the showers?" Turner asked.

"Who's crazier, Berkowski or Krupp?" Zack asked.

"Berkowski's crazy funny; Krupp's crazy scary," answered Turner.

Berkowski sat in the grass in right field near Shaky Metz and Bible Skinner; Krupp returned to the sideline. Smiling Hardy prepared to pitch, but the game was interrupted again, this time by a four-legged barking visitor. From outside the fence on the third base side, a dog barked loudly.

Zack's attention went first to a boy who peered through the fence. *The boy couldn't be more than nine or ten,* Zack thought. And then Zack's attention went to the dog. The dog paced back and forth and barked. The size of the boy, and the dog's movement, chin up, and tail practically pointing to the sky was remarkably familiar to the tech. *Why?* Zack was confused. *The dog looks nothing like Midnight.* Midnight was Zack's dog when he was a young boy. Maybe it was the boy and the dog and the woods, all of it together. Zack's happier days before his father's failing business; the family forced to move; and his father giving Midnight away to a farmer. Was that when it all started for Zack, his distrust of authority?

"Get away from the fence!" Tech Krupp on the sidelines turned and yelled to the boy. And the boy did. He disappeared back into the forest with his dog.

A patient from 3A, the only other Closed Ward in the building, stepped to the plate and began taking practice swings. The batter had an athlete's thick neck and broad shoulders. He was streamlined from the shoulders to his narrow hips, an inverted triangle on athletic legs. Even from where the techs were sitting, they heard the swish of the bat as it cut through the air. He bent slightly at the knees. Smiling Hardy delivered the pitch. The patient didn't wait for it; he anticipated the pitch. With the rotation of his shoulders, and the smooth fast snap of the bat, the patient walloped the ball.

The ball soared outward and upward, forcing a flock of birds to change direction. Some of the 3A patients cheered, others paid little attention. The ball sailed deep over the heads of Shaky Metz and Bible Skinner. By the time the two soldiers reached the ball, the batter had rounded second base and headed for third. Metz retrieved the ball and handed it to Skinner. Skinner looked at it and handed it back. The batter, coming around third, dust flying, slapped the hands of the 3A patients who had gathered on the third base line.

The batter increased speed as he approached home plate. He sped over the bag and kept moving even faster, both arms pumping. He raced toward the chain-link fence. His black Army shoes turned brown from the dust. When he reached the fence, he started his climb that continued his run. The patient ran up the fence.

The patients and techs, as if in a silent movie, were eerily still while the home run hitter ascended the Great Wall. Left foot first, then the right, then left, then right, and clutching the top rail he arched his back, his legs together, the soldier, now perpendicular soared over the fence. He dropped toward the grass and landed upright, knees bent, arms outstretched; Olympic tens; the patient had stuck the landing. He scrambled up the freshly cut grassy bank and took off down the road toward the back gate.

And along with all the others, Zack and Turner stood and watched as the patient ran out of sight. The only sound was the warm breeze in the trees.

And then, "You Prick! You come back here!" Krupp's useless command ignited an explosion from the soldiers: cheers and shouts of "All right!" "Unbelievable!" "Hey! Hey! Hey!" "Go! Go!" The soldiers thrust their hands skyward; ran in circles, rolled in the grass. Even Catatonic Cart raised his arms slightly from his sides, dropped them and raised them again. The soldiers on the sidelines and the ones in the field, all of them, Mumbling Grier, Obsessive Godwin, Paranoid Firenza, Shaky Metz and Bible Skinner sprinted to the pitcher's mound where the soldiers jumped and hollered, thrusting their arms skyward, they hugged each other. They performed the universal dance of freedom.

• • • •

The patient Womer scanned ahead as he ran the narrow blacktop. With the name Womer, Tonakis and Turner may have tagged him with the rhyming moniker of Homer Womer. Womer saw the guardhouse at the back gate. The gate was open.

"Go-go-go-go. Go-go-go-go. Go-go-go-go." Womer said it aloud, a mantra, as his legs pounded the pavement. Two MPs stepped out from the guardhouse and moved to the center, setting up a human blockade. The older and larger one with a puzzled look reached to his side and removed a black, shiny billy club.

The athlete turned right off the road and sprinted across the field toward the fence. "Go-go-go-go. Go-go-go-go."

As far back as elementary school, then junior high, and recent high school years, Womer could always do it. Run faster; jump higher; hit the ball farther; and the teammates knew it, and the coaches knew it. He was their shining example and his parent's praised him and and told him so. In school, the underclassmen looked up to him and gave him compliments, and the girls, even the older ones, flirted. And when the country asked for volunteers to serve and protect, he stepped up to be the best that one could be. And things changed.

In basic training there was no praise, no compliments, no pats on the back, instead he got his first kick-in-the-ass, and yelling, constant yelling. The drill instructors weren't satisfied with how fast he ran; they wanted faster. And when he ran faster, the instructors yelled: "Faster!" And when the recruit learned the low crawl the instructors yelled, "The low crawl will save your life!" And he low crawled and they yelled "lower!" And with his knees and feet and chin in the dirt he pushed forward and he went lower, and then they yelled "Faster!" And when he finished ahead of the others in the platoon, a sergeant screamed at him "Go back and do it again, this time correctly!"

But he had done it correctly, he knew he had. And for him it wasn't enough to low crawl to save his life in the bush because he couldn't imagine the jungle; he couldn't relate to the battle; and he couldn't relate to the yelling. He hated how the instructors' yelled at everyone. Why yell at him? He ran faster; he jumped higher; he low-crawled lower and faster than anyone else, he just didn't get it, not the Army way. So he began to dog it; to hold back; instead of pushing for first in anything, he fell to the back on everything. Slower in running; slower in crawling; slower on the obstacle course; slower for formations; last for morning reveille, and even last in line for chow.

The sergeants saw it; the captain saw it; and they decided Private Womer needed an attitude fix. He was falling into the most common category the Army faced with recruits: "A Failure to Adjust." So to straighten him out, and to preserve the fighting strength, Private Womer was sent to the psych wards.

"Go-go-go-go. Go-go-go-go" Soldier Womer ran through the mowed grass, dodging several shrubs on his race to the fence.

The MPs took off on a diagonal route to intercept him. The MPs were trained, if someone runs, they chase. The MPs must have had a mantra of "No-no-no-no."

If Womer could have heard the cheers from teammates, or if the patients could have been there on the sidelines to root him on, it's possible his body wouldn't have tired or his legs wouldn't have slowed, and his lungs wouldn't have gasped for air. He reached the fence, planted his right foot and pushed upwards.

An MP, running with his club out front, like a sprinter's baton, arrived at the fence a second behind Womer. The MP planted his feet and swung his billy club the way Womer had swung the bat. Something cracked on Womer's left side. He continued to climb. His fingers grasped the links of the fence; his upward movement stopped; his legs held in a vice grip by the MP's partner. 'And swing batter'—and Womer's left knee popped. Womer surmised that the MP was a southpaw. The next swing and Homer Womer saw flashes of light with a hissing, static noise, and then nothing.

The call from the MPs to the main office of the psychiatric building was received within minutes of the apprehending of Womer. It came at the same time Tech Krupp was reporting the escape to Sergeant First Class Helms who immediately reported to his superior, Major Vann. Sergeant Helms nervously waited at the foot of the major's desk as his superior stared from his office window to the ballfield where the soldiers celebrated. The major tried to mentally measure the height of the chain-link fence that surrounded the psychiatric grounds. "That fence is almost fifteen feet high," the major said. "And you're telling me that during the ballgame, with techs watching, a patient goes over that fence."

"Yes, sir."

"Unfucking believable. Did he fly? Was the guy superman?"

"Yes, sir, I mean no, sir."

"And superman? Where is he now?"

"MPs took him to emergency. Broken bones. He'll go to the stockade, not back here."

"Do those techs even know what their job is? Do they know?"

"Well, sir, I'm not certain whether . . ." Sergeant Helms initially went up on his toes but lowered back down when he wasn't certain what answer the major wanted. The first sergeant had a severe buzz cut. He also had a forever tan from years of standing in formation. He held shoulders back as if it would be a sin to insult appropriate posture. His khaki shirt and pants were heavily starched and held the crease even in late afternoon. Sergeant Helms was an administrator, not a medic. When he believed he had something important to say he tried to appear taller believing taller people got more respect. He would go up on his toes to punctuate a word or sentence. But for now, he remained grounded and listened to the major.

"I shouldn't be here." The major said matter-of-factly. He turned back exposing the unbuttoned collar, shirt partially tucked in, and a black belt loosened to ease pressure on a slightly protruding belly, something he worked at controlling by periodically abstaining from sweets. He placed his hands on the wrinkled jacket with its gold leaf clusters that hung over the back of the chair.

"I'm a Quartermaster, twenty years, a numbers man, and damn good at it." The major's body reinforced the notion that he had sat behind a desk for years instead of out in the field. The major moved his hands to the jacket's lapels and stroked the insignia pinned there as if paying homage to its parts:

An Eagle, the symbol of our nation; a Sword signifying control of supplies; a Key, symbolizing responsibility for the store; all on a Wheel, for delivering the goods. Soldiers and supplies, one and the same for Major Vann.

"Today is the eleventh of October."

"It is the eleventh, yes sir."

"I know the damn date," He snapped. "I wasn't asking. I was telling."

"Sorry, sir."

"I retire in two months, eight days . . ." He looked at his watch. "Seven hours and thirty-four . . . thirty-three minutes. I'll be home by Christmas!"

"Yes, sir." The sergeant agreed with the major's march of time.

"Temporary, that's what the commander said. Just till they can get a medical man." The major turned quickly to the window, looked left and right, as if searching for something. He practically shouted, "SO WHERE IS HE?"

"Well, sir, you know the Army. It is . . ."

"I'm here less than two weeks and I've had to deal with a brawl over a TV show. Like little kids. I had to make the TV room off limits."

"Yes—"

"And now," the major shook his head, "an escape." The major spoke resignedly to the window. "This will go on my record." Suddenly a burst of energy, the major pivoted back to Sergeant Helms and pointed repeatedly and emphatically. "I want the ball field off limits. No outdoor activities, none. You hear me?"

"Yes sir."

"They can cross the street to the mess hall and for medical appointments but no outdoor activities until I say. Get the memo out."

"Yes sir."

And then on that day of the ball game between soldiers of Closed Wards 2A and 3A the line that existed between the sane and the insane was crossed.

"If another patient tries to get off this base," the major growled through clenched teeth, "you tell the MPs to shoot the crazy bastard!"

"Yes, sir!"

Sergeant Helm's returned to his office where he began to type the memo that would be delivered to the Closed Wards.

Date: 10/11/67
  To: Sergeant McCabe, Closed Ward 2A
       Sergeant Suhre, Closed Ward 3A
From: Major R. Vann

Neuropsychiatric Unit
Subject: Until further notice
All outdoor activities are off limits for
the Closed Wards.

But at that moment on that sunny Indian summer playground afternoon the celebration continued. The soldiers cheered, laughed, slapped hands, and hugged, as if they were the ones who had escaped not only their situation but what had brought them here in the first place. Zack saw it and wished he could feel what they did. He couldn't. He knew this escape didn't bode well. It was bad for the techs, and especially for the patients. As the tech's watched, the soldiers culminated their celebration by converging on the pitcher's mound and piling on top of each other as if they had won the seventh game of the World Series. And maybe they had.

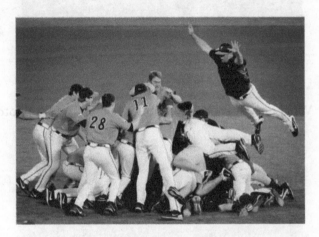

Take me out to the ballgame,
Take me out with the crowd,

Zack hadn't expected what the soldier Homer Womer had done. But this he should have expected. That voice outside the fence was Frank Sinatra's, his mother's favorite singer.

Buy me some peanuts and Cracker Jack,
I don't care if I never get back,

Years of hearing his mother play Sinatra's albums and *Damn,* Zack thought, *now the singer shows up here.* Zack wasn't going to turn around to look for him. He wasn't delusional. Zack knew the singer wasn't really there. None of them ever were. Besides Zack never acknowledged them. They were hallucinations or the word he preferred: apparitions. Apparitions didn't sound as crazy to Zack since the word was seldom used. The singers, the songs, it was his secret, and it was harmless, sometimes actually helpful. And Frank, entertainer that he was, knew just when to fade out.

Let's root, root, root for the home team,

If they don't win it's a shame.

For it's one, two, three strikes you're out at the old ball game.

What once was the psych unit's ballfield. (2014 photo.)

What once was the road the soldier ran on after climbing the psych unit's ballfield fence. (2014 photo.)

The road the soldier ran on to get to the back gate of the base.
(2014 photo.)

Valley Forge General Hospital
Neuropsychiatric Unit

DAILY LOG - Ward 2A and 2B
October 11, 1967

DAY SHIFT

Another day - just like the other day.

EVENING SHIFT

The same.

NIGHT SHIFT

Same

Midnight . . . and Zack

When I was a kid, probably like most kids, I seldom got in trouble, nothing to get in trouble for. I went to school, did most of my homework, helped in the store and around the house, worked in the yard, played sports, went to the movies, went swimming and fishing, and only griped a little about going to church on Sundays. And I took care of Midnight.

Midnight was my dog. And I mean mine. I had picked him from a litter of pups when I was seven years old. He was a gift from my dad for being a good boy and helping in his grocery store.

When I caught the school bus in the morning Midnight would scurry along, and bark "goodbye, see you later" as the bus drove off. That's what I told the other school kids he was barking. Sure enough, later when the bus brought us home, there was Midnight waiting in the yard to lead me down the gravel lane to our home.

That's when I would sing the latest hits I'd learned from the radio.

When the moon hits you eye like a big pizza pie,
That's amore.

I crooned in my Dean Martin voice, at least I thought I did. I loved pizza.

When the world seems to shine
like you've had too much wine,
That's amore.

As for wine, I had only tasted a spoonful during communions when the priest said, "blood of Christ." . . . Yuuuk blood.

I was a happy kid, and happiness lasted throughout my summers and elementary school days. That's not a long time if you were young as me.

The grocery store was losing money, bankrupt. Dad took an offer in a big city, hundreds of miles away, to manage a restaurant for a highly successful Greek businessman. My father would no longer be his own boss.

The way I saw it my dad had failed, but I was being punished. I was eleven years old, just finished the fifth grade, and my family was moving.

I said goodbyes to Eddie, my human best friend, and to the other neighborhood boys, and to classmates, Frank, Robert, and Spanky, and Diane, who I liked in a different way than the other girls. Goodbye to Mr. Shepard, my gym teacher, and Mrs. Brown and the glee club, and then there was one more goodbye.

The lamp from the picture window of our home cast light mixed with shadows across the front lawn. I stood in the darkness of the apple tree. My chest was tight, something was in there and wanted to break through and scream, THIS IS NOT FAIR!

I watched my dad lift Midnight awkwardly in his arms and hand him up to the farmer in the back of a pickup truck. Both men were strong and lifting Midnight they needed to be. I turned and looked back to the house and there was mom on the porch, watching; one hand gripped the porch railing, the other covered her mouth. She was holding tight to the railing. *Was it to keep her from coming forward?* She had covered her mouth. *Was it so as not to say something to stop this?*

It had only been an hour ago that they had told me. Our family was moving, and Midnight wasn't coming with us.

"We wanted to make it easier for you," Mom said. Then, dad, with that firmness in his voice that it's already decided, no discussion, "Son, this is for the best."

They leaned closer to me from across the kitchen table. I stared and their faces transformed, grotesque, as their mouths and lips moved and shaped words with voices that came from somewhere in a tunnel.

"Your dog was bred and raised for the outdoors," Dad said. "Fields, forests, not a small fenced-in backyard in the city." Spittle sprayed from my father's mouth, each word louder as if he were arguing with himself. "He's not a city dog!"

Then another voice. "Your father and I have discussed this. And we are both in agreement." I looked at the woman who was talking, her lips cracked and dry with flecks of yesterday's pink lipstick at the corners of her mouth, she was ugly. She couldn't be my mother.

I struck back. "Oh yeah, well this may be the first time you've been in agreement about anything. Ever!" Dad stiffened; mom looked away. I rushed outside, stood under the darkness of the tree, and did the only thing I could do, I watched.

Midnight moved around in a circle in the flatbed of the truck while the farmer shook dad's hand. The man got in the truck, started the engine, and Midnight began barking. The dog kept looking to the house, I knew he was searching for me. The light from the house caught the gold of Midnight's eyes. The truck gear's shifted; the truck pulled away slowly. Midnight barked, yipped, and whimpered, barked and whimpered. It didn't sound the same as when Midnight wanted me to run with him through the woods; or throw a ball and play fetch, when Midnight would run a few steps, turn and comeback, take off, comeback, bark with that higher pitch, almost saying, "Please, please let's play." . . . No, the sound, a whimper, the last I heard from Midnight.

That night I learned eleven-year-olds have little say in life-changing events. Parents made the decisions and then validated their choices with hackneyed expressions.

"It's part of growing-up."

"Disappointment is part of life."

"You'll get over it. Trust us. You'll get over it."

My first year in our new home in the big city; new neighborhood; new school; and new friends didn't go as my parent's expected. My grades suffered and I failed; the friends I chose were the type good parents would want a son to stay away from. And what my parents had told me, they were wrong . . . I didn't get over it.

Eat Your Beets

The dining room table had an extra leaf put in to accommodate the two families for this occasion, a going away dinner. Our family was leaving the hills of West Virginia to a home I had only seen in photos, a country of concrete, the city of Baltimore. My father's grocery, now closed, he would no longer be his own boss. He had taken a job in a steel mill. I was to be separated by hundreds of miles from my cousins and my friends. Dad had even given my dog, Midnight, to some farmer. "The city," dad said, "was no place for an animal." This evening an image flashed through my mind of The Last Supper. Is this what they were feeling, not exactly sure about the occasion?

My uncle, the host, this was his home, sat at the head of the table. My aunt and her two boys and my mother were around the table somewhere. If someone could be excited and unhappy at the same time, it was me. I was sitting to the right of my uncle, the man I wanted to be like when I grew up. My dad's place was at the far end of the table, the man I didn't want to be like.

The table was filled with my favorite Greek food: green beans in tomato sauce and onions; baked chicken rubbed with oregano and garlic; roasted sliced potatoes in olive oil and lemon juice; a salad of cucumbers, tomatoes, onions, black olives, and topped with Feta cheese; and plenty of crusty baked bread and butter. But for me there was one bowl that barely got a passing glance: beets in their bloody juice. No way would those deep red, shadowy pieces get on my plate. I crinkled my nose and turned to see a possible antidote. Below a large ornate mirror on the buffet sat small bowls of rice pudding sprinkled with cinnamon.

My uncle was successful. He was respected. My mother said it so often and especially in front of my dad that once he banged the kitchen table with his fist and shouted, "Your brother is successful. All right. Enough! Enough!" And then he left. When dad was upset with mom, he always left the house, got in his car and drove somewhere and didn't return until hours later. She would especially get dad upset if she asked about our market, and whether we could pay our bills. "It's none of your God damn business." He would say, "It's my business." Well, I knew one thing. Dad wasn't successful. He had failed. Bankrupt. I got punished.

My uncle was an attorney. Mom never called him a lawyer, always attorney. I thought lawyer and attorney were different professions. Uncle was a prosecuting attorney. He sent the bad guys to jail. Superman, Batman, the Green Hornet and all those other comic book heroes were make-believe; my uncle was the real thing.

Although I wanted to be like my uncle, I didn't want to look like my uncle. My uncle's skin wasn't tanned. Mine was. His was typical of someone who spent more time inside than out. He had brown hair, sparse; you could see the dome of his head. Uncle was a short man and had a bit of a paunch. He wasn't muscular, but he sure had a grip. When he shook my hand he'd look me in the eye, tilt his head slightly to the side, and with a devilish kind of grin, he would squeeze and squeeze and squeeze my hand compressing the bones until I felt a sharp pain run up my arm to the back of my head. *Don't let him know*, I thought. I knew he was testing me, always testing me. He wanted to see if I was tough; how I would handle the pain. Could I take it? I took it.

But even if uncle didn't look tough, he had an attitude of someone you wouldn't want to mess with. What we boys called "a scrapper." I thought of myself as a scrapper. I wouldn't give up until you proved it to me. You had to beat me: in games, in sports, in wrestling, racing, climbing a tree, or even in a school spelling bee.

Uncle signed papers with the immigration department and brought relatives from Greece, family on his mother's side. He found jobs for the new immigrants with painting contractors operated mainly by Greeks, or working in one of the Greek diners. Uncle donated a hefty amount of money to the local Greek Orthodox Church and served on its board of directors. In his large family room with its picture window overlooking the valley, the framed awards dominated an entire knotty pine wall. Awards from local civic groups. Kiwanis; Rotary; Elks; the Lion's Club; and there was the March of Dimes award which I knew helped those crippled kids that had polio. Every time I visited his home, I'd look at the awards and think *That's what I would do, be successful; make money; and help others. I would be respected.*

Respect, now there was a word you would think I understood.

"Respect your elders."

"Respect your teachers"

"You boys. Stop the giggling and show respect. You're in church."

"Do not talk back." Whack! "You have no respect." That was dad's line as his right hand smacked some respect into me. But that came later, after we moved to Baltimore. For now, on this evening I sat next to my uncle bursting with admiration as he reached over and rubbed my head. I was special.

Food was served, the bowls passed around, everyone except me taking portions because my uncle took my plate and filled it. Beans, chicken, salad, everything, even butter on the plate along with a slice of baked bread. And then there on my plate, menacingly, beets with blood inching toward my potatoes.

Whoa, my mind started racing I'd heard it all before, from dad, mom, other visits with relatives, beets are good for you. Beets will improve your eyesight. Beets will do this for you and beets will do that for you. Well for me, no nice way to put it, but beets will make me puke. I just knew it. No, it hadn't happened but some things even an eleven-year-old just knows.

We lowered our heads briefly for my aunt's quick prayer of thanks, we made the sign of the cross, and we began to eat. I maneuvered food away from the beets making certain the oozed blood didn't contaminate anything on my plate and dug in. I watched as my uncle cut a slice of beet in half, spear it with his fork and paint his teeth red as he held court on subjects where the words "politics" and "foreign policy" were mentioned repeatedly. No others around the table shared an opinion other than asking a question or two that uncle answered without hesitation and in that tone that reinforced my long-held belief that he was smarter than anyone I had ever known, especially my own father.

Eventually I had eaten everything on my plate, except the beets. Uncle smiled at me with that sort of devilish grin and said matter-of-factly, "Good boy, now eat your beets." And then he returned to some other subject about the community and the Greek church and the many projects they were working on to improve Greek lives in the community.

My uncle had only to announce the directive for any issue and it was followed. He had power of presentation; charisma; authority; the quality of generals. The opposite of my dad. My dad was more a dictator and never to be disagreed with by anyone in the family. If dad said the sky was red and I saw the sky was clearly blue, it was red. No discussion, no disagreement, no opinion of your own. I knew it and my mother knew that too.

But this wasn't my dad telling me to eat the beets. This was my idol: my uncle. I took a breath and made the decision: I'll eat the beets. That will please him. I can do it. I could eat dirt for him. But just then at the far end of the table, my dad made a mess. He had poured milk into his glass but far too much and the milk overflowed and soaked the tablecloth. Milk ran off the table and dripped to the floor. My mother sprung to her feet and using her napkin, not paper but cloth, began to soak up the mess on the table. Meanwhile my aunt rushed to the kitchen to get a towel. My dad held the carton up as if he were examining it. I could see it wasn't a carton container that I was familiar with in our home. It was a brand that I guess attorneys knew to buy, not failed dads with fourth grade educations. I was embarrassed for him.

Dad stuttered, "This c,c,c,carton opens on the corner, not in the middle, that's not good, too easy to over pour." He looked across the table at my uncle the attorney as if he needed to convince him of his innocence. "It wasn't my fault," dad said. He sounded whining. "This carton is not as good as the milk cartons we get."

And that's when uncle responded to my dad in a sing-song tone as if he were talking to a child, "Yes, I'm sure your right, has to be the carton. Has to be the carton."

"The spout should be in the middle," No more whining, my father had returned to that certainty that he knew best, down is up, up is down.

"Yes, I'm sure it has to be the carton, not your fault." And then my uncle winked at me. It was our little joke; our little secret. "You're right, your cartons are better," as if speaking to a child. But the law school educated, godfather of the community, the uncle I wanted to be like, EUREKA, I wanted to be like no more. In an eye blink, he lost my respect. And I learned a forever lesson: I can say something bad about my dad, but don't you say something bad about him. There had to be a price to pay.

I didn't touch the beets.

Dinner was finished and the small bowls of rice pudding were passed around. As I ate the dessert, it was the first time that my aunt's rice pudding, that sweet creamy substance with cinnamon and raisins, was flavorless. No specialness on my spoon, tasteless. Then my sense of sight was affected. My eyes refused to even acknowledge that the beets were still on my plate. When my aunt and mom started to clear the table, my uncle tested me again, earlier it had been the handshake, now came the taste test.

"You will not leave this table until you eat your beets." Uncle stated it as a matter-of fact, the same as "the sun will come up tomorrow," expecting it to happen. He then tilted his head slightly to the side and raised eyebrows and gave me that grin as if that should be enough. Nothing more to say, he had spoken.

My dad didn't interfere. I didn't expect him to. He knew how angry I was for his failure. The entire family left me at the table and proceeded to the recreation room to watch television. Several hours later, with my lower back aching and a sore neck, I stared straight ahead as both families passed the table and went to their designated bedrooms. Not a goodnight from any of them, not from my own mother, probably the general had issued orders. My aunt left a lamp on for me and I sat there, me and my beets. My thoughts raced! *Trust! Respect! Respect! Trust! Respect! Trust! Trust! Respect!* They both lost.

I don't know how many hours later it was when someone shook me awake. I'd fallen asleep with my head on the table and, fortunately, not on the plate and the beets. My aunt said, "Go to bed now, no more will be said about this."

The "N" Word

"A WOP-BOP-A-LULA-A-WOP-BAM-BOOM!" Like a speeding hot rod with sound exploding from duel mufflers. **"1-got-a-girl-named-Sue. She-know-just-what-to-do."** The words raced one to another. So different from the Pat Boone "Tutti Frutti" version played on the majority of radio stations, "White" stations. Pat Boone's version was comparable to a quiet, slow riding limousine: A wop bop a lula a wop bam boom. No explosion. No action. No pounding rhythm.

Boone's version was known as a "clean sound." A sound even "white" mothers and "white" ministers thought was sweet. And Pat Boone's looks, "What a sweet voice and a sweet young man" my mother said.

But not Little Richard.

The adults in my life never said something positive about "Tutti Frutti" or Little Richard himself. That could be why, when I wasn't even a teenager yet, I adopted Richard Penniman as my rock 'n' roll idol.

My way of getting back at the adults in my life, especially my father. Dad's failure in business, forced to close his grocery store, must have made him feel that way, a failure. His next decision didn't solve things for the family either, at least not for me or for him. Our move from West Virginia to Baltimore for his new job in a steel mill, working the night shift wasn't working out for Dad either. I got over my sadness at having to give up my friends and my dog, Midnight, by turning sadness into anger. And the new sound of rock 'n' roll music let me express it. But I took it a step further.

It wasn't the "White" artists, except for the very few, that gave me the outlet for my frustration, my powerlessness. Instead it was the "Black" singers. The music industry called the Black artists' "Rhythm & Blues" performers. And it was these singers who helped me through the tough times surviving an often violent father. That violence was the origin of my Condition of Peculiarity. I would sometimes imagine that the singers were performing just for me. To get me through a hard time.

The violence stopped. Was it because dad had accepted his fate that he was no longer his own boss? Or, had he realized that smacking me around didn't make me less rebellious or more respectful. That wasn't going to happen, at least not then. Just maybe the hitting stopped because I got older.

By the time I graduated from high school I knew I didn't want to stay close to home or him. So in 1965 of all the colleges to enroll into I chose one back from where we had come from . . . in the hills of West Virginia. Back to the place, where as a young boy, I had those wonderful growing-up memories.

Back in the 1960's and before, West Virginia liked to proclaim the slogan West "By God" Virginia. After all, my home state was formed out of the slave state of Virginia and sided with the north during the civil war. Plantations were hard to come by in the hills and there wasn't a slave economy. By the 1960's West Virginia was no closer to God than any of the states that had practiced segregation, officially or unofficially. But I didn't know that. After all, I was "White," and racial discrimination wasn't my issue anyway. My concern was getting far away from home. Concord College in the southern hills of West Virginia here I come.

When I arrived to the parking lot of the dorm, I unpacked my car of my most valuable items, a phonograph and a box of records. The dorm room was identical to the photos in the college catalogue. A room divided in half. Each half with its small single bed, small dresser, and small desk. I didn't know it yet, but the college was also small-minded.

The college dorm

My unknown roommate hadn't checked in so I fired up the phonograph with an album by James Brown: "Live at the Apollo." I left the door open and headed back out to my car to bring in other items, my clothes, that were not as important to me as the music I had carried in first.

Back in my room, I was surprised that several visitors were seated on the empty bed across from the one I had chosen. They were going through my box of albums. First thing I noticed was that they were Black guys. I do see color. Second, they were tall, very tall. I do see size. They seemed surprised to see me and even commented, "Hey, we expected someone Black." I guessed it was because of the James Brown sound coming from my room and my albums they were flipping through: Otis Redding; Ray Charles; Solomon Burke; they were especially surprised when they came across my Nina Simone albums. This White and Black musical bonding encouraged all three of them to go out to my car to help bring in the remainder of my belongings.

My car got laughs from my new acquaintances. The car was a convertible Alpine Sunbeam, a very small sports car, baby blue with a black leather top. I had purchased it already used from the only foreign motors lot in Baltimore. What can I say? It was an impulse buy with money I had earned working summers. The laughter from me and my fellow students was because none of these tall guys could fit into the front seat without scrunching their bodies, knees against the steering wheel, making them unable to raise a foot to press on the brakes.

1962 Alpine Sunbeam

Once we completed the move of my property into the dorm, we parted ways. It was evening and I left the campus to drive to a nearby local restaurant, hungry for a burger. Returning later I pulled into a spot next to my dorm. No streetlights. It was dark. Almost the same time a car pulled into a spot next to mine. The driver revved the engine. Not just once but twice, three times. The car had a doctored muffler or a rotten tailpipe and sounded similar to a go-cart that teenagers raced around small tracks.

I looked over to acknowledge who I assumed was a fellow student. The car was packed with guys. Guys sitting on the laps of other guys and brought to mind a miniature circus car at center ring that magically empties clown after clown after clown after . . . .

As a way to reply a "hello," I revved my car's engine. Now there was a difference. My Alpine Sunbeam had two mufflers, a necessary part of the sports car image. When revved my little Alpine became a long distance, tractor trailer. It said HELLO! BROOOM! HELLO! BROOOM, BROOOM!

Just as I turned off the engine, my car door was suddenly opened and someone, a very strong someone, grabbed my shoulder and jerked me out of the front seat. I fell to the pavement. Confused, I scrambled away from the car and quickly got to my feet. I then found myself in a circle of young guys who looked similar to me, "White" students except that they were big guys. Not as tall as the "Black" students but very large and wide.

I didn't have time to ask what this was all about because they began throwing me from one large guy to another around the circle. One to the other—to the other—to the other, *Was it because I showed-off my sports car?* to the other—to the other—I stayed on my feet—to the other—to the other, a scene from a Hollywood movie.

And then I heard good and loud. **"Who the hell do you think you are!"** A statement yelled at me not a question to answer. **"Yankee!"** That one threw me for a second, but I had no time to dwell on it. And then the words came loud and fast as I was spun from one large guy to another. **"Nigger lover! Nigger lover! Nigger lover!"** They all took up the chant. **"Nigger lover! Nigger lover!"** *Whoa,* I thought, *that's what it is. It's not the Alpine.* No time to dwell on it. I had completed a second round of the circle and was starting a third of one to the other—to the other—when I selected the only student close to my size and punched him in the face.

• • • • •

I woke up in my dorm room in my bed. I was hurting. My side hurt. My head hurt. Even my right hand knuckles hurt.

"Hey, I'm your roommate. You okay?" A student was on the floor between our beds and was taping a cardboard sign to a crudely made wooden post with a wooden base about three foot high.

"A couple students in the dorm saw what happened and helped you stagger into the dorm and into your bed."

"I don't remember that part," I said.

"Well, I don't want you to get the wrong idea, and I'm not at all sure of what happened out in the parking lot but . . . just in case."

I watched as he wrapped a large amount of masking tape around the wooden pieces with its wider base. It appeared to me that the tape worked in place of a hammer and nails.

"Those guys are a little crazy. Typical jocks. I was told it was the football team."

"They were big."

"I also heard that you had guys from the basketball team in our room earlier today."

"They were big too."

"Yeah, and they were Colored guys."

My head was clearing. "Yeah, they were."

"I guess the football players were not too happy about that."

"Yeah, you guessed right there."

"I don't have any issues on whether Coloreds should be coming to our school." He finished wrapping the base to the post with enough tape to wrap an Egyptian mummy. "You're my roommate. What you do is your thing. My thing is to get my teaching degree and get back home."

"Going back home isn't exactly why I chose to come here."

"But just in case those jocks decide to come into this room tonight, and I sure hope they don't, to finish whatever it is . . . anyway, it's not personal. I just don't want them making a mistake."

My roommate had creatively wrapped the tape in an X pattern to hold a piece of cardboard onto the post. I watched as he then took a large black magic marker and proceeded to draw on the cardboard. *What the hell was he drawing?* He finished his art project and turned the sign so I could see. It was an arrow.

• • • • •

The racists didn't show that night. I got some sleep probably because my body required it after the beating I had gotten. Early in the morning my roommate was still asleep as I dressed, and I was careful not to disturb his insurance policy as I hustled out of the dorm. I wasn't sure of what would transpire from last evening's craziness. Classes weren't scheduled to start for another day so I thought a walk around the campus would help me. I was angry. And then I became even angrier. The convertible top to my car was slashed, one long cut, front to back. The tear gave me my marching orders. I got in my car and headed off campus to find a hardware store. Sure enough, the small town nearby had a store and it was open. Unexpected events can teach life lessons. My lesson was that heavy duct tape, black to match the top of the Alpine, can provide a temporary bandage to almost any rainfall.

Back on campus as I was taping the Alpine's torn top a student approached. "The dean wants to see you." He shook his head slowly and said, almost in a whisper. "I'm sorry that happened to you." And walked away.

Damn, I thought, *called to the dean's office even before I had a chance to go to class.* This broke my record. Even when I failed in junior high and got in all kinds of trouble, I at least made a few weeks before the call to the principal's office.

Sitting in the office's reception area I was unsure as to whether to tell the dean what I knew and what I had heard. *Why not just let things settle? Why bring grief to the football players that were involved. They couldn't help it that they were racist.* At least that's what my mom had said so many times as an excuse for a number of our relatives and neighbors who never wanted anything to do with Negroes. Most of the time my mother used the word "Coloreds" instead of "Negroes." I believe she thought the word Negro sounded too close to that curse word we were never ever to speak.

The secretary told me the dean would see me now. I entered and stood at the foot of his desk. The dean sat in a wide, high-backed leather chair. He wore a dark blue sport coat, a white shirt with a solid red tie. He had dark hair that was streaked with gray that made him appear experienced . . . responsible. He didn't hesitate. "I have a quick message for you."

Quick, l thought, r*eally quick.* He hadn't introduced himself or even asked my name. The Dean's throne rocked a bit forward as he spoke, his hands placed solidly on the desk as if he were going to jump out at me. "l want you to get this and get it the first time l tell you."

This was not the start l expected. *But perhaps,* l thought, *here comes an apology for what happened to me. Maybe l won't have to say anything.*

"You young men come down here from up north and think you can change us, our culture." He rocked back in his leather throne and swiveled slightly to the side. He stared off somewhere but not at me. "And mistakenly think you can change history." It seemed he was just warming up in his "quick" message. "We may be forced to do things because of the government or the courts but it won't be because of you people." At "you" he turned to point a finger my way. "l do not want to hear any more about what happened."

Wow, he sure didn't hear it from me.

"You brought it on yourself. Now learn from it."

End of message, not quite. The Dean's tone softened, he leaned in closer. His expression concerned as if he were now my mentor. "Be a good student and pay attention to your grades. Now head to the cafeteria and get yourself lunch. We serve excellent food here." He swiveled the chair to the left, reached and picked up the phone and punched some numbers. He nodded and motioned for me to leave. Our meeting was over.

• • • • • •

l was now even more confused than l was from the beating l got from the racists. It just didn't feel right to refer to them as fellow students. l didn't think l had anything in common with them, except that l liked football. l could smell the food as l approached the cafeteria and entered to a long line of burgers, sloppy joes, macaroni and cheese, green beans, salad, pies, cakes, all the good for you college staples. l pointed to whatever and filled my plate not thinking of anything except trying to figure out what had just happened at the dean's office. What the hell had he meant with "our culture" and "change history."

l stepped out to the main room almost as large as any auditorium and it was then that "culture" and "history" hit me like a cafeteria pie in the face. There must have been a couple hundred hungry students eating lunch. But only one table in the brightly lit room stood out: the one that seated seven or eight Black students. l perused the room and didn't see another dark face anywhere. My focus returned to what I now realized was a very special table. I recognized the guys who helped me from the night before. Or I should say the nightmare before. There were two other guys there, as well as two females. I guess the college didn't see a need to paint a sign "Colored Students Sit Here."

I didn't hesitate and my legs directed me towards that special table. No time to sort out my feelings, too many going at one time. I stood next to the table with my own tray of "college cooking." I looked at the guys I knew. I asked, almost implored, "Can I sit with you at your table? I need to, just this time. I won't do it again." The reason for wanting to do this I hadn't even thought about. It was spontaneous. "I got to show them they can't scare me. Just this once."

In the cafeteria, more than a hundred students stopped eating. No sounds of clinking glasses or forks and knives on plates. The table where I stood took center stage. Several of the Black guys, ones I had not met, got up and left. The three students who had been in my room, who had helped me move in, who had wished me a 'good night' and a 'see you again,' they stayed. The women stayed. I took their response as a "Yes" and sat. We didn't talk. I never realized this could put them in harm's way. Too selfish about my own ego, my own stubbornness, my world. I never sat with them again.

• • • •

It took me little over a month to find a student, a White guy to move off campus and share the expenses for an apartment. My dorm roommate supported my move not for his own safety but because he saw how ostracized I was by the other students. The word had gone out immediately: "Steer clear of the Greek guy from up north." Maryland?

While others steered clear of me I stayed clear of studying. I spent more time in a neighborhood bar where I drank beer and fed quarters into the jukebox. The few miles to the college seemed not worth the gas or the class. Was I going along with my father's alcoholic journey? I don't know.

The courses I was supposed to be attending had little to do with what was taking place on the evening news. Every night on my roommates small black-and-white TV there were stories and news clips of marchers, Black and White, young and old, chanting and carrying signs about voting and justice. A number of signs read, "I am a Man." This was the first time I had paid attention to the news since the assassination of President Kennedy.

Civil rights wasn't my issue, if I even had an issue other than my father. And then came Selma.

Selma, Alabama, March 7, 1965 Known as "Bloody Sunday"

The Sunday news was dominated by the site of civil rights marchers getting beaten. I got beat-up for having Black students in my room listening to music. These people were bloodied for trying to get what was rightfully theirs, the right to vote. The news all the next week was about the marches and Selma.

But in my Sociology 101 class not a mention of the events. The professor, a man not that old, in his '40s, dressed in a white shirt, unbuttoned collar, an open black sweater and pressed gray slacks. What students called "a cool look" for a teacher. Today he had begun the class by drawing on the board concentric circles, beginning with the smallest circle and moving outward to a larger one, and outward to another larger circle while he droned on and on about the movements of people from cities to suburbs.

This, I thought, *had nothing to do with what was happening now in Selma or in other cities.* I grabbed my books, stood and asked, "May I be excused?" No response. He continued to drone on still drawing circles on the board, so I left. I headed to the student lounge where I found my only competition for a comfortable seat was another guy who was asleep. The television was on. On the screen something was happening that I guess the professor didn't know about or didn't want to talk about. It sure looked like a big deal. I took a seat, watched and listened.

March 25, 1965 Martin Luther King, Jr. on the steps of Alabama Capital.

> Like an idea whose time has come,
> not even the marching of mighty armies can halt us.
> We are moving to the land of freedom.
> How long? Not long,
> because no lie can live forever.
> How long? Not long,
> because you shall reap what you sow.
> How long? Not long,
> because the arc of the moral universe is long,
> but it bends toward justice.

The first semester would be my last semester. I flunked out. When I got the news I was faced with the task of telling my father, which in some strange way I looked forward to. A college degree was the one dream my father wanted for me. Disappointing him felt like I was getting even with him for letting me down.

"Dad," I held the phone tightly to my ear trying to muffle the local dive's jukebox playing in the background.

"Son?"

"Dad, I didn't make it. My grades . . . I have to sit out a semester."

No response, nothing. I pictured dad holding a can of beer. *Was he already wasted for the evening?*

Finally, "Come on home boy." A sigh. "You tried," he slurred, "that's what counts."

But I hadn't tried. And it didn't seem to make me feel any better that I had disappointed my father, even though I believed the man deserved it. I left the phone booth and walked past the jukebox where next to it, and I know he wasn't really there, it was country star Buck Owens. He was dressed to the nines as if he were on stage at the Gran' Ole Opry.

What song would Buck sing to help me through this trying time?
We'll . . it's . . crying time again,
you're going to leave me.
Damn, I thought, *trying time and crying time, it rhymes. Buck knew just the right song.*
I can see that far-away look
in your eye.
A customer got off his barstool, walked through Buck Owens, put a quarter in the machine and punched a few numbers. I nodded to the bartender, pushed open the door to the street while behind me "Crying Time" played on the jukebox.

You Must Pass the Physical

The room, large as a gymnasium, could have been a warehouse for Army supplies. And in a way it was. The supplies were fresh young men, civilians all, including me, Zack Tonakis. I wasn't yet officially in the Army. First, I had to pass a physical: eyes, ears, nose and throat, as well as other body parts. "Bend over and spread 'em." If the Army's going to invest in you, they absolutely want to know that the goods aren't defective. So far I had completed half-a-day of going in one room and out another while carrying a folder that showed the results of my passing the physical with flying colors. I didn't want to be healthy, not today, but my body betrayed me. That was even after staying up all night drinking every concoction of alcohol my buddies swore would have me fail the physical.

Now, still hungover, I had entered the hangar and was standing near the head of a line of recruits that led to a soldier who was seated behind a desk. Lines of recruits were everywhere, an initiation of more lines to come. We looked stupid wearing shoes and socks, no pants, just underwear. Being civilians, we didn't call them skivvies yet. We each carried our shirt and pants rolled up so we could ensure looking like crap when we put them back on later. I don't recall any of those guys that took the physical with me. None of us wanted to look at each other because we knew we looked stupid.

Across the hangar floor young men were seated at tables answering questions, nodding "yes" or "no" to whatever the soldier who sat across from them was asking. Quiz completed they took their folders and were replaced by another young man in skivvies. Watching the other recruits I couldn't help but think how much of a little boy I was, we all were.

My turn came. I took a seat and handed the folder to the soldier across from me. The soldier opened the folder and studied the main questionnaire we all had answered when we checked in this morning. I knew what was coming but what the hell it was worth a shot.

"Toe-na-kiss, Am I saying that right? Greek isn't it?"

"Yes sir. Greek."

"I'm not a sir, son." The soldier paused to ponder the questionnaire, then continued, "Tonakis, you checked 'Yes' to a hell of a lot of illness," He wrinkled his brow.

"Well, off and on, I've had a number of—"

"It appears when you were a child you had Measles, Mumps, even Smallpox. Must have been tough on your parents."

"Well, yeah, they—"

"You checked here you damn near have broken every bone in your body at least once."

"Well, what with sports and football and—"

"And, I see here that you're a queer?"

I was ready for this one. While I stood in line I had gone over the possible exam questions time and again. Which check mark would they focus on? This one, that one, all of them, I couldn't be certain. I had checked "Yes" to so many questions I really hoped in the end I would just plain flunk the Army physical and not know which test: eyes, ears, nose, throat, or whatever had succeeded. For me, failing was success. Now I launched into my rehearsed explanation.

"That's not what the question asks," I corrected. "It asks "Do you have homosexual tendencies? Tendencies."

The soldier didn't stand corrected. "Are you queer?" he continued.

I leaned in a little closer and tried to keep this part of the exam just between the two of us and not between us and the three hundred or so other guys in skivvies.

"I took a college psychology class and I learned that tendencies can run the gamut from exhibitionists, who are obviously those persons in the entertainment profession who have a need for public limelight, and I was in a band, to those others who—"

"Answer my question." He leaned across the desk until we were almost nose-to-nose. He was intense. "Are you—"

"But that's not the question on the form," I shot back. Now I was getting pissed at this representative for our military that insisted on rewriting the question.

The soldier sat back. Was that a retreat? He didn't have the expression of someone who had given up.

"Do you suck dicks?"

Could he have announced it any louder? I doubt it. Could any place reverberate with the sound as clearly? I doubt it. This medical amateur announced it only once but his question bounced and echoed off the walls of the hangar.

"Do you suck dicks?" "You suck **dicks?**" "Suck **dicks?**" "**dicks?**" "**dicks?**" "**dicks?**"

God, I thought, *it was like a flat rock bouncing across a lake, the sound had to stop bouncing, eventually.* Has any person received the unasked for attention of so many young men in skivvies as I did that moment? I turned over my king and resigned the match, checkmate.

"No," I said. In case he didn't hear me, I moved my head in an exaggerated left and right, left and right that I believed even he would understand. And the three hundred others in the room looking my way.

The soldier smirked, leaned forward, took a pen and scratched heavily through the "Yes" check mark and then he became me for the moment and clearly circled "No" next to: "Do you have Homosexual tendencies?" He tossed the folder back to me with that smirk still on his face.

"Get to the next station," he said.

As I rose from the chair, I couldn't help but wonder, *how would a Homosexual have answered the Army's questionnaire?*

"Tendencies? That's an inclination, a propensity, I have no tendency; I am. So . . . No, I don't have homosexual tendencies." Go figure.

Postscript: Almost three years later when I was processing the papers necessary for my discharge from the Army I went to the records office to pick up my medical history. It was required that soldiers upon leaving the Army had to sign-off that our bodies hadn't acquired something that wasn't there when inducted. The clerk, a corporal I'd known for over a year in the barracks, stood next to me as I opened the folder. There on that first sheet were the numerous medical questions I had checked off for my physical almost three years ago. One stood out with its multiple lines scratched through the checked box of that infamous question: Do you Have Homosexual Tendencies? The corporal saw it. Perplexed, he asked, "So Greek, what was that all about?"

Zero Week

The bleachers in the base gymnasium were filled with fresh Army recruits. There was a war going on and job applicants were wanted, those who wanted to apply and those who didn't. Robert Turner and I were one of many already seated at small tables on the gymnasium floor. Recruiters in brown khakis sat across from us while we wore our spanking new Army issued too-damn-large green fatigues. What did the recruiters know about us? Nothing. Nada. Zero. Okay, conceivably what the days of testing had supposedly revealed. Serious life discussions were taking place at every table.

A sergeant walked to the center of the floor and announced, "Keep it moving—as a chair empties—get down here and fill it. Don't forget your folder."

My folder was currently being studied by a soldier, an older guy. *He must be in his '30s,* I thought. I was about to learn how much intelligence and skill I brought to the service of my country. I was anxious. I could feel it. Just yesterday I registered a disastrous result in a test that was for the signal corps. Sitting in a booth with earphones and a sheet of paper when the sound emanating gave one beep or two-then one-then three-then two-and faster with three-then one-two-one-three-faster-three-two-two-two-one-two and you had to mark the sheet for each sound that came over the earphones and I hesitated while one-three-two continued at a breathtaking pace and I lost track, lost my place and couldn't finish the test. I placed my pencil on the desk, rose slightly and looked over the edge of my booth and saw other faces peering out of the top of their cubicle. Lost in the maze of beep-beeps. No signal corps for us.

Suddenly my recruiter leaned forward and pointed at me. He must have discovered something important.

"Son."

In my short time in the Army every soldier with stripes seemed to refer to me as son.

"Son, you scored very high on our tests, and I mean very high. You qualified for an elite position." He reached across the table and poked my chest. "The Army wants to invest in you."

Invest . . . in me? I thought. *That was a good thing.*

"If you extend your Army time for one year, we," he nodded, then emphasized "I" and paused "can get" paused "you" paused "into Helicopter Pilot School." The Recruiter said the "we" the "I" and the "you" as if the we, he, and me were heading there together.

He sat back, a smug look, nodded again with an exaggerated affirmative.

I had a question. "Excuse me, aren't helicopter pilots getting killed every day in Vietnam?"

I looked around the gym searching for Bobby Turner. He also was one week into the draft and was my newly assigned Army barracks bunkmate, he in the lower and me in the upper.

"Son," my recruiter leaned forward, "You've been watching too much TV."

I spotted my bunkmate at a table on the other side of the gym. "Hey Bob, Bobby. Hey Turner!" My call disrupted any number of life discussions. Turner saw me and raised his hand.

I yelled, "What did you qualify for?"

He yelled back, "Helicopter pilot school!"

"So did I." I yelled back.

Suddenly from other tables everywhere in the room, "So did I!" "Hey, me too!" "Far out, I did too!" "Top score over here!" "I did too!" "Same here!" "I did!"

The outburst provided a much needed escape from the serious life decisions that we recent high school grads and college dropouts were being asked to make. While we at the tables contained our amusement, the recruits in the bleachers fell-out with laughter.

My recruiter stared disgustedly at me and tossed me the folder. "Boy," He said. I guess I was disowned as his son, "unless you want to walk in rice paddies you'd better pick an MO before the Army picks it for you."

An MO, I thought, *Military Occupation. My life had come to this.*

Later that week, my bunkmate Bobby Turner and I picked an MO. Medic Training. Turner wanted to help soldiers who were wounded. I just didn't want to shoot somebody.

Tests, tests and more tests.

A Condition of Peculiarity

"Out of your bunks. Out! Out! Out! Now!"

"Get down in the dirt, head down."

"Crawl! Crawl! Crawl! Now!"

"Hit the floor and give me twenty. Now!"

Basic training was synonymous with deadlines and yelling. Hurry-hurry-hurry, run-run-run. And it was in basic when my platoon was on a march, and the South Carolina temperature neared one hundred degrees that my jukebox of the mind went haywire, and instead of my seeing one singing group or singer and playing one song, the jukebox played three, four, five snippets of songs from the past, one after another so connected, not one beat missed, and I started singing to myself to keep up with my peculiarity:

> Pretty pretty pretty pretty Peggie Sue, Tutti-frutti oh Rudy,
> You ain't nothing but a hound dog, Bye bye love, bye bye
> happiness, Chantilly lace and a pretty face, Tell me what I say
> tell me what I say, Lover please, please come back,
> Goodness gracious great balls of fire . . .

When the grueling march completed, I was finally able to get a sense of control. That night back in the barracks exhaustion had its way and I slept.

By morning at the mess hall, I had come to grips with what had happened the previous day. My peculiarity had gone into overdrive. This was a first for me. Normally, if I can use the word normal, singers and their songs were part of me. I grew up with them. It wasn't until my first year in college in a psychology 101 text that I read that the singers and songs in my jukebox of the mind were a defense mechanism. The kind of protection I didn't want to tell anyone about. Especially now, I could imagine how a discussion with an Army psychiatrist would proceed if it was known.

"So, Private when did you start hearing these voices?" the psychiatrist would probably begin. "They're not just voices," I would respond, "they're singers." And as to when I first developed this marvelous ability I would say,

"Oh, when I was about twelve years old." What I did know was that my peculiarity, this jukebox of the mind, had helped me survive the worst of things.

As so many teenagers I had spent an inordinate amount of time listening to the radio. The music, not for parents, was rock n' roll. But as for my peculiarity, I knew that the songs and singers couldn't take full credit; my dad deserved his share. It was, after all, one of those times when my father slapped me around that I noticed I wasn't paying a whole lot of attention to what he was doing. I usually watched dad's right hand, the hand that delivered most of the pain. But not on that night. Instead, I found myself focusing on the sounds emanating from the radio next to my bed. And to the question the Coasters asked,

Who walks in the classroom, cool and slow?
Who calls the English teacher, Daddy-O?

Before the Coasters answered their own question, Dad did his part.
Whack!

Charlie Brown.

Whack!

Charlie Brown.

You got to love those Coasters, I thought. Singers took center stage while somewhere off behind the curtains my father delivered his lines.

"God damn you," dad said. That was another night.

Oh, Oh, Oh yes, I'm the great pretender.

"Do . . . not . . . talk . . . back!" Whack! Dad smacked. But no pain, the Platters were singing.

Pretending that I'm doing well.

The songs on the radio were called into action so often that I soon could conjure up songs even without a radio nearby. I first became aware of this ability the day I was putting trash into the garbage can by the side of the garage. My father drove up and I hurried toward the house.

"Hey, where the hell you going?" Dad slammed the car door. "Freeze, Mister!"

I froze.

"You'd better get back here."

I turned around but stayed where I was.

"Go back there and put that lid on right!"

I turned and saw the lid to the can was askew. I looked back to my father who was moving toward me—and then he was there—almost pressing his face against mine. His cheeks and lips vibrated; his eyes flashed like lights on a pinball machine. My dad reached for me but instead of grabbing hold of my arm, he latched on to my chest, the fleshy part around the left nipple. His look of rage told me that he didn't know what he had hold of.

Fingers dug into my flesh right through the T-shirt. *My father is going to tear off my nipple.* I thought. *God, how am I going to take showers in gym class with no nipple?* With dad's fingers implanted in my chest, He yanked me back to the garbage cans. I tried to keep close to his right claw in hopes that I might save the nipple. I felt a burning sensation. I thought of the old western movies I'd watched on TV. *This must be what it feels to be branded by a white-hot poker.* And just then I became a DJ and spun a record. *Ooo-popla-tee, Ooo-popla-toe, here we go, here we go.* But this time more than just a song there were the singers. Right in the back yard, side by side, looking cool in their black suits, red vests, and black bow ties was the singing group, The Olympics:

My baby loves western movies.
"God damnit! Can't you do anything right?"
My baby loves western movies.
"You want garbage spread all over the alley?"
Bow; Bow; A-shoe-be-do-bow,
uuh-huh-huh,
My baby loves western movies.

Why that song? I wondered. And my DJ answered, *The stranger the selection the greater the protection.*

I quickly replaced the lid on the garbage can, and I received five deep indentations, black, blue and strangely grayish with specks of blood that circled my left nipple. Sure enough, on Monday afternoon in the shower after gym class, came the questions, "What happened to your chest?" And I responded, "I was attacked by a werewolf."

But it wasn't the full moon that transformed my father, unhappiness did. But I didn't know that, at least not then. I believed it was my own doing. My father was angry at me for not being better, better in school, better at everything, a better son. And the same as Lawrence Talbot of the Wolfman movies, I was convinced my father had no control over his own horrific transformation. Proof of that always followed an attack. After the garbage can incident, that night dad came into my bedroom with a jar of cooling cream.

"You be still now," my father said with a brusque voice.

He raised my pajama top and spread the healing salve over the dad-inflicted hurt. No other words were said, but I knew the man was sorry.

I got older, and the hitting stopped. And although I no longer needed protection from my dad, I knew that my peculiarity, this jukebox of the mind, was again helping me survive the worst of things . . . war.

David . . . and Zack

"Medic. Meeedic. Medic!"

I entered the ward quickly as the high-pitched plea came from the patient, David.

"Pee! I have to Pee!"

I reached underneath the bed for a metal urinal.

"Okay, Okay, soldier, Here you go." I raised the blue blanket and positioned the urinal, all part of my training as a medic. Only after this assignment would I go on to more training and become a neuropsychiatric technician, an impressive title. Sure didn't sound like a guy who had failed out of college.

"Take care of the soldier in bed one," the nurse had said, "That is your daily responsibility."

I didn't know it but my daily responsibility, David, was dying.

David knew he was dying. He was a daily witness to the thinning of his arms, chest, stomach, legs, even his toes, fingers and pads of his hands. The few times David looked at his reflection in a mirror he saw that his mop of dusty brown hair was gone. His skin transparent, blue veins mapped his nineteen-year-old body and shown through the sparse fuzz on his white egg-shaped head.

When I lowered the soldier's pajama bottom so the patient could empty his bladder into the urinal, David saw he had lost much of his pubic hair. It was as if every part of David's body had stopped growing, including his now limp and shriveled penis. No more morning erections; no erections anytime.

David watched and listened as the Army doctors came by for rounds in the early morning. They stopped and read his chart while I, the patient's caretaker, stood by. The doctors' spoke loudly so the group of interns could hear the patient's prognosis. They spoke as if on automatic pilot and David could hear what his body had in store for him.

"The shrapnel perforated this soldier's lower gastrointestinal tract and the patient is no longer able to absorb necessary nutrients. The additional damage gives his prognosis less than a month or, at the most—"

49

David heard the blah, blah, blah, and because his vocal chords had taken an early retirement, the soldier responded in his newly acquired high tenor vocalization, "I'm here. And I hear you. I can fucking hear you." And the professorial doctors apologized in a superior tone as if David were a child.

Eventually, the patient, a soldier still, won this battle and the doctors stopped using David as a chalkboard. Instead, they would pass through the ward stopping briefly to glance at his chart, initialize their approval of whatever inconsequential treatment was in order and move on without comment. And David who more and more had given up on niceties would call after them "I'm here! I'm still here!"

Weeks later I wheeled David, still here, into a windowless room that was filled with a multiplicity of wounds and illness. The soldiers saw the wheelchair first, and then David, slumped sideways, an emaciated body, strapped in to keep him from sliding off to the floor. The soldiers returned their attention to magazines, stared at the ceiling, at the floor, at their fingernails, at the backs of their hands, anywhere but at David.

A nurse entered from an office door. She wore a severely starched white uniform; her expression as sterile as the room's décor. She called a name, and David called out in a high-pitched monotone: "I got to shit!"

Startled, the audience looked at David.

"I got to shit!"

They looked away.

I wheeled David from the room and raced through the corridor. David's head bobbled like a plastic doll in the back window of a Chevy.

"Zack! Zack! Hurry Zack. hurry hurry! Zack, Zack!"

In a latrine I untied David's blue pajama bottom, lifted him from the chair, and lowered his skeleton to the seat.

"Not so tight. Not so tight. Zack, not on the seat, it hurts." David whimpered. "Hold me. It hurts. It hurts. Zack, hold me. Hold me. Hold me."

"I'm here, David. I got you, David."

"Mommy. Mommy."

I held David while outside of the stall I could hear Smoky Robinson and the Miracles singing:

> You really got a hold on me.
> You really got a hold on me.

That night I woke abruptly when I heard David's bones snapping, cracking, and splintering as I held him. For me, a medic-in-training, it was a dream; the rest was real. A week later David died.

The Grassy Knoll

Zack arrived at the cavernous Philadelphia train station at the same time a military plane carrying wounded soldiers back from Vietnam landed at the Philadelphia airport. Zack wore his dress uniform, shined black shoes, marksmanship and good conduct medals on his jacket, and medic insignia on his collar. If not for the military ticket rate to his assignment, he would have worn civilian clothes.

The domed center of the station had tentacles of corridors and Zack's short-term memory bank refused to register the information on his ticket: He read it, and then he'd forget it. He had to repeatedly check the slip of paper for the appropriate corridor. When he did locate the entrance, he stopped and took a needed deep breath before entering. Suddenly they were there, off to the side of the corridor, Peter, Paul and Mary, the folk singers. Peter and Paul strummed guitars and harmonized with Mary of the long, golden hair. She moved her head to the rhythm. Her hair tossed across her face as she sang.

This train she's bound for glory,
if you want to get to heaven,
you've got to stay holy,
this train she's bound for glory,
this train.

What a send-off, Zack thought. *Peter, Paul and Mary are here just for me.* Once again, Zack's prescription for high anxiety, his peculiarity had worked its magic. He entered the corridor.

From the city of the cracked Liberty Bell, the PFC boarded an old-fashioned commuter train, the Little Engine That Could as it chug-chugged through the Pennsylvania countryside. Before every small town stop a conductor came through the two-car train announcing with a nasal twang, "Norristown, Norristown," until finally, "Phoenixville, Phoenixville."

Along with a few locals, Zack exited the train to a platform with two benches. The wooden building with a shingled roof resembled a train garden's miniature station. A ticket window had a sign that read: **Purchase Tickets Inside.**

Zack headed to a taxi and joined his duffel bag in the back seat. The taxi weaved its way on a secluded road past forests and cornfields. The cabbie was a talker.

"I'll tell you what they ought to do with Vietnam. Bomb the whole effin place. Make it a parking lot. Know what I mean? Know what I mean?" The cabbie could have been an auctioneer as his words spewed forth, "Knowwhatlmean-Knowwhatlmean?"

The cabbie looked in the mirror. Zack looked away not wanting the driver to think he agreed with those war plans. The cabbies head, with a bald spot, rocked forward, then back, and seemed to speak to Zack.

"I feel bad when I pick up the moms-dads-wives, bring 'em out here to see their boys. It's a damn shame-damn shame."

Zack agreed with the bald spot.

"Maybe we should drop one of our 'tomic bombs, that would get their 'tention. Boom!" The cabbie slapped the dash.

Zack flinched and looked away again.

The driver deposited Zack at the hospital's front gate and drove off muttering something about "Why have a 'newclor' bomb if we won't use it?"

The hospital base was surrounded by a high chain-link fence. Bushes and evergreens outlined the inside of the fence and softened the "off limits to civilians" look. Two MPs stood at the front gatehouse. Zack handed orders to an MP to validate that he was supposed to be here and not in another state.

"Too naa kiss," the MP's voice faded at "kiss."

"Toe nah kiss," Zack spoke it phonetically for him.

"Whatever. Check in at the barracks, rear of the hospital." The MP returned the orders.

Zack picked up his duffel bag and headed towards the hospital that was a short distance from the gate. The two-story red brick structure had windows that lined both floors, some curtained some not. Directly in front of the hospital was the customary freshly cut grassy circle with its flagpole and stars and stripes. Today, Zack noticed the Flag hung lifelessly. The hospital's white, double door entrance welcomed the wounded.

As Zack neared the circle, a brown Army bus passed by, belched, and stopped at the front entrance. As if on cue, medics in white and soldiers in green fatigues exited the hospital's double doors. They hustled to the rear door of the bus.

"Okay, careful, careful." A corporal in green fatigues stood to the side of the opened back door giving directions. "Keep 'em level. Don't tip 'em. Careful. Careful."

Medics in the bus lowered patients on stretchers to the waiting crew who immediately carried them into the hospital, a speedy and efficient operation. The walking wounded followed the stretcher cases out the bus's rear door. Most patients wore Army black dress shoes; a few wore combat boots, while others wore white cotton open-back slippers. They all wore light blue scrubs under heavier dark blue shirts and pants.

Like cattle, each soldier had a brand. Faces partially adorned by bandages; A sling for a lucky-to-have-not-lost-the-arm; another soldier not-so-lucky missing an arm; forearm crutches, underarm crutches; and canes that should only be for the very old. The flow of patients slowed for a couple of minutes while two patients were handed down, babes-in-arms to waiting arms below, and placed into wheelchairs and then rolled into the hospital. And throughout "Careful, careful" was the corporal's reminder. "Careful, careful."

Finally, the bus was emptied; the engine started; the bus exhaled smoke and headed to the garage for oil, gas, and a disinfectant scrubbing until another run to the airport. Left behind was a small group of patients who wore no bandages and no casts, used no crutches, and showed no visible body part wound. They had exited the bus from the side door under the watchful eye of two medics. The soldiers wore the customary patient blue scrubs and white plastic wristbands. To Zack most looked younger than his twenty-two years. The two medics tried to move the patients into a line. They tried, but it wasn't going to happen. A medic in front repeatedly checked a clipboard. Zack knew it immediately: these were soldiers for the psych wards and the medics were psych techs.

"All right, do we, do we have everyone? Do we..." The tech's tone betrayed his own uncertainty to command. "Come on now, I need to know, do we have everyone?" He practically pleaded for an answer and probably would have accepted a "yes" from one of the patients. "I'm asking . . . do we have–?"

"Off! They're off. Everyone's off!" responded the other tech.

"Yeah, but do we have everyone?" The tech said almost whining.

"For Christ's sake, Grey, we counted at the airport!" The other tech shook his head in disgust. And then under his breath but not that under that several patients didn't hear, "I never should have let you take the lead." Then back to loud with, "No one jumped off the fucking bus while it was moving."

"Okay, Krupp, okay. Take it easy," Grey said.

"Damn it," Tech Krupp snapped, "line 'em up and get 'em to the crazy house."

Stepping in and out of line was a wiry little guy. His mouth and body constantly in motion, he stepped out of line, back in line, then out again. His chin raised high he pointed to one patient or another and then turned and gestured to a nonexistent audience and lectured.

"Don't I have rights—I'm a citizen—we all have rights—how about the Bill of Rights—the Constitution—If I were a lawyer I'd file a charge . . ." The patient, name tag Lucas, raised a finger to emphasize a point and went on and on as if he were a lawyer. Getting the patient Lucas to stop talking had been a major problem as far back as elementary school when one teacher resorted to placing masking tape over the boy's mouth.

The two techs continued to push, pull and place the patients but finally, surrender.

"I say fuck it, move them out, let's go!" Krupp took control of the flawed formation.

The patients as if they were one long blue slithering snake followed Tech Krupp as he led them away from the front of the hospital. Suddenly, from the rear of the line the snake shredded a patch of skin; a patient wearing slippers shuffled away from the group. "You, hey you, soldier," Tech Grey implored, "please come back here."

The soldier had the looks for the cover of a teenage fan magazine. Dark hair, cleft chin, and straight polished teeth. His handsome head jerked slightly every few seconds as if on a timer. He shuffled across the grass. Zack hustled after him and fell into a shuffling rhythm next to him. The patient's eyelids appeared to be glued open.

"Hey soldier, where you going?" Zack asked, as they both now headed toward the evergreens at the fence. Zack read the patient's nametag and spoke softly. "Godwin," Zack said. He trusted that the first syllable of the patient's name was pronounced identical to our Supreme Commander's. *Godwin, WIN WITH GOD,* Zack said to himself, *Now there's a can't lose war slogan.*

"There's nothing over there, nowhere to go," Zack said.

Godwin stopped, and wide-eyed, looked to the trees and bushes. Then, with that jerky head movement, he turned and looked at Zack.

"Walk with me," Zack told him. And then almost in a whisper as if speaking to himself, "It's going to be okay." *Is it really?* He thought.

As they returned to the group, Zack saw, standing on the hospital steps, three young Black women as if dressed for the high school prom wearing green satin, with white gloves to their elbows, with hair coifed. It was the R&B group, The Shirelles. With beauty shop hairdos and their ruby lips that highlighted symmetrical smiles, the trio raised their right hands, held a salute, and sang their promise,

> Soldier boy. Oh my little soldier boy.
> I'll be true to you.

Then, salute and song, the Shirelles were gone. Zack thought, *if Godwin could have been a witness to that I know he would have felt better. I feel better.*

Tech Krupp welcomed the patient Godwin back. "Stay in line, asshole."

"Listen up," Tech Krupp said, "we're heading to a different building. Your new home is over the hill." Krupp turned and pointed the direction as he moved out.

The Lawyer Lucas had something to say about that. "Over the hill—over the hill—that's a violation of Army regulations." Lucas pointed an index finger upwards.

Medic and psych tech Zack Tonakis watched as Tech Krupp led the procession away from the main hospital and across a narrow base road. The soldiers headed toward a red brick building partially visible below a tree-lined grassy knoll. Secrets, secrets, the grassy knoll hid secrets.

Building that once housed the psych unit
at Valley Forge Army hospital (2014 photo)

The Bogeyman

The top half of the Dutch door to Ward 2A's Nurses Station was open. In the office, the space on one wall was smothered by a glass and chrome cabinet that contained the bottled magical elixirs to cure or control the soldiers on psych ward 2A. Memos were posted everywhere. The back wall was filled with an erasable chart listing the patients' names from both the Closed and Open Wards in black marker. In the corner a wooden rickety table held numerous folders and a green journal with "Daily Log" written in a black marker on the cover. Directly in front of an office window that looked out to the ward, a gray metal desk and gray swivel chair dominated half the room.

Sergeant McCabe, an Army lifer in his late forties, was a big man, over six feet, broad shoulders, wide neck, wide face with a wide set of uppers and lowers for a wide smile. He looked up from reading Zack's folder and then to Zack's nametag.

"To . . . na...nah, help me out here, Tech."

"Sergeant, it sounds like it looks, Toe-na-kiss."

"What is that, Italian or Greek?"

"Greek, Sergeant."

"You got some college, Greek boy."

"One year, Sergeant."

"So you screwed around and got drafted." Sgt. McCabe opened Tech Turner's folder.

"What are you, Turner? Colored, Negro, or you call yourself Black?"

"Black, sir. Sergeant." Turner answered."

"So you didn't finish high school. Was it trouble?"

"No, Sergeant. I had to help the family. I'm first born."

Sgt. McCabe pauses, nods at Turner, and closes the folder.

"Okay, it's Orientation Time. Now the first thing is call me Sarge. The second thing is I'm not your momma, and I'm not your daddy. But I will do right by you. And maybe some things I say will help you, just maybe. Now look at those soldiers out there."

Zack and Turner looked out the office window in front of the sergeant's desk. On the ward some patients' pace, others are reading, some writing, two patients are working on a jigsaw puzzle, and at a table closest to the office four soldiers are playing cards.

"For some it's hard to see them as soldiers because now they're sick and wearing patient blues. Call them patients or soldiers but don't ever refer to them as crazies."

"Crazies?" Zack and Turner repeated it but seemed confused.

"And you have two primary duties," Sgt. McCabe continued, "your safety and the safety of others. Cause you just never know what one of these soldiers will do. Got it?"

"Yes, Sergeant. I mean Sarge." Both techs responded.

"A soldier may try to hurt you or try to hurt someone else. That could happen. And one will damn sure try to hurt himself. You already know these soldiers have some serious issues. The docs give them labels: Schizophrenics, Manic-depressives. We have a catatonic. And upstairs on 3A a Jesus holds court."

Now Zack and Turner looked really confused.

Sergeant McCabe continued, "Those guys at that table are playing Crazy 8's. You will learn how to play Crazy 8's."

Sgt. McCabe rose from his chair, his white smock was tight across his broad shoulders, the top shrunk from too many visits to the base laundry. He exited the office and the techs followed.

"That closed door at the back of the ward was the TV room. Was. Our new major just closed it after there was a near riot over what program to watch. So no TV. I don't know for how long. I am doing my best to get that room opened."

He points back off the ward across the main corridor.

"That's our open ward where they wait for duty orders or discharge, a Medical or a Failure to Adjust. This spot here between the office and the latrine is a tech's most important position. We call this the Watchtower, the best place to watch for the Bogeyman. For most soldiers, the meds have chased him away. But it's our job to watch for the Bogeyman," he said.

"The Bogeyman."

Rise and Shine

Monday morning in Sioux City, Iowa, Big John Cart drove to the only hill in sight to begin the day as usual at the Hilltop Diner. When he entered and sat at the counter, he removed his cap with the John Deere logo and placed it on the red vinyl stool next to him. Because other customers sat next to each other their caps sat on the countertop. The men's caps displayed a variety of logos, but the men all wore blue jeans or blue coveralls. That's the same color John's son wore, blues, patient blues.

Big John gave the slightest of smiles to acknowledge the nods and hellos of the other regulars. The deep smile lines on his face had not seen much use lately. This morning, he would drink the usual cup of black coffee; no sugar; order two eggs over easy; bacon; and a side of home fries and buttered toast, plenty of toast.

In the diner the father no longer talked about his son, or the war. The regulars knew young John Jr., knew him all his life. Knew he had enlisted and how proud his dad was. But something had changed. The father had stopped bragging about his son. He didn't mention his son, about where he was stationed, or when he was coming home. And no one asked.

• • • • • •

"Why do I need pills? Twice a freaking day. Pills-pills-pills-pills-pills!" Lawyer Lucas ranted then he quieted to a whisper as if he were speaking to himself, "Pills-pills-pills-pills . . . ."

For soldiers on the psychiatric wards, this was a time of new pharmaceuticals and old technology. Lieutenant Emma Hill, a nurse, and the only female assigned to the psychiatric wards, rolled a squeaky-wheeled stainless steel cart next to the door. The cart was filled with the tiniest of paper cups containing pills of various sizes, shapes and colors. The orange one, the time-tested Thorazine; the white one, Valium; the cream-colored, Mellaril; the smallest of the small red one, Prolixin. And the not so tested, swallow this one and let's see the reaction, Stelazine.

Nurse Hill looked the part in her white uniform, white stockings and white shoes of the traditional caretaker. On her collar the star-shined bars that announced her rank of Second Lieutenant. The army brought a lot of nurses into the ranks as second Louie's. Most came because they wanted to help. But as for Nurse Hill, after fifteen years of work in civilian hospitals, one couldn't be sure. There was something about the nurse's mouth and jawline. It was clenched, but not angry, more like disgusted. She was a tough-looking forty-year-old. Her hair was cut not much longer than a recruit's. Her shoulders barely came to the opened section of the Dutch door. Zack thought, *if she were any shorter, she could have been a munchkin from Lollipop Land.*

"This isn't right!" Lawyer Lucas said as he paced at the rear of a long queue that had formed first thing in the morning. "And speaking of rights! Don't we have rights! Rights!" Then back to a whisper, "Rights-rights-rights . . ."

The haphazard line of patients snaked from the office back through the ward and around several tables in the center. Narrow beds lined both sides of the room, each with a blue blanket and its territory marked with a brown metal nightstand. The morning sun lit the ward through the opened windows and thick-wired grids that were screwed into the frame casting crisscrossed shadows across the waxed floor. Patients may open a window but cannot go out a window.

Surprisingly this morning Paranoid Firenza was the first in line. Without hesitation he tossed the pill from the cup into his mouth as if it were candy.

"Pill check. Please open your mouth," Tech Zack asked.

When it was pill popping time on the ward, Zack was always polite when eyeballing the personal space under the patient's tongue. A task made even worse because there were drugs that dried-out a soldier's mouth, as if during the night a spider wove a web from the patient's lower lip to the upper, to the lower, to the upper in a zigzag pattern that stretched but never completely disintegrated as the mouth opened.

"Please open," the tech said again. Paranoid Firenza knew the drill and complied. He opened wide and placed his tongue to the roof of his mouth so Zack could play "I Spy." Firenza passed the inspection, and Zack who had other responsibilities this morning was replaced for pill watch duty by another tech. Returning to his bed Firenza raised his hand covered his mouth and coughed, just once, a sharp burst and the saliva coated pill was in his hand. He quickly tucked it under his pillow. The techs knew you could lead a soldier to pills but you couldn't make them swallow.

"Why are we here? Why pills? Why? Why?" Lawyer Lucas burst forth again. He paced left, then right, and then back to a position behind the others. He got quiet and then loud, his index finger pointed upwards, "Can someone tell me why?"

No one answered, and the assembly line of soldiers moved forward.

"Excuse us, excuse us, coming through." Zack and Tech Turner wheeled a gurney through the pill line. Strapped on the rolling bed was the soldier, Cart, the catatonic. Cart's feet in his cotton slippers hung over the gurney's edge. Some patients watched as they headed up the hallway while others pretended not to even notice.

The patient on the gurney was always expressionless but not always motionless. The soldier Cart would walk with or follow a tech or a patient if given a directional tug or a push in the right direction. Sometimes if nature called, he'd walk alone. You might spot him standing at the far end of the ward and he would move toward the latrine in his slippers slowly sliding his left foot forward, then the right, then the left, making a scrapping sound along the highly glossed floors.

The route through the ward 2A hallway had the trio pass by the utility room with its cleaning supplies and where the always popular doughnuts, juice and coffee were kept. Another room with the towels, blankets and sheets, patient light blue scrubs and heavier dark blue outer wear, and white cotton slippers. On the left were two rooms, closed doors with narrow, clear, thick plastic windows for those outside the room to see in. The Army bureaucracy hadn't yet approved a euphemism for seclusion rooms. Techs used various names: quiet rooms, meditation rooms, contemplate-your-navel rooms, and jerk off rooms. The only furniture was a gray rubber mat. Each room had a window with a view of the same ancient Sycamore tree, a view disrupted by a thick wired grid.

Before they exited the ward, they passed by the last two rooms. On the right was the closed door of the ward psychiatrist, Captain R. Lane, MD. Directly across his room was the always opened because there was no door but there was a sign, Family Room. Sparsely furnished with a long worn green couch, several chairs, coffee table, and a stand for the small television. Thick green drapes that somehow failed to blend with the green couch and substantially blocked the view from the sole window made even more useless by the grid that slashed the horizon.

The techs left behind them the line of soldiers that continued to grow at the pill station: a long line of panic attacks; sleeping disorders; eating disorders; irritable bowel syndromes; severe anxiety reactions; one with lack of impulse control; one sociopath; and two who had attempted suicide. A cup of juice and meds, a cup of juice and meds, one after another, a cup of juice and meds, there seemed to be a pill for everything. But sometimes, as in the catatonic's case, other treatment was ordered.

Zack and Turner wheeled the soldier up the narrow corridor. This morning Cart was headed for his inaugural ECT treatment, one that would be repeated every Monday, Wednesday and Friday for fifteen sessions, or depending on the results, another five to reach the twenty mark. Catatonic Cart had also begun the day with a pill, a valium to relax him. It was the cooperation of the new science of pharmacology with the old. The old was Electroconvulsive therapy; invented by physicians back in the '30s and first tested on a homeless man, a schizophrenic who had no voice in the approval process, the same as soldiers. It was the physician's mistaken belief that epileptics did not suffer from schizophrenia. And by inducing seizures, subsequent convulsions would cure schizophrenia.

Other doctors administered the treatment on sick soldiers in World War II, then others again during the Korean War, and the machine was kept oiled and ready for action during the new war. Doctors who administered the procedure swore by it. But at times it was the patients who swore at them.

"Fuck you!" A patient would curse the doctor. "Fuck all of you!" adding the same instructions for the techs. "Please . . . don't . . . please." A soldier would call out, "Somebody! Anybody!" And then, almost pleading, "Help me." Sometimes a patient would thrash about on the gurney straining at the straps that held him down in the belief that he could, like Frankenstein, snap the straps and save himself from the mad doctor. Zack never ever saw a patient smiling or singing on his way to treatment. Most patients were stoic, asked no questions, and did what they were told. It was still the Army and they were still soldiers. But there were exceptions; escape attempts from the wards were frequent on shock treatment days.

ECT was known to briefly erase the patient's memory, especially the short term. The patient would forget the things that hurt him, the things that put him here. By the time he did remember perhaps the things that brought him here would no longer be an issue. Electro, that's electricity. Convulsive, that's convulsions. "Therapy," Zack liked to proclaim, "was a misnomer, why not just call it shock treatment and get on with it."

Today, as Zack and his partner Turner wheeled the patient Cart up the corridor, the wheels of the gurney on the waxed hardwood floor made a continuous rolling R's sound, a miniature motorbike. The rolling R's took Zack back to that first time.

Zack stood over him. The patient looked up at Zack. The patient was pitifully sad, tear-jerking sad. He didn't speak but his eyes asked "Why?" The soldier had soft cheeks with freckles and buckteeth. He resembled the boy on the TV series; he was the Beaver.

Other techs had warned Zack, "It's not easy, not the first time." They always added, "But you'll get used to it."

Zack looked down at the Beav and he wondered, *Do we get used to everything?*

And the Beav spit in Zack's face. The spit dribbled down Zack's forehead. Just before the saliva reached his eyes, Zack wiped it with his sleeve. Zack felt hated. He was hated. The Beav would forget he spit on Zack.

· · · ·

The techs, Zack and Turner, with their patient entered the ward reserved solely for these weekly rituals. Half a dozen beds lined the right side of the ward. No tables, the center of the ward was open to allow for a wait station for patients on gurneys. A section of the room on the left was separated from the main area by a curtained divider. Behind the divider the techs would tell you, "Was the mad scientist's invention."

The techs guided Cart's gurney behind curtains where fixings were in place for the procedure. Zack moved to a stand at the head of the gurney that held a black box with electrical wires that protruded from two sides. He checked the outlet. The black box was ready. Turner tightened the worn leather straps buckled across Cart's chest and moved to the foot of the gurney where he attached straps around each ankle.

From a tube Zack squeezed gel on his fingers. "You know this stuff is cold," Zack said quietly to Cart, "but only for a minute." It was hard to be certain what Cart knew. The tech smeared the gooey ointment on Cart's temples and attached the electrodes from the black box.

The psychiatrist, Captain Lane, entered quickly and disconcerted as if interrupted from something much more important. His long, white medical smock was buttoned, straining to cover a body that was too wide for the man wearing it. His black tie was askew with an opened Army brown shirt collar allowing the folds of his double chin to spread comfortably. The collar was damp as if his walk from the Closed Ward was a major workout. The psychiatrist moved to the head of the gurney but with a quizzical expression, not someone who would be in charge. Captain Lane was a beginner, new to the profession, new to the Army, and new to the psych wards. Other than his limited training on ECT's in medical school, this was his first solo performance.

"Let's get on with it," the captain said.

Zack placed his hand on Cart's chin and opened the patient's mouth putting the mouthpiece in place. Cart responded by trying to suck air and made a wheezing sound.

"Breath through your nose, through your nose," Zack said, "that's it, breathe, breathe."

Captain Lane adjusted dials on the black box. He glanced at the patient and then moved a switch and delivered an electrical current from the apparatus through the wires to the electrodes on Cart's temples. The electrical current then took a side road from its planned destination and landed in the pain center of Cart's brain.

Cart's head jerked backwards, eyes opening wide as if he were a comic strip character. His frame wrenched and twisted. Suddenly his arms and body shot upward straining the strap that held him. He fell back to the gurney minus a white slipper flung to the ceiling. And Cart was awake. From his nose a burst of mucous joined the saliva that escaped from the sides of his mouthpiece. He wasn't supposed to be awake. The electrical jolt should have initiated the convulsions. Cart wasn't having convulsions. He was a soldier who had just been burned.

Captain Lane was confused. He hit the switch again. Cart stiffened again, and if it were possible for a human to produce the sound of a dying elephant, Cart did just that. "MMMMMFFFFFFFFUUUUUU!"

Captain Lane looked at the patient as if he wasn't following the rules.

"Sir. Sir!" Zack started but stopped. He reminded himself, Lane is a captain, a doctor, a risk to challenge either one. "Sir, he's still conscious. Adjust the voltage, he's hurting." Zack blurted directions as if he were in charge. It was no wonder since during Zack's on-the-job training at Walter Reed he had assisted sometimes with two or more patients for three times a week for any number of sessions and as he admitted, "delivered a hell of a lot of electricity."

"Excuse me, sir," Zack said as if he were asking for permission.

The captain didn't move; Zack did. He nudged the transfixed captain aside. Zack adjusted the voltage and hit the switch. The catatonic's eyes were first to respond, the iris's rolled upwards showing more white than brown, the eyelids fluttered, his body stiffened. One thousand one, one thousand two, he vibrated, one thousand five, he shuddered, one thousand seven, Tech Turner held the ankles, Zack held the soldier's head, one thousand ten, Cart shook and continued to shake, one thousand thirteen, one thousand fourteen . . . Captain Lane stared, stuck in his own catatonic state, one thousand twenty-one. Cart stopped shaking, body limp. His face shiny from drool, his blue collar soaked, darkened from sweat. He was in a deep sleep, exhausted by the dance.

Zack removed the electrodes and the mouthpiece, and with a tissue wiped the gel from the patient's temples. Turner loosened the leather restraints and returned the missing slipper to the patient's foot. They wheeled the soldier Cart from behind the screen. Momentarily, Zack was distracted by music coming from the back of the ward. Tickling the ivories on a honky-tonk piano was the "Fat Man" Domino.

Fats leaned in slightly, and with a mellow delivery, he sang:

Blue Monday, Oh, how I hate Blue Monday.

Gotta work, gotta slave all day."

The techs exited the ward with their patient who was now in an exhausted sleep and behind them they could hear Captain Lane yelling, "Who gave you the right to interfere? Who? Do you hear me! I'm the doctor. I was prepared to make the necessary adjustments . . ."

The techs caught just part of "You insubordinate" reverberating through the corridor as they again rolled gurney and soldier by the MP who gave them a quizzical look.

When Zack and Turner returned to the ward the Lawyer Lucas, manic as usual, last in line, still hadn't taken his meds. He stood at the Nurses office for one last stand.

"Twice a freaking day—Pills—I'm going to be a lawyer—Use the GI bill— Get a law degree—Sue the Army for giving us pills. I want an answer, any answer will do. Why do I need pills?"

Lucas got his answer just as Zack and Turner wheeled the soldier Cart past the office. Nurse Hill handed the future lawyer his pills. "Quit squawking" she said. "Pills help you swallow the crap life hands you."

Valley Forge General Hospital
Neuropsychiatric Unit

DAILY LOG - Ward 2A and 2B
October 16, 1967

DAY SHIFT

Another day - just like the other day.

EVENING SHIFT

The same.

NIGHT SHIFT

Same

Smiling Private Hardy

Private Hardy had a bladder problem. The nineteen-year-old Army recruit had the problem for as long as he could remember. Years ago, his mother had explained it to him using medical terms he didn't understand.

"You have overactive bladder syndrome," she said.

"Why?" the child asked her.

"It's not your fault," she said in a resigned manner. "It was your father's fault."

"Why?"

The young child was confused that it was his father who had done this to him since he couldn't even recall his father's face. The long-gone dad had left when the boy was just two years old. At that age wetting his diaper was not an issue. But now at the age of four the boy knew what his mother knew: he had an "I pee in my pants" problem.

"It was all that yelling" his mother said. "Constantly yelling at me . . . me, your mother. And my precious baby, you heard it all."

"But I don't remem—"

"Yes, but the place that keeps your pee does. And then she returned to using medical terms beyond the child's comprehension, "Your bladder remembers." His mother shut her eyes and seemed to talk to herself, almost a whisper, "As if it wasn't tough enough for us, a Black man and a White woman, and a son that's both."

She focused back on him and leaned closer across the kitchen table. "Your father's inability to control his anger caused stress in your little body and that's why you've been unable to control your urge to urinate, to pee."

The child couldn't recall the yelling but he accepted his mother's explanation that the place that kept his pee, his bladder did remember. The urge to urinate and the inability to control it wasn't an issue for the child so long as the day went well: no crisis to face, no difficult decisions to make, and the access to a bathroom was nearby. By the time the boy was five years old he had learned something on his own. As long as he was involved in an activity, busy, writing the alphabet, drawing pictures, playing with his toy soldiers, or engaged in any physical exercise, playing ball or tag with the neighborhood boys, his urge to "urinate," by now he had learned that was the grown-up word for pee, he could control his problem . . . until the activity ended. But then, look-out, run for the bathroom. And at night if tired from playing all day, other than an occasional "accident," his problem was almost under control. Until it was time to go to kindergarten.

Hardy's mother filled out the school's registration form and was relieved she could finally go to work full-time knowing her son was in a safe place. Of course, in filling out the application form she would have to lie. The first question and the only one in bold type read: **Does your child have any physical issues or medical needs we should be aware of?** Without hesitation she checked **No**.

"Okay," She said to her boy, "now let's get a game plan. Okay?"

"Okay!" He said with enthusiasm. His mother always insisted on a positive approach to his condition, even though her son felt nothing but disappointment.

"First, when you are in class you will have to sit still for long periods of time with little to occupy yourself. That happens in school. Sometimes it's boring. For the next few weeks you will practice just sitting, doing nothing but counting to a hundred and back to zero. This will help you get your mind on something else besides needing to go to the bathroom. And remember to sit up straight in your chair. That will also help keep your mind on other things. You must keep busy."

"Got it!" he said recognizing the keep busy part of the plan.

"Second, I know this will be difficult, but it will be our little secret. Okay?"

"Okay," he said. "A secret." The boy was used to secrets.

His mother reached into a paper bag and removed a blue and white cardboard box. She opened it and handed him a rectangle-shaped thick white napkin. At least, that's what it resembled to him.

"You will put this in your underpants in the morning when you head off to school." She said this matter-of-factly, the same as when she took his temperature and instructed him to put the thermometer under his tongue.

"And if, and I mean if, because I don't think it will happen," that was his positive mother speaking, "your bladder lets loose then this pad will absorb the liquid."

"What's absorb?"

"Soak it up." She snapped. For the briefest moment she closed her eyes, her hands opened outward, her fingers stiffened, and then she exhaled slowly. She continued "This will soak it up."

He wasn't used to his mother being upset with him. He felt like he would cry. "What do, what do I do with it after it's wet?"

"I'm sorry, dear." She returned to her instructional mode. "When you get the regular bathroom break, you take the pad off in a stall where no one can see you. Throw it into the trash can. I will have an extra pad in your lunch box if you need it." Then she reassured him, "but you won't need it."

She returned the napkin to the box. She raised both index fingers and pointed to him across the table. "And now for the most important part of the plan. You know when they flash the bat sign in the night sky to have . . . Ah, what's Batman's real name?"

"Bruce Wayne!"

"Yes, and Bruce Wayne puts on his Batman disguise. You will have your own disguise. And this disguise will rescue you when you're in trouble. Just in case."

"Where is it?" he looked toward the paper bag on the table.

"You'll have it with you always. If others make fun of you, put on your dis . . . guise." she emphasized guise, "right in front of their eyes."

"Hey, mom that rhymes." He loved words and how they sounded.

She placed her hands over her face and in slow motion removed them. Her mouth was opened wide, teeth clenched, and her cheeks raised upward in an exaggerated manner that made her eyes squint. The boy had never ever seen his mother smile this way. Her smile reminded the boy not of Batman but instead the hero's enemy, the Joker.

"Your disguise is your smile," she said. Her face had returned to normal. "When they are being nasty, you will smile." His mom gave him another wide smile but a quick one. "And that tells them that you . . . are . . . not the joke, you are in on the joke." This confused the boy, but he didn't interrupt. "And," she continued, "being embarrassed is not a big deal. You may blush . . . that's what you feel when you have a fever. But that will last just for a minute and go away if you give a big, big smile."

She moved around the table, knelt down, face to face with her son. "Watch me and practice." She smiled and looked like the Joker again.

So he practiced. He practiced so often those few weeks leading up to his foray into the world of preschool his cheeks hurt. So armed with the knowledge to keep his mind occupied, his extra layer of protection, and his secret disguise, he went off to school. And on that first day he had an accident. The class had quiet time, nothing to do but sit. Some napped, heads on their desks. He tried counting to a hundred and back from a hundred. But on the backside at sixty-eight almost to sixty-seven he felt his belly would explode and then he felt warmth in his pants. He immediately put on his disguise and smiled, and no others knew he had a problem.

In the evening the boy devised what he believed was a better plan than his mom's extremely boring instructions of counting and sitting up straight. He would write. Or think of writing. After all, what he loved more than anything were words. He loved words. His mother even bragged to her friends that he had a "marvelous vocabulary." He guessed that meant he knew lots of words. So the rest of the week in class when nothing of interest was going on he wrote words. He copied the words on the bulletin board. He would use what words he knew to describe the scene outside the windows. Then he'd describe the room, the teacher, the other kids. "The trees are very green." "The room is yellow." "The teacher is fat. Not real fat but fat." "Fat, Cat, Hat, Sat." "The teacher is nice." "The kids are nice." "My desk is brown." "Bob is brown." "Bob will be my friend."

When he couldn't use his pencil and paper, he wrote words in his head. And when his mother picked him up after school, he showed her his writing, told her his pants were dry, and she applauded both accomplishments.

But sometimes, the boy learned, something you work so hard to avoid happens. It was an afternoon, outside recess had been vigorous and he was tired. Others around him, including his friend, Bob, had their heads down on desks, naptime, so he joined them. And then, he leaked. Could anything be worse? He had worn khaki pants that day. A wide, dark brown circle spread outward and down to his knees. He jumped up, raised his hand and frantically shouted, "May I go to the boy's room? I have to go to the boy's room!"

It seemed to him that everyone in the room had been waiting for this moment, the moment his mother had warned him about. The other boys, awake now, gathered around and pointed to his pants. And there was laughter. The girls covered their eyes or turned away so as not to look. There were giggles. The boy saw that even his friend Bob laughed. Quickly, he put on his disguise. He smiled.

The teacher told him to go to the boy's room, and he did, and he smiled as he left the room. In the empty hallway he stopped, the floor seemed to move. He looked up, the ceiling spun. He closed his eyes and leaned against the lockers so as not to fall. This was not what his mother had described about being embarrassed. This was something else. This was absolutely the worst feeling. He had nothing to compare it too. Even when he had the flu and threw-up for an entire day and night, he hadn't felt this awful. It would be several years later as he continued to expand his vocabulary that he would find the word that described what he felt—Humiliation.

When he returned to the classroom, he entered smiling.

• • • • •

Hardy's smile was there throughout elementary and secondary school. It was even more pronounced in high school. His light brown complexion and curly, reddish hair served as a backdrop to his wide smile reminiscent of a clown's face on a box that kids threw beanbags at when the carnival was in town. His smile was there for years where anyone who wanted to notice could have.

He smiled when he sat across from the Army recruiter who was a bit confused when the quiet, red-headed young man checked Negro where the enlistment papers asked the "Race" question. He smiled throughout the drills in basic training, and as he stood in line to the mess hall. He smiled as he shined his boots and oiled his rifle in the barracks at night. He was smiling on that stifling summer day when his platoon was out on bivouac.

"Private, who the hell gave you permission to . . . your in ate."

"No one, Sergeant. I had to go real bad."

"Well, that's just too damn bad." The sergeant turned up the volume to include the recruits in Bravo Company in his lesson plan.

"So private, what should we do about it now that you've already . . . your in ated in that dirt."

"I don't know, Sergeant. I . . ."

"Well, I know what to do about it." The sergeant said. "You have to remove that foulness from the earth and return it to where it came."

"Sergeant?" Hardy's smile was joined briefly by slight furrows on his sweat-beaded forehead practically hid under his camouflage helmet.

"Private, you scoop up that puddle of dirt, and put it in your pocket. You will take it to the barracks and dispose of it in the garbage. You will not leave it here to contaminate our forest."

Private Hardy looked to the only spot of ground that wasn't parched.

"You do it now. You obey my order, or you will face the consequences."

"Yes, Sergeant."

Private Hardy knelt to the ground. He scooped handfuls of urine-soaked dirt and deposited the foulness into his pockets. He stood and smiled as the dampness darkened his fatigues.

"Now fall in with the others. And wipe that damn smile off your face."

Hardy joined the line of soldiers but continued to smile. And it was his smile that gained Hardy a new respect from those who were witnesses. For the recruits, the smile represented Hardy's way of giving the finger to the sergeant, something the privates wished they had the nerve to do.

That night in the barracks Private Hardy wrote a poem. He'd been writing poems since before high school, sometimes to control the urge to urinate, and sometimes it helped to put into words how he felt about himself. And he wrote:

> Once I was nothing,
> but then I grew,
> and **grew**,
> and **grew**,
> into nothing.

The delivery of Private Hardy to the psychiatric ward occurred the following day after the noon formation when the sergeant walked the line inspecting the soldiers and saw a widening dark wet spot on Hardy's fatigues at the private's privates, and Hardy was smiling.

Mail Call

"Mail call! Mail call!" The soldier entered the barracks and announced the information as if he were speaking through his nose. He wore a khaki uniform and carried a gray cloth mail bag with stenciled black letters that read "U.S. Army." He walked to the center of the barracks that was home for the medics and other military personnel charged with taking care of the wounded. "Mail call!" He twanged again. "Mail call!"

Soldiers, wearing fatigues, a few in skivvies, hustled to the center of the room confident their names would be called. Other soldiers moved almost leisurely to the action, their body language indicating the likelihood they wouldn't hear their names, but just maybe, maybe, so they came forward anyway. And then there were those soldiers that never came forward. They continued to shine belt buckles and boots as if shined shoes were more important than a letter from home. Don't let them know you care; don't let anyone know.

The mail carrier held a stack of envelopes and read aloud the last names, and sometimes if the envelope was pink, flowery and perfumed, he'd comment, "Ooooooeeeee!" eliciting the laughter he anticipated. Other times he stumbled through names trying his best to make out the handwriting scribbled the same as a doctor's prescription that only a pharmacist could decipher. And sometimes it was the name itself, foreign to his eyes. "Zor . . . Gor . . . Zors—"

"ZZZ . . . gorski! ZZZ . . . gorski!" A soldier, barefooted, barechested, wearing only skivvies, reached-out and snatched the envelope from the hands of the delivery man. "Seven effin letters. How hard can that be?" The soldier clamped the valuable to his hairless chest. Then with his left hand he rattled the dog tags that hung around his neck and walked away muttering "Zgorski. Just like it looks, Zgorski."

That was normal routine for the barracks but not so at that other location on the hospital grounds, the psych building. Mail delivery here had to be done differently. Here were soldiers suffering war-time traumas. The term shell shock wasn't used. Instead other medical terminology identified these patients: manic-depressives; paranoid schizophrenics; catatonics; obsessive-compulsives; and those who joined the army with personality disorders; the Smiths and the Joneses. No Zgorski on the psych ward, instead there were soldiers with the military's most common problem, FTA, a "Failure to Adjust." to Army life.

The accepted procedure for mail delivery, unwritten but common knowledge for the veterans that managed psych wards, was for the mail carrier, usually a psych tech, the one dressed in white smock and white pants, to discreetly locate the patient, usually at his bed or a table, sometimes in the TV room, or on the porch playing ping pong, call him aside and hand the soldier his correspondence. The tech waited patiently to determine whether the delivery was accepted without an unpredictable reaction, like the soldier who immediately tore his letter in half, then in quarters, and stuffed the contents into his mouth. Damage to self was one reason to monitor the delivery.

But so was the possibility of damage to others. The new tech, still in training, brought the letters out from the office and mistakenly mimicked how it was done in the barracks. He called out the names for patients to come forward. No call for a soldier named Sanders. Patient Sanders was of average height and weight, not especially muscular but when fueled by frustration seemed capable of leaping tall buildings. Sanders, whose name wasn't called, and never had been called, and never would be called, swept his average arm across a table and cleared the almost completed 1,000 piece puzzle; grabbed a chair threw it against the wall; grabbed another and threw it across the room and over the heads of patients who hit the floor. Sanders started with a third chair but was subdued by several techs.

"Fuck the mail! And fuck this place. And fuck the Army!" Sanders was held down by the techs until he quieted. He was then escorted to the seclusion room where the ward nurse gave him a shot of Thorazine that helped him sleep, a deep, deep sleep.

Anger acted out by one soldier created the potential for a wildfire, flames from dry kindling, bush to bush, tree to tree. Every patient on the ward felt the heat and sometimes a few exploded in kind and repeated another's profanity. "Yeah, fuck this place; fuck the major; and fuck the Army; fuck this war!" One "fuck" seemed to lead to another "fuck," until even those who had never even thought the word now said "fuck."

Today, in the Nurses Station, Zack removed several envelopes from the Army's gray cloth postal bag, and with the sun's rays streaming through the ward windows, he made the rounds without fanfare. Four soldiers were playing cards at the first table, a table that seemed reserved for a specific card game in particular, Crazy 8's. It wasn't so much as an easy game to learn as the importance placed on the ending of the game. The soldier who got rid of his cards first, who goes out first, is the winner. And getting out of this place was something these soldiers wanted more than money or fame.

They saw Zack coming out of the office with the mail. and ended their card game and headed to their beds. Nothing said . . . just a silent agreement between soldiers that for some of them this was more important than a card game.

Shaky Metz nodded left and right, left, then right as if his head were a metronome; he took an envelope from Zack. It was from his mother.

Jimmy,

It seems weeks and no letters from you. I pray every night that you will be coming home. Are you eating? Are you sleeping? Are you still having crying spells? I'm sure if you were here it would be better for you than being in the hospital. I'll write tomorrow.

Mom and Dad love you

Patient Tabor rose from the floor next to his bed and interrupted his daily sit-ups routine and without a hint of satisfaction or dissatisfaction took the letter Zack extended to him. Tabor opened the drawer of the nightstand and placed the letter on a stack of letters, all unopened.

Lawyer Lucas accepted his letter, an official looking legal-sized envelope with the embossed return address of James C. Lucas, Esq. The soldier took a seat and for one of the few times this morning he quieted. He opened the letter. It began with a demand:

Son,

TAKE YOUR MEDS!

And then for the patient Lucas whatever was written morphed into a chaotic alphabet, dancing on the page while over the ward speaker came his father's voice, gruff, demanding:

"Can't you ever do what you're told. Do you hear me?"

Lucas closed his eyes and responded mouthing the words, "Dad, I hear you."

"Then damnit for once do what you are told. Now take the stand."

Lucas opened his eyes to a ward that had transformed to a courtroom. He sat at the table and listened.

"Ladies and gentlemen of the jury, I am the prosecutor on this case. And I must tell you I am also this young man's father. But I don't want that to prejudice your decision in any way. The evidence will prove beyond a shadow of a doubt that this young man, my son, is guilty. Guilty of failure! He failed to take advantage of the opportunities that I, his father, provided. I have a successful law firm. I had a position for him. I pulled strings, got him into my alma mater. But my boy couldn't cut it. He couldn't take the pressure. He failed. He has always failed."

Lucas rubbed his hands as if he could erase the damned spot. He squirmed.

"Son, didn't I give you a beautiful home? Buy your clothes? Feed you? Pay for your education?"

Lucas looked upwards to the voice coming from the speakers, to his father.

"Well, answer the question."

"Yes," Lucas said softly

"Say it louder so the jury can hear you."

"Yes. Yes, Dad, Yes! Yes! Yes!" Lucas cringed. He hung his head. Others on the ward were distracted by the outburst but just for a moment since it was Lucas.

"And my son, even as a soldier, has been nothing more than mediocre—average—-he's not even an officer. Ladies and gentlemen of the jury I ask you . . . How could a father be proud of a mediocre son? I say, absolutely not."

The speaker turned to static and then quieted. Lucas wiped his wet eyes. He stood and began to pace. Finger raised he made demands that no others paid attention to. "Why are we here? Why? I **will** be a lawyer. I'll **sue** someone, **I'll sue everyone!**"

While Lucas ranted Zack had completed his rounds except for his final delivery. Obsessive Godwin accepted his letter in an envelope that announced upperclass. Godwin opened to its perfect penmanship.

Dear Robert, Jr.

Your father, Robert, Sr. and I plan to visit you as soon as we return from our cruise to the Greek islands. The travel arrangements were made several months prior and we've been so looking forward to it. We are confident that you understand the situation. As soon as we return, we will come spend a bit of time with you.

Now for good news. The club held a successful fundraiser for the township's animal shelter, and your father's foursome won the golf tournament. He was not the only one who claimed a trophy. You will be pleased to learn that my group won the club's bridge tournament.

I've got to run now. We will be in touch.

Fondly,

Mother

With eyes downcast, pensive, Godwin ripped the letter of half-lies in half and placed it on the table. The cruise was real; the tournaments were real; but the son had never asked them to visit and didn't expect it. He went to his nightstand and opened the drawer that revealed every item had a special place. He removed an unopened, pack of filtered cigarettes, Winstons. He returned to the table and took the last cigarette from the pack he had in his shirt pocket, struck a match, took a deep drag of tobacco and set the cigarette in a metal ashtray. From the used pack, he removed a piece of paper. He unfolded the paper, and unfolded, and unfolded again and again until he held a deeply creased, typed sheet of paper. He read, whispering the words, even those that were discolored and spotted that no other eyes could distinguish.

September 21, 1967

Hello my Cupcake, ----Why HAVEN'T YOU WRITTEN???

Well cupcake, I know you don't want anyone to know that's what I call you but you are. this is going to be a boring letter. I'm at work, and nothing exciting has happened. Gads, I'm going crazy honey. Come and take me away from all this. Have you told your parents about us? NO NO don't. they won't believe you could love me. A high school graduate, a clerk-typist. Who can't type so good. They would die. I've never been in a country club. But that'll change one day. You do love me. I know it.

*I do have news!!! I cooked myself dinner last night.
I made Spaghetti and meatbals. It was delicious!!!
After we get married, that's all we will eat.*

*Honey I am getting GROUCHY! BECAUSE YOU HAVEN'T
WRITTN BACK.*

*WhAT no mail boxes in Vitenam.I know I know it's
Vietnam. I'm not stupid. I think you're stupid. Marry
me!!! I'm desparate. No I'M NOT desparate, I'm lonely
and inlove. Oh well, breaks over. Id better learn to
typ before I get fired. AND ID BETTER GET A LETTER
SOON!!! LOVE YOU CUPCAKE.*

Patient Godwin picked up the fresh pack of Winstons and stripped off
the cellophane and meticulously peeled the top foil that contained the
twenty fresh cigarettes. He folded the letter, refolded it again, each fold
accomplished in a precise and almost tender manner until the letter had
returned to its creased state, and then, painstakingly, placed it inside the
cigarette pack and tucked the pack into his shirt pocket. The soldier
returned to the lit cigarette, took a drag, exhaled, and stared into his past.

If Desserts Weren't First

Private Stover was escorted into the psych building by two MP's. The taller of the MP's, not nearly as tall as Stover, led the way while the shorter MP walked behind. Stover was dressed in patient blues, but instead of black dress shoes or cotton slippers he wore black combat boots that made him appear even taller. Inside the entrance a fellow MP at a desk directed them to the nearby office. It was noon on a Monday. The patient Stover figured it was around noon since the trip had begun in the wee hours from Fort Jackson, South Carolina and he was, as he kept telling the MP's, "God awful, awful hungry."

The MP's and Stover made the first right pushing open the thick glass door, one of the few modern additions to this aged building. Stenciled on the glass in black letters was "Administrative Office." Below were the names: "Major Vann" and "Sergeant Helms." The transparent door provided a view of a hallway with several offices and a rear door with an exit sign.

The clerk sat at a desk in a file-clogged office with a door on each side that separated the offices of the major and the sergeant. He entered the time of entrance of the visitors on the sign-in sheet. "SOP is that weapons need to be locked up here unless the major orders differently," the clerk said. "And the major's not here so let's lock 'em up."

"Hey," the shorter of the two MP's nodded to the clerk and then with an upwards glance to Stover who was taking in his surroundings, the new kid in class. The MP had reservations about being disarmed given the size of the delivery. His partner felt no such concern since Stover was limited in movement by the leather restraints on his wrists and ankles. Standard operating procedure prevailed and they entered the sergeant's office and the clerk locked their weapons in the bottom drawer of the desk.

The MP's followed the clerk's directions back through the glass doors and the dimly lit corridor with its sweet smell of recently applied wax on the dark, worn hardwood floors. Several windows along the way interrupted the shadowy corridor with irregular squares of afternoon sunlight. The floors shuddered with each footfall of the soldiers' boots with slight squeals of pain, the floor an old person with arthritic knees. The door stood open to ward 2A and they entered, proceeded down the hallway and arrived at the Nurses Station.

"Got a new patient for you" the less cautious of the MP's said. He handed a manila folder through the opened Dutch door to Sergeant McCabe. The sergeant handed the manila folder back without opening it.

"The doc has to evaluate him before I enter him in our roles. Take him back up the hallway to the door on the right. He's expecting him. And stay with him until the doc says it's okay."

A voice behind Stover said, "I'll be crazy before this detail's over."

"First crew, chow time, line up! Mystery train leaves in five minutes." Tech Krupp, being his usual obnoxious self, made a "Woo, Woo" sound and played conductor as he raised and lowered his hand as if pulling on a cord. "Woo, Woo."

The line immediately formed at the exit of ward 2A. As usual, the Family Room was empty but the office door of the psychiatrist, Captain Lane opened and two MPs excused their way through the line, their detail completed, package delivered. The patients couldn't help but notice the leather restraints, familiar to a few of them, draped over each MP's shoulder as the two left the ward.

Inside the psychiatrist's office, the patient Stover's stomach growled when the call to the mess hall was made. He implored, "Doc, I am God awful hungry."

Meanwhile on the ward Tech Zack Tonakis watched Patient Godwin who was stuck in first gear at his bed. Godwin ran his hands over the blue blanket. He smoothed it. He tucked the corners. He tightened the sides of the blanket. He smoothed it. He tucked the corners. He tightened the sides of the blanket. He took a quarter from a pocket of his patient blues and held it over his bed. He let it fall. He picked it up. He let it fall. He picked it up.

"You are having a bad bed day," Zack said as he approached the patient. "Go to lunch. The bed is made. Perfect. Now lunch!"

Obsessive Godwin shook his head, disappointed. "This quarter will not bounce." He returned the quarter back to his pocket and hustled to join the mess hall line.

The patient Shumacher saw his meticulous neighbor Godwin move toward the chow line so he doubled his efforts to complete his chores.

Shumacher's morning had started with his self-inflicted "barber school dropout" shave. And now, the soldier, half-shaven with blood spots where he had nicked himself, quickly tucked in two sheet corners on his bed, covered the sheets with a rumpled blue blanket that left two ends touching the floor. He shook a pillow and tossed it near the head of the bed, missed, and it fell to the floor. He took off quickly for his favorite line of the day.

"Whoa there, Shumacher, hold on a second." Zack stopped him. "Let me help you out here." The soldier Shumacher broke out in a sweat. When he was anxious Shumacher sweat. He sweat at other times, as well. For him, walks to or from the mess hall were physically an uphill climb, and he'd sweat. It wasn't that the soldier had always been out of shape. During basic training that famous line "The Army will whip you into shape" was true for Shumacher. It was only after basic when he was in advanced training and destined for Vietnam that he ate his way to obesity. It was familiar territory for this soldier returning him to his earlier ways and days of childhood. The Army decided a trip to the psych wards could curtail the soldier's appetite.

Zack rebuttoned Shumacher's misbuttoned shirt made difficult because of the patient constantly wiping the perspiration from his forehead with his sleeve. The tech tied the patient's scuffed shoes. The soldier wasn't wearing socks. Shumacher anxiously watched the mess hall entourage as more patients lined up. Shoes tied, Shumacher, his pants barely hanging on his big butt, broke into a trot.

Tech Krupp was having the usual get-the-patients-in-some-semblance-of-a-line experience. "Hey, Grey! Grey! Get that catatonic moving in the right direction." Krupp called out the instruction to Tech Grey who was the designated bring-up-the-rear for this afternoon's walk to the mess hall. Obsessive Godwin responded before Tech Grey, and he turned the catatonic Cart in the right direction. Tech Grey was usually late in responding to anything. If it wasn't the Army one could wonder how he had passed the training requirements to get this military occupation. Tech Grey did follow directions but had no idea what the word initiative meant.

"Let's go. Stay in line. No talking. And I do mean no talking in the corridors at the main hospital." Krupp, no longer a train conductor was now the wagon master. He waved his arm overhead and motioned for the wagon train to move forward. "Move out! Now!"

The phone rang in the Nurses Station.

"Yes sir," Sergeant McCabe responded military style. "Right now, sir." He stepped from the office and located Zack.

"Hey Tonakis, Greek boy, pick up the new patient from doc's office and take him to mess. Doc said he's not a problem, but you stay one-on-one."

Zack hustled to Dr. Lane's office and knocked. The door opened. Zack's eyes scanned upwards. He read the nametag. Stover looked down at Zack and with a wide grin surrounded by a fresh case of acne said, "Man let's go eat! I am God awful hungry."

The soldier's patient blues didn't fit. Stover's shirtsleeves didn't reach his protruding wrists; his pant legs ended well above his ankles and exposed what Zack estimated were size twelve boots. The two of them traveled the corridor and Stover gave the MP at the door a half salute and a "See you later, Alligator!"

Outside Stover looked to the sky raised his arms high over his head and took in as much sun and breeze as he could get hold of. This added additional spring to his stride that challenged Zack to keep up. Stover was that overgrown gawky kid at school recess.

"Wow, look at that soldier out there!" Stover almost shouted. In the ballfield, a patient pushed a whirring mower. "I love cutting grass. Grass smells the same here as it does back in . . ." He looked upwards and pointed both index fingers to the sky, "West by God Virginia!"

They walked up the tree-lined sidewalk to the top of the knoll when Stover stopped abruptly. "You know what today is?" Stover asked looking down at Zack.

"Today?"

"My birthday." Stover smiled broadly.

"Okay, happy birthday," Zack responded shaking his head. "Let's keep going."

"Bet you can't guess how old I am."

"Okay, tell me, but keep walking."

"Can't tell you." Stover said and made a motion that his lips were sealed. He resumed his stride and Zack quickened his pace to stay by the patient's side. It was as if Stover had no need for Zack to lead, he could smell the trail to the mess hall. At the crosswalk to the main hospital stood a psych patient from the Open Ward 2B. He held a wide bristled paint brush. Next to him a soldier with two yellow corporal stripes on his green fatigues waited as the two passed. He held a bucket of white paint.

Zack was the tech who had assigned this Open Ward patient to base maintenance. These soldiers were limited to painting, cutting grass and washing Army vehicles. Carpentry or electrical work was for regular soldiers, not those on psych wards. According to the psychiatrists the half day work assignments were therapeutic. More realistically it helped keep the soldiers from getting into trouble before their orders came through.

"Hey, soldier, how's it going?" Zack couldn't think of this new patient's name.

"Fuck you. How do you think it's going?" The patient named Leaverton shot back.

Zack and his assignment, Stover, entered the side door of the main hospital, the route the psych patients walked for breakfast, lunch and dinner. Immediately to the left was the hospital lobby. New arrivals of the physically wounded soldiers and any civilian visitors entered through the lobby's white double doors at the front of the hospital. There they were greeted by WACS who checked the sheets and instructed the medics as to what rooms to deliver the soldiers. Medics and patients would then enter the main corridor that snaked through the hospital. A sign overhead gave directions to ward locations: room numbers, the pharmacy, the mess hall, the laundromat, and the barracks.

Different voices spilled out from the lobby to the corridor as a WAC searched for the needle-in-the-haystack for the frustrated visitors. "What room did you say?" "How do we get there?" "Patience? Patience!? This is my son we're talking about here!"

The corridor was a rush of doctors, nurses and medics who cut across Zack and Stover's path from one side of the wards to the other. Voices in the corridor sounded like changing stations on the radio. "Did you get the antibiotics from the pharmacy?" "What time is the game Sunday?" "Have you checked on the amputee on ten?" "What about a drink later at the club?" "Medic, clean up the mess at the back bed on eight. It stinks back there."

Patient Stover's persistent pace narrowed the gap and Zack and his patient joined the rear of Tech Krupp's group that had slowed to comment on another soldier's handiwork. A soldier in fatigues held a can of paint in one hand and a yellowed brush in the other. The painter stepped back and cocked his head and examined what he had already accomplished. The Army usually painted most things green or brown, but this was a hospital and yellow projected optimism and cheerfulness. There was a drawback. On yellow walls a single coat of yellow paint wasn't going to hide the black letters **FTA** that had been haphazardly stamped on the wall. The letters, approximately one inch high, waited for the second coat to complete the task.

For the soldiers on the psych wards FTA had two meanings: the first, A Failure to Adjust, was grounds for being sent to the wards and for discharge from the Army. The second meaning of FTA was known by almost all soldiers: Fuck the Army. For some soldiers the stamper was a strange sort of hero.

The patients encountered another soldier who had ascended a ladder and carried a bucket and brush to reach black-marked graffiti: **Make Love Not War.** This was also accompanied by the smaller stamped **FTA**, as if it were the artist's signature. Doctors, nurses, and medics, everyone that walked the corridor, except for Catatonic Cart, looked upwards.

"How about Have sex and Not war?" Joker Berkowski laughed at his own joke.

"Someone's been busy," Paranoid Firenza said as he eyeballed the message and everyone else who passed him in the corridor.

"Yeah, well I smell court martial for a loser," smelled Tech Krupp.

"This is America. This is free speech." Lawyer Lucas began his daily lecture. "This is a protected act in the Constitution of the—"

"Hey motormouth." Tech Krupp turned back and motioned to his crotch, "I got your freedom of choice between my legs. Knock it off."

In the corridor a contingent of officers and civilians were coming in their direction. The group acted as if they were tourists taking in an art gallery. The tour leader was the commander of the base hospital. The tour group came to a stop and gathered around two patients who had posted themselves at the entrance of a ward. One leaned against the wall; the other slouched in a wheelchair. They were smokers, not sentries. It was an Army regulation, "No smoking on the wards." The soldier in the wheelchair was missing a lower part of his right leg. The other patient had both legs, but the right leg no longer performed to Army specifications. He stood with the help of a forearm crutch. They flicked ashes from donated filtered cigarettes into a tall, round, sand-filled ashtray. The tour group closed in on the smokers.

Techs and patients from 2A, except for Zack and Stover, managed to work their way through the group before the corridor was blocked by bodies. Forced to wait as the other patients continued ahead the two settled in as part of the audience. The commander addressed the patients without waiting for a salute that may or may not arrive. "Boys, the congressman wants to know how we're treating everyone. Here's a chance to complain about the food." The tour group nodded and chuckled at the commander's sense of humor. A young second lieutenant at the commander's shoulder laughed out loud. The patients showed little interest and sucked in as much nicotine as their lungs would allow.

The center of attention shifted from the commander to a civilian, a much older man, retirement age with wrinkled face and wrinkled trousers, a loosely knotted striped tie, and an opened-collar white shirt with rolled-up sleeves. A younger man wearing a light blue blazer carried the older man's dark blue suit coat. Zack noted that there were a couple of photographers, one civilian and one Army, and two reporters with notepads, one civilian and one Army.

The rolled-up-shirtsleeves congressman got to work quickly, mixing an ad lib response with a scripted line. "These aren't boys, colonel. They're men who've proven themselves in battle. Heroes." The "heroes" was definitely from a script. The congressman spoke in a deliberate speechifying tone. There were affirmative nods from the visitors but nothing from the patients. For the wounded soldiers it was watching a TV show that held little interest for them, and these visitors were just actors in the series. The TV just happened to be tuned to this channel.

"As your representative in Congress," the man spoke as if he were on the floor of Congress, "you know you can call on me if there is anything you or your families may need." His promise projected through the long corridor.

The wheelchair patient extinguished his smoke, but before his hand even left the rim of the ashtray, the congressman held it in a firm grasp. The politician vigorously shook the patient's hand and turned and profiled for the photographers. The camera flashed.

"Any snafus on benefits, I can cut through the red tape for you." The congressman froze his vote-getting smile. The camera flashed again.

"Now you tell your parents and friends I'll be there for you."

The politician moved to the other patient, extended his hand, but there was no handshake. The patient's right hand held a cigarette that he would rather have burn his fingers than surrender it to the grasp of the vote seeker. His left hand tightly clutched the crutch that held him upright. Undeterred, the congressman placed his hand on the patient's shoulder and smiled for the camera as the photographers captured the congressman's posturing.

As the cameras flashed, the civilian reporter turned and looked at Zack. Zack thought the reporter looked almost embarrassed as he turned back and continued to write in a notebook. Tomorrow's local newspaper would be filled with the congressman's words such as "heroes," "must honor the sacrifice," "We have to stop the communists before . . ."

"Excuse us, excuse us." Zack politely moved a gawking patient Stover through the crowd. The congressman's baritone followed them. "America won't forget your sacrifice. The veterans of this war are going to get the best medical treatment that can be provided." The congressman's promises "This nation will always" faded and were replaced by a strange sound from the very last ward on the corridor. A soldier sat next to a bed, his neck wrapped in white gauze except for the dime-sized metal opening below his Adam's apple. The soldier's chest rose as the hole sucked air inward: Wheeezzz. And then like a practical jokester's deflated puffy cushion the hole exhaled, Wheeezzz. Zack took a deep breath as if that would somehow help the soldier get the air he needed.

At the mess hall entrance a crowd had gathered. Two very confused MPs stood between two boisterous groups of soldiers. There were patients in their blues while others wore fatigues or khaki uniforms. A soldier in fatigues ascended a ladder towards a symbol painted on the ceiling.

PEACE

The symbol, a circle, although a bit irregular with three lines interjected, was easily recognized. The word Peace next to the circle as if the artist wanted to make certain everyone knew it was the symbol of the anti-war movement.

"Get rid of that shit!" a soldier in uniform yelled.

"Leave it up!" A patient in blue yelled.

"Bullshit!" A uniform yelled.

"Leave it!"

"Chicken-shit protest, fucking Hippies!" the yes-paint-over-it group's position plainly stated.

An order in the Army is not to be questioned unless the order violates a much higher moral authority. For some soldiers the peace message was a moral override. "Leave it up! Leave it up!"

The psych patients led by Tech Krupp worked their way through the unorganized noisy debate and entered the mess hall. Lawyer Lucas paid tribute to both groups as he passed by. "Excellent! Excellent! Freedom of Assembly and Freedom of Speech what's more American than that? What's more American than that? Excellent, excellent . . ."

Pick up a food tray and life becomes a series of choices between sight and smell, a test of sanity for Ward 2A that began in the morning and continued at lunch and dinner. It was about choices. For them breakfast had gone fairly well. Choices: eggs scrambled or sunny side. Choices: bacon or sausage. Choices: pancakes or waffles. Choices: Oatmeal or cereal. Choices: Grits or hash browns. Choose, choose, come on, soldiers are waiting. Choices: grapefruit or orange. Pick-a-little-talk-a-little-pick-a-little-talk-a-little. To pass the sanity test several psych ward soldiers watched and mimicked others. Take a fork, take a spoon, take a knife. Move along. Choices. Ice water for the thirsty, milk for the health minded, iced tea for the sweet tooth.

But this was lunchtime. And lunchtime in the army meant the desserts came first. Choices: Pick a dessert: Cherry, blueberry, or peach pie, or perhaps chocolate cake with vanilla icing, or yellow cake with chocolate icing? And farther down the line, choices: Baked chicken or meatloaf; baked potato or mashed potatoes; mushed creamed corn; overcooked limp green beans; apple sauce; and don't forget the gravy, no choice there, always the gravy.

This afternoon, as usual, Tech Krupp, led the patients with trays filled to one of the few empty tables. They were picnic tables painted a cheerful sky blue, as if this were a summer lodge and the patients were campers. They stood for a moment and contemplated a message in black marker scrawled across the table's surface. **Does anyone know what's going on?**

Still to complete the food circuit was Obsessive Godwin who advised Catatonic Cart on what nourishment to select. At the rear of the line the boy-giant Stover picked up his tray. Zack followed. At the glass sky scrapper of desserts Stover reached in and selected one, two, then three pieces of cherry pie and then reached for a fourth.

"Stover, easy on the pies," Zack said with authority. "Later you can—"

Stover turned quickly from the pies and glared down at Zack. If looks could, Stover's would have. Zack shrugged. His look said Stover could have as many damn pies as he wanted. The patient reached for additional cherry pies. Behind Zack other soldiers in line chuckled and enjoyed the show. Stover's sweet tooth was contagious. Zack took a pie: blueberry. They were out of cherry.

The two continued down the line and there, dolling out the chow, her nametag askew on her gravy-stained white outfit was the civilian, Shirley. Short Shirley with the round flushed face, pursed mouth, forehead beaded with sweat, hair in a tight bun and net. Shirley who reminded soldiers of all the Shirley's that had served up cafeteria food throughout their school years.

"Son," Shirley paused and with the back of her hand wiped away sweat that had worked a glistened trail from her forehead to the tip of her nose. "What will it be? Meatloaf or chicken?" She looked at Stover's tray. She leaned forward on the counter on miniature hands that didn't seem capable of holding her heavy upper body. Surplus skin hung under her arms and jiggled. Her prodigious breasts strained trying to pop buttons and escape. She nodded once, twice, again, and again, four, five, six, an adding machine, her head registered the number of pies on Stover's tray. She looked up at the soldier and launched into a high-pitched scold. "Young man! You will put those pies back! You take one pie like any normal pers—"

Stover's left hand flashed. He grabbed Shirley at the back of her head and pulled her forward to meet his ascending right hand that held a cherry pie. Flash and smash.

Shirley said, "Aaaauuughhhh!"

Zack grabbed Stover's right arm and held on as the patient flung him in whatever direction he chose to fling. Other soldiers in line reached for the same arm that Zack held on to. Someone in the mess hall yelled "Food Fight!" at the same time the two MP's joined the fray. Stover was wrestled to the floor where the gang of them slipped and slid and rolled around in cherry syrup. The MPs finally flipped the patient onto his stomach and Stover suddenly stopped resisting.

"I give up," he said calmly. He smiled. "You win." The cheerful patient Stover was back. It had been as if another Stover had taken over briefly, a rabid don't-tell-me-what-to-do-or-I-will-bite-your-face-off Stover. And now that dog was gone.

MPs take few suggestions other than from other MPs but when Zack said, "Let's get him back to the psych wards." They mistakenly agreed, saving Stover a trip to the stockade. Zack again tried to look in charge as they hustled their way through the corridors but this time with rear guard accompaniment. The MPs directly behind them muttered something about "Messed-up uniforms" and "Mess you up." But Stover was back to being the gawking teenager taking everything in except what the MPs were saying. He didn't have a care in the world.

Patients in the corridor watched as they walked by in cherry-stained uniforms. No jokes, no comments. The red of the stained uniforms was familiar.

The four of them crossed the road to the psych building and delivered Stover directly into a Ward 2A's seclusion room. Stover entered peacefully as if this was another place to explore. Before Zack could close and lock the door, an MP blurted "Catch you outside, you'd better look out." Stover grinned and went to look out the grated window. Zack headed to the office to report the incident to the sergeant.

Back at the mess hall the Ward 2A patients along with the rest of the soldiers had returned attention to their meals. Joker Berkowski at the opposite end from Tech Krupp initiated the conversation. He tapped the table's graffiti. "Hey Krupp, do you really know what's going on?"

"Protest is bullshit, that's what's going on," Krupp said. "Bullshit protest." He scowled across to Berkowski. "I know one other thing. It would have been nice if those MP's had your ass on the floor."

"I know what's going on," Paranoid Firenza said. "They're trying to kill me. That's what's going on,"

"What's on my plate? Under this gravy?" Obsessive Godwin moved the conversation to a more agreeable topic, the non-agreeable food.

"On my plate, same thing, Que ' Que ' " Patient Perez said.

"It's some kind of gravy," Slob Shumacher suggested. He spooned mashed potatoes into his mouth and some kind of gravy rolled down his chin.

"What if they don't want us to know what's underneath?" Paranoid Firenza cautiously probed into the potatoes and gravy with his fork as if he might touch a trip-wire.

"Hey, lawyer," Tech Krupp said, "What if we locked up the protesters until the war was over? Is that in the Constitution?"

"The Constitution guarantees every citizen the right to . . ." Lucas chewed the words through a mouthful of food.

"Here we go; got him started." Krupp was satisfied.

"Why protest the war." Obsessive Godwin said. "That's yesterday for us." Godwin rotated his plate to eat the mashed potatoes, all of the potatoes. Next on the plate were the green beans. He would eat all the green beans before rotating the plate to eat whatever food portion came next. Again, rotating to the right, never skipping by a portion even if it was not to his liking. This just seemed more orderly, finish one thing on his plate before moving on to another. "I'm not worried about this war," Godwin said and rotated his plate to the green beans, "I'm worried about the next war, going home."

"Gentlemen." Joker Berkowski stood and held his plate outwards. "The answer is to protest what affects us today, not yesterday and not tomorrow."

"Yeah, getting your ass out of this nuthouse on to a civilian one," Tech Krupp said.

"The answer my friends," Joker Berkowski announced as he used the cartoon voice of Foghorn Leghorn, an exaggerated southern voice that sounded as if he were speaking through a megaphone, "And I do call you my friends, the answer is not blowing in the wind. The answer is on our plate. It covers whatever they feed us. Be it, chicken!" He punched out the word **"chicken!"** then modulated lower for "covered with gravy." Then louder, **"meatloaf!"** lower again, "covered with gravy." **"Potatoes! with gravy." "Gravy and more gravy!"**

The mess hall of patients, sane and insane, lifers and short-timers, medics and techs, and those who served the food that was covered with gravy stopped feeding and eating as Berkowski began to chant: **"Save me from the gravy! Save me from the gravy! Save me from the gravy! Save me from the gravy!"**

"Ffffrom the gravy." Shaky Metz was the first to join in.

"Save me from the gravy! Save me from the gravy!" Berkowski continued in a rhythmic pace. The patients of 2A joined the protest. "Save me from the gravy!" Voices: high, low and in-between. "Save me from the gravy!" The chant by Berkowski and the soldiers of 2A was contagious and even the catatonic Cart nodded his head. The psych techs and everyone else in the mess hall watched as the enthusiasm of the patients rocked their table like a séance.

Meanwhile at the front side of the hospital in a second floor office, in his personal bathroom, the base commander lifted the seat of the commode, unzipped his fly and reached for his—This is my weapon this is my gun. Satisfied that he was hitting what he aimed for the commander noted a message at eye level: **I M C N U R P N FTA**. The colonel peed on his shoe.

In the mess hall, Berkowski led the sellout crowd as the entire audience, sane, insane and in-between, picked up the chant, "Save me from the gravy! Save me from the gravy!" The chant grew louder. Dishes shook on the tables. Pots and pans rattled in the kitchen.

"Save me from the gravy!"

Bible Skinner bowed his head, "Lord, please save these men—"

"Save me from the gravy!"

"and send them home—"

"Save me from the gravy!"

"safely and—"
"Save me from the gravy!"
"save them from the gravy. Amen."
And all of this would not have happened if the desserts weren't first.

Once was the main hospital for physically wounded soldiers.
(2014 photo)

Valley Forge General Hospital
Neuropsychiatric Unit

DAILY LOG - Ward 2A and 2B
October 24, 1967

DAY SHIFT

Another day - just like the other day.

EVENING SHIFT

The same.

NIGHT SHIFT

Same

Redeemed — A One Act Play

Obsessive Godwin's Family

MOTHER: Women in her early forties.

FATHER: Man in his early fifties, graying at the temples.

SON: Teenager

A kitchen, modern, upscale. Mother is well dressed, every hair in place, as if she visited a salon that day. She wears a colorful apron. She stirs a pot on the stove with a wooden spoon. The father wears a white shirt, loosened dark red silk tie, expensive dress pants and shoes. He sits at the table, legs crossed, sipping a martini as he reads the Wall Street Journal. The teenage boy wears gray slacks, sleeves rolled-up on his white shirt, and sits on a couch reading a hardcover book.

Doorbell chimes.

(The father ignores it. The mother looks back at him, frustrated. She places the spoon in a holder, wipes hands on her apron, and leaves the room. The father and son can hear the mother as she opens the front door.

MOTHER. (Politely.) Oh, there are two of you. Yes, may I help you?
(Pause)

MOTHER. The church of the what?
(Shorter pause)

No, I have no time now. (Very frustrated.) Pamphlet? No, please, I don't want your literature. Must you come at dinnertime? It's dinnertime! (She closes door abruptly and returns to the stove. She mutters and stirs the pot vigorously.)

How offensive; what gall—

FATHER. Honey, weren't you a bit harsh with them? They're just doing what their religious beliefs require. It's the same as a job. It's not their fault that—

MOTHER. (Mutters.) Not their fault? No, they have no responsibility; it's no one's fault. (She turns from the stove. She holds the spoon that drips gravy.) I expect that's what you want. You want me to say it's not your fault. No, not your fault . . . How could you? How could you? She's got to be twenty years younger than you.

FATHER. Hon—

MOTHER. Don't you say Hon to me.
    (She bites off every word as she walks towards him and uses the spoon to emphasize each word.)

MOTHER. Don't. You. Ever. Say. Hon. To. Me.
    (The gravy flies off the spoon and hits him in the face and onto his white shirt.)

MOTHER. I want you out of here—Out! Tonight—Go to a hotel. Go to one where you slept with her. Out now!
    (The father rises slowly and takes his monogrammed handkerchief from his pocket and wipes gravy from his face. He leaves the room. She returns to the stove and stirs the pot.)

Epilogue
It was as if the boy wasn't there, but he watched it all. The father never left the house, and the mother stayed. She needed the security. His father needed the image of normalcy. A restructuring of the corporation was agreed on and an unwritten parental long-term contract was negotiated. The young boy didn't experience what other children of divorce had. Godwin, Jr. never heard his parents argue again. No raised voices, never even a disagreement. For the parents, a successful arrangement.

The Inspection

"One and ah-two and ah-three and ah-four-ah, one and ah-get in sync and ah-three and four-ah. . ." The soldier counted cadence with a southern drawl reinforcing the patient's belief that all drill instructors were from the south. "One and ah-two and ah-three and ah-four-ah and ah-one and ah-two and a . . ."

The psychiatric patients of Closed Wards 2A and 3A filled the activities room as they did every morning following breakfast at the mess hall. Daily sessions of jumping jacks, deep knee bends, pushups and other exercises were meant to stave-off atrophy. Their keepers, the psych techs, liked to say that the Army's goal for the patients was to ensure "a healthy body with a crazy mind."

"One and ah-two and ah-three and ah-four-ah . . ."

Those patients following or trying to follow the instructor's count stood in their usual uneven lines. For the patients that wore cotton slippers the jumping jacks exercise provided a special challenge. The instructor facing them was tanned, a burned-in-forever-look that contrasted with his crisp white T-shirt tucked into his fatigue pants, tucked into his laced-to-the-top buffed combat boots. As the muscled GI jumped, his untucked metal dog tags jangled around his neck. His way of reminding these soldiers that he'd been to battle.

The patients stood too close to each other even though the room offered ample space. Toes were stepped on and patients accidentally pushed each other left and right, or unintentionally slapped a face or head of a neighbor when hands extended into the other's territory.

Bible Skinner, Good Book tucked into his pants, raised his hands upward. His arms looked like reeds in a pond blown by a confused wind. This was an improvement from the previous month when he held the Bible and clapped his hands at the top of the jump resembling a bible-thumping preacher.

Immediately behind and towering over Skinner was Cherry Pie Stover. Sweat on his forehead rolled down his elongated face. His six-foot-four frame soared high. He clapped his hands rhythmically with the instructor's cadence reminiscent of a percussionist in the last row of an orchestra striking symbols. With each clap he exhaled a mission accomplished "Ah-yes-ah."

Patient Stover was enthusiastic about everything. Other than his first day explosion at the mess hall the gangly teenager seemed happy to be here. Even when taking his meds in the morning he smiled as if he were a playful puppy. He would sing out, "Goood Morning, Nurse Hill." He'd take the paper cup that held a pill and another cup with juice; pop the pill into his mouth and swallow with the juice chaser. He'd drop the paper cups into a trash can and return to the ward but not before an exaggerated "Thank Yooouuu" to Nurse Hill. The pill assisted Cherry Pie Stover in dealing with his explosive anger. The leather ankle and wrist restraints were no longer needed. For now, the pill worked.

Stover's exclamations didn't seem to interfere with his neighbor the Puerto Rican, Perez. "Uno, dos, tres, quatro, uno, dos, tres, quarto," Perez counted along with the drill instructor's Alabama English. His Spanish translation was of course for the benefit of his compatriot Vasquez who no longer could or would count to ten in English.

Joker Berkowski in the back row moved his arms over his bald dome to the count of the instructor and nothing more. The Joker seemed content to play a minor role in this morning's calisthenics, a fortunate situation for the drill instructor and the techs.

Almost forgotten by the others, a few steps behind the rest of the group was Firenza. His dark brown eyes peered suspiciously from under black caterpillar eyebrows making certain no others had taken up a position behind him. "Do you smell something?" Firenza directed his question to those closest. "I smell something." A few patients looked back expecting to see what it was the paranoid soldier smelled. "Something in the chow this morning? Huh? A chemical?" As he jumped, he brought his right hand to his nose and sniffed. "Do you smell me?" He asked even louder. He undid several buttons of his shirt, tucked his chin and brought his nose under the garment. He took a whiff, re-buttoned his shirt and whispered to himself, "I smell me."

The closest patient, Grier, turned back toward Firenza but not looking directly at him instead somewhere over his shoulder mumbled words of encouragement. "Gonbeawrigh." Seldom could Firenza nor anyone else make out what Mumbling Grier said.

Voices that weren't counting were complaining. "I didn't get to sleep last night, I'm exhausted." "I hate this." "The sarge said I didn't have to exercise today, I'm sick." "I hurt myself, I pulled a muscle."

"The fucking 'Cong didn't kill us but you will." Even after his morning meds Lawyer Lucas was in a hyper state, veins pulsing energy over his bony frame. And in the same manner as an attorney he presented his complaints to the court. "Where does the Army get the right to make patients exercise? We're not on active duty." He pointed his finger upwards and shook it to release more electricity into the room. "This is cruel and unreasonable punishment—that's the legal term—it's daily harassment. And when's the major going to let us use our ballfield? We want to play ball!" The last part of the rant by the ward ombudsman drew a boisterous response from the jury. "Right-on!" "Tell it like it is." "Play ball!" "Si! Si!"

The drill instructor stopped. He waited with a look of disgust. He thought of the complainers as losers, selected by the Army to go to war and then, unsatisfied with the results, the Army shipped them here.

• • • • •

The marching band of buses, buses, buses sat empty on an airport tarmac close behind a military cargo plane. Several brown military vans and dark green ambulances also stood in formation. The vehicles could have used the humongous plane as a garage. A delegation of medics, including psych techs, Zack Tonakis and Robert Turner, along with other soldiers in fatigues gathered outside of the vehicles. Some smoked Winstons or Marlboros. And mentholated Newports were popular having replaced the previous war's Pall Malls, Camels, and the "Oh, so lucky you, Lucky Strikes." Most soldiers stood silently while a few tried to hold conversations that were impossible to hear over the roar of the plane's engines.

A safe distance from the plane behind a metal gate a number of families also waited. A wife held a baby; a teenage daughter held a bouquet of flowers; a small boy waved a small Flag; and anxious parents waved. The side door of the plane opened, stairs dropped, and several officers descended. An officer stopped halfway on the steps, waved to his family, then continued to the foot of the stairs where he was greeted by salutes and handshakes from fellow officers. These returning soldiers were safe and well. Tears and cheers, tears and cheers.

At the rear of the cargo plane, the wait was over. The obese belly of the plane yawned and lowered its tongue to the tarmac. The tongue became a ramp, a ramp that one month ago served as the entrance for jeeps, trucks, supplies, and all things imaginable or unimaginable used for war. But now it was soldiers who exited the bowels of the plane.

These soldiers didn't charge gung-ho down the ramp as if attacking an enemy's beachhead. They came out tentative, unsure of their footing on the down slope. A number of the wounded wore fatigues, but most wore patient blues, the uniform of the wounded. The sun was blinding. They raised hands over eyes as a shield and to get their bearings. "Where am I?" "Are we home yet?" "What airport is this?" "Damn, why don't they shut those engines off?" Questions, unheard and unanswered.

The soldiers' bodies had been accessorized: slings for arms, crutches for legs, tape and gauze over eyes. A familiar sight for those medics waiting. The soldiers helped their brothers. One served as the eyes for another. One lost his balance, but another grabbed his elbow and walked with him. Some disoriented. Some resigned. Another airport, another stop, another somewhere, any place but back there.

As the patients exited the plane, Zack and Turner and other medics with clipboards greeted them. They checked nametags and ID bracelets and directed the patients to the appropriate vehicle. This would be the last time the mentally wounded and the physically wounded would sit side-by-side. Other medics rushed into the grotto of the plane. Their eyes adjusted to the darkness. Stretchers lined the walls of the plane, attached like bunk beds in a ship, two and three levels high on each side of the plane's cavernous interior. Ladders were set between the rows. The plane was a library of biographies.

Medics climbed to the stretchers and carefully lowered patients. They carried them from the dark to the light and loaded them into military busses and on to the specially rigged supports for the winding road trip to the hospital. A bus departed. A bus took its place. Pickup and delivery was an efficient operation made so much easier by repetition.

• • • •

"Ah-one and ah-two and ah-call it out, let's hear it." The drill instructor counted. Protest over, the patients had returned to the rhythm of the exercise. "You, soldier, and ah-two, and ah-three, come on up here and lead the group. Show'em how it's done." The instructor motioned to a patient in the front row.

"and ah-four . . ." the patients continued the count.

Patient Tabor of the sculpted body was a drill instructor's dream. The D.I. would call out the drill and he'd execute, equal to any instructor. Tabor had spent a major part of hospitalization doing sit-ups and pushups. Pushups his favorite. He'd get down and count-out pushups whenever he had to stand in line for any length of time, and in the 'hurry-up-and-wait' Army that was often. Pushups Tabor moved to the front and commenced to perform perfect jumping jacks.

"I'll yell the cadence and you do the drill," the instructor said. "And ah-one and ah-two and ah-three and ah . . ."

Morning exercises were something soldier Tabor had been raised on.

•   •   •   •   •

"Let's go, up and at 'em! Out of bed, on the floor!" The major was the boy's morning alarm. "Got to pump you up for the day. Crunches time," Major said as he held his six-year-old son's ankles. "And one and touch-the-knees and down and two and touch-the-knees and down and three . . ."

The boy, with a crew cut that matched the major's military cut, rose from the floor, arms locked behind his head, elbows touched knees, back down to the floor, back up, elbows touched knees, back down, and he swallowed and swallowed because something inside his chest was about to rush upwards and out his mouth and he forced his lips together to keep his mouth shut to keep it inside and tears formed as he rose to touch his elbows to knees, and his dad saw.

"What the hell you upset about?"

"I'm not upset," was the boy's snapped-rubberband response.

"Then why are you crying?"

"I'm . . . not . . . crying."

But he was.

And the boy continued the sit-ups and the major continued, "one and two and don't-be-a-sissy and three and . . ."

The boy knew if he could do this today maybe tomorrow he wouldn't have to because the major would be gone on assignment to another country, maybe to Korea because that sounded far away.

•   •   •   •   •

Obsessive Godwin was impressed that one of Ward 2A's own was leading the calisthenics. He gave him undivided attention. Godwin's hands met above his head at the precise time as Tabor's. When Godwin's hands returned to his sides instead of slapping his legs, he touched his pants lightly not wanting to transfer any moisture from his hands to his blues.

Next to Godwin, Shaky Metz vibrated like a Flamenco player's guitar string. While for his neighbor, Smiling Hardy, jumping in rhythm was especially difficult because Hardy needed to get to the latrine. He believed it was the constant necessity to empty his bladder that had him sent to the psych wards in the first place. But it wasn't, it was Hardy's smile. To distract himself from the pressure on his bladder Hardy initiated his defense mechanism and worked on a five-seven-five haiku:

> See Tabor's muscles
> he rises and soars stretching
> upwards to—

He tried again:

> See Tabor's muscles
> He raises his arms upwards—

He settled on:

> The soldier soars high
> his arms stretching upwards to
> reach beyond his pain

Hardy repeated the haiku over and over to himself, not satisfied. But it served its purpose. He forgot he had to pee.

Slob Shumacher, black shoes scuffed, blue shirt misbuttoned, no string tie or belt for his blue pants that were held up only by his large ass. He smacked his hands over his head and his pants fell. He dropped his hands to catch the pants and fell sideways bumping the ward's catatonic who lost his balance and struck Skinner who then tripped over his Bible and lurched into the back of the giant Stover who was on his way upwards but now transformed into a six-foot-four high diver and with both hands out front pushed the shaking Metz completely off his feet crashing into metal chairs stacked on the side of the room. Proof to the drill instructor that if Vietnam fell so would Cambodia, Laos, and Pennsylvania.

"What the fuck?" "Hey, I'll smack you." "Watch out. You're on my foot."

"Get back Jack, before I punch you." The patients, many confused, and some angry, tried to get their bearings. Shaky Metz worked to disengage himself from the chairs that he had invaded while Paranoid Firenza who intentionally stood a distance from everyone and watched the cataclysm unfold.

"Sessions over." "Sessions Over." The techs, Zack and Turner, made their announcements almost simultaneously. "Line up, back to the ward," Zack said. "We're out of here," Turner said. "Let's go," Zack said. "It's Inspection day," Turner said. And then with an ominous tone both Zack and Turner said, "Let's get ready for the major."

• • • • •

"Cleanliness is next to Godliness." Sergeant McCabe proclaimed, serving as an example with his starched white smock and polished black shoes. The techs trusted him, and the patients trusted him. The sergeant greeted new patients with a handshake that gave the impression of equality, opposite of a few of those of higher rank who squeezed tightly to signify dominance.

They had all heard his reassuring line and some had heard it more than once, 'I'm not your momma, and I'm not your daddy. But I will do right by you.' And they all called him "Sarge."

"Get this ward ready for inspection." And then in one single breath Sarge said, "Strip the beds, make the beds, empty the nightstands, throw out food and trash, wipe 'em clean, refill the nightstands." Sarge was a veteran of a thousand inspections. "Move everything that can be moved, wash the baseboards, the tables, the chairs, wash the windows, wash everything, and move everything back to where it was." He then returned to the office leaving the psych techs to monitor the patients.

"I don't do windows." Patient Perez muttered surprising himself at his immediate response. His mother had to wash windows for women in the suburbs. Washing windows was the only complaint she ever shared with him. He wiped clean the windowsill and moved on giving the smiling Hardy room to take on the task. Hardy, holding a damp cloth, maneuvered his arm in the narrow space between the window and the thick-wired outer grid to clean off the dust and dirt that accumulated from last week's cleaning. On this pleasant autumn afternoon, Hardy stopped to give attention to the surrounding forest of oak, maple and elms with their yellow, gold and splash of fiery red leaves. Hardy imagined himself following a deer path and away from this place.

"Okay, guys, move those tables and chairs to the side." Tech Turner took charge. "You, Tabor, get the buffer going."

From the opened latrine door, a strong odor of pine escaped to the ward. Inside Tech Krupp, in his usual foul mood, acted as a plantation overseer. "Check those shower walls. Are those soap streaks? Do 'em over. And pay special attention to your close friends the commodes and urinals."

The overseer's instructions were interrupted when Sarge revisited the ward holding a clipboard. "Listen up." He spoke loud enough for several soldiers to hear knowing they'd pass the word to the rest. The ward quieted; the men in the latrine exited; and most of the patients moved closer to the front.

"I've got a memo from Command. And you will pay attention to what it says." Sarge looked at the clipboard. "If you have discharge in your skivvies or pajamas," he looked up and ad-libbed, "and I'm not talking about normal stuff here," then back to the memo, "I mean if it burns when you urinate, if you have sores or blisters on your penis," he looked up again, "let me or the techs know immediately." And then, as if he were reading a public service announcement, Sarge said, "Venereal disease can be treated."

"Ppppenis?" A shaky Metz stuttered, his voice matching his tremors.

"That's dick, dickhead," the overseer Tech Krupp replied.

Sarge continued reading. "You are to check your genital area for lice or crabs." He looked up from the clipboard. "If you suspect someone may be infected because they're scratching their—ah, ah,—well, anyway, tell us immediately."

Joker Berkowski scratched his bald head, his chin, and then under his arms, and moved in a circle imitating a chimpanzee. For a moment the patients switched attention from the Sarge to Berkowski and then back. Sarge ignored the distraction.

"Crabs and lice are easily treated," Sarge said reading from the memo, "lotions and shampoos can treat the problem." Sarge paused, looked down at his shoes then to the patients. "Guys, don't be embarrassed about asking for help." Sarge rolled through "mbarest" as if uncomfortable with the word and the topic.

"One final matter," Sarge said, "we shouldn't have to remind you guys to take showers and change pjs. If someone next to you is starting to smell rank, tell us so we can get him cleaned up." Sarge looked pointedly at the slob Shumacher who was stuffing the last bite of a Reese's cup into his mouth savoring the taste of peanut butter and chocolate. Shumacher had the smallest ears, biscuits that failed to rise. With his candy filled mouth his pinkish cheeks appeared to be two wads of inflated bubble gum.

"Shumacher, get those wrappers under your bed. You've had breakfast, how much more can you eat?" Sarge asked with the perplexed tone of someone who had never had a weight problem.

What Sarge said was all too familiar for Shumacher. In Sarge's voice he could hear his mother's disappointment. "Lawrence, I found cake crumbs in your bed this morning. Don't you ever get enough to eat?"

"And soldier, get a shower and change clothes." Sarge's directive brought cheers and whistles. A suddenly self-conscious Shumacher tugged his pants up that had fallen below round buttocks.

"Now everyone, back to work." Sarge returned to the office.

At a window the perpetually smiling Hardy reached high to remove several water marks with a dry rag when suddenly a body dropped from the sky briefly blocking his view of the forest. Hardy watched as a patient from upstairs 3A writhed in the grass, rose, hobbled, fell, rose again, then dragged his left leg as if it were a busted tree limb across the grounds. No fence on this side of the building, only the windows thick-wired grids that hadn't stopped this soldier from entering the woods.

Two techs and an MP came into Hardy's view running in the direction the patient had taken. Hardy had a thought that fit the smile on his face. *Maybe the soldier will take a whizz in the woods before they catch him. Wizz in the woods, alliteration, I can use that in a poem.* When pursued and pursuers were out of sight Hardy moved on to another window leaving water spots as the only other witnesses to the escape.

In the middle of the ward the tables had been cleared enabling the athletic Tabor to easily glide the buffing machine across the floor resulting in the sheen necessary to pass the weekly inspection. Just then patient Vasquez, having deserted an assignment in the latrine and his translator Perez, found himself in the proverbial wrong place at the wrong time. Tabor had to relieve himself, and to relieve him from the buffing machine he drafted Vasquez. "Hey," Tabor said and stopped Vasquez's forward progress by stopping the machine in his path. Tabor motioned toward the buffer. "Take over while I go to the John."

Vasquez looked at him but that's all he did.

"TAKE OVER WHILE I GO TO THE JOHN," Tabor yelled believing this translated the words to Spanish.

Vasquez looked at Tabor and then at the buffer with its giant doughnut brushes. He gave his own doughnut face a negative expression and shook his head "no."

"JUST HOLD THE HANDLE AND SQUEEZE." Tabor, losing patience, took Vasquez's wide hands and placed them on the buffer's handle.

"Yo no entiendo," Vasquez said, still shaking his head.

Tabor issued a last instruction, "JUST SQUEEZE THE LEVER, THE MACHINE WILL DO THE REST." He hastily departed to the latrine muttering, "When you got to go, you got to go."

Patient Vasquez looked at the piece of heavy metal and brushes as if it would fulfill its purpose on its own volition. All he had to do was watch. So he watched. About that time, the Smiling Hardy saw the befuddled look on Vasquez's face.

"What's the problem?" Hardy asked.

Vasquez answered, "Esta maquina no esta funcianando."

"No comprende," Hardy said smiling. He'd learned Spanish from cowboy movies on TV.

Vasquez looked at the buffer and back to the patient with a look that said, "This machine does not work."

Hardy clearly understood this cross-cultural communication and demonstrated what needed to be done by holding his own hands outward and making a squeezing motion. Vasquez decided to take the suggestion of his fellow soldier even though he believed that Hardy's perpetual smile certainly qualified him as loco. Vasquez squeezed the lever on the handle. The buffer rocketed to the right and took Vasquez with it. Smiling Hardy jumped onto a bed. The buffer crashed into a table, then knocked over a chair.

Vasquez, strength a strongpoint, believed he could hold the machine from wreaking more havoc by pulling it in the opposite direction. This initiated the buffer's movement to the other side of the ward pulling Vasquez along and shining the floor as it went.

Patients saw the whirring rollers speeding their way and jumped on beds. The buffer hit the legs of one bed, bounced off, and dragged Vasquez along. Up the ward the two went. The brushes bounced off another bed. Patients were knocked around and down like passengers on a small boat on high waves. The buffer moved up the aisle with the unintentional assistance of the operator. Every time Vasquez jerked the machine to obey, the buffer knocked over more chairs and attacked more patients.

"Socorro! Socorro!" Vasquez was a tough Puerto Rican and had been through too much in life to be scared of this machine. But he recognized when he needed help. Help is what he called for. "Socorro! Socorro!"

Zack came out of the office the same time Patient Perez raced out of the latrine to answer his adopted brother's call for help. Vasquez saw him and yelled, "Socorro! Socorro!"

Perez yelled, "Suelta la maquina! Suelta la maquina!"

Zack and the patients, as if in a high school Spanish class, responded in unison and unknowingly translated Perez's words, "Let go of the machine! Let go of the machine!"

The chaos initiated Zack's peculiar condition and the Coasters appeared at the rear of the ward.

Now finish cleaning up that roooom,
Clean that dust up with that broooom,
And when you finish doing thaaaat,
Bring in the dog and put out the cat.

Vasquez let go of the buffer. The chaos over, the Coasters disappeared. And the patients prepared for the inspection.

• • • • • •

Beds made, nightstands dusted, tables cleared and chairs in place as the patients stood in their territory and the techs did their last walk through. Major Vann entered. Today, he was all spit and polish. Other days, as best he could, the major sequestered himself in his office waiting out his retirement. For the ward rounds, as always, he was accompanied by his right-hand-man Sergeant Helms.

"Ward, tention!" Sarge said decisively. "Ward, ready for inspection, sir." The patients, at the foot of their beds, responded to Sarge's "tention" as soldiers do whether they have one week's basic training or five years of combat, whether drug-free or drugged; they straightened their stance, some more than others, shoulders back, arms at their sides.

The major returned Sarge's salute almost as an afterthought and continued to the freshly waxed ward that smelled like overripe cantaloupes. With Sergeant Helms at the major's right, Sarge followed and took a position to the left. They stopped at the first bed. Standing at the foot of the bed was the soldier Metz. His hands shook and his feet shuffled in place.

"How are you, soldier?" the major asked.

"Fffffffine, sir, fine, sir, Ffffffff . . ."

On one of the "F's" the major moved to the next patient. He glanced at the nametag. The patient, a soldier still, looked away. "Where are you from, Grier?" Major Vann leaned left to try to catch the soldier's eye.

"Michigan, sir." Grier mumbled sounding like "Mishcansu." And leaned right to avoid the major's gaze.

The major moved his white face closer to Grier's black one. "Where's that again, soldier?" The major cocked an ear.

"Mishcansu." Now looking somewhere over the major's left shoulder.

"Ah," the major stepped back, "City boy from Motor City Detroit."

"No suh, I'm from upper-Mishcan, never been to Detroi." Grier mumbled, but the major had already moved on, thereby maintaining the major's misconception that if you were Black and lived in Michigan, you lived in Detroit.

The White Sergeant Helms, born and raised in Mississippi, which may have had something to do with his suspicion of all blacks, moved to soldier Grier's nightstand where he opened the drawer and quickly looked through its contents. Satisfied there were no illicit drugs or revolutionary Black Panther literature, he rejoined the major.

Major Vann stopped in front of Smiling Hardy. Hardy held a slightly angled salute. "At ease, soldier." He hastily returned Hardy's salute. "Son, you're what all officers want to see: a satisfied soldier." The major turned to Sarge. "This man's obviously getting well." He turned back to Hardy. "Son," the major chuckled, "that smile is contagious."

Sergeant Helms took note that Hardy was bunked next to the not-to-be-mistaken-for-anything-but-a-Negro, Grier, something Helms considered inadvisable to a productive squad or ward. His floor plan would have had Colored soldiers spaced around the room. He believed having two of the

Negro race bunk together was bad enough, but three or more would lead to boisterous behavior, gambling, and just plain goofing-off. Helms learned this sociological information from years of personal observation. He knew he wasn't a racist because he felt the same way about Mexicans, Puerto Ricans, Okies and Hillbillies.

Push-ups Tabor, the star patient of morning calisthenics, was the major's next stop. Tabor personified strict military attention. Eyes focused straight ahead; arms at his sides with hands pressed to the seams of his pants; heels together and black shoes shined to a high gloss. The major was impressed.

"So you're Tabor." The major said reading the patient's nametag.

"Sir." The soldier snapped his response, "I am Corporal Tabor, sir." He continued looking straight ahead; chin thrust forward.

The major turned to Sergeant Helms. "This is Major Richard Tabor's son. I told you about him." Helms nodded in agreement whether he remembered being told or not.

"His father phoned me ... when was that, a week, two weeks? Right after his son was admitted. His dad was one pissed off officer." The major turned back to Tabor.

"I promised your father I'd check on you." The major then offered his diagnosis. "It's hard for the major and me to believe you belong here. After all," the major paused to stare into Tabor's eyes, "You are of military blood."

Tabor held to attention and looked straight ahead.

"Your dad and I agreed. All you needed was a couple weeks R&R. You should not have been sent here." The major's version of rest and relaxation for soldiers was a week at the beach and then back to duty. "How long has it been now?" The major turned for an answer to Sarge.

"Sir, the soldier Tabor's been here approximately one month."

"Four weeks, that's plenty of rest. There's a war going on," the major said.

Every soldier on the ward agreed a war was going on. They did take exception to the major's assessment of earned vacation time.

"I told your dad I'd get you back to your unit, and that's what I'm going to do." The major said it as if it were a done deal. "I'll get the doc to sign-off and get orders cut. Your dad is a fine officer and that's the least he deserves. Now carry on."

Tabor raised his right hand and held a tight salute. The major returned the salute. Tabor snapped his hand downward, executed a precise about face, and strode to the watermarked window next to his bed. He clenched his right hand to a fist, drew it straight back, elbow tight to his side, muscles loaded, a coiled spring. He released the fist and punched forward through the glass continuing on to hit the metal grid that made a clanging sound announcing the end of round one. Tabor's fist lodged in the broken windowpane. Blood squirted upwards. The ward erupted.

Sarge moved immediately to help Tabor. Major Vann turned and hurried off the ward. Patients yelled, cried, cursed, shook, rocked, fell on their beds, jumped on their beds, turned over beds. Shaky Metz hid under his bed. Paranoid Firenza hid under a table. Zack saw that the Isley Brothers had appeared at the head of the ward. They wore white suits that contrasted with their dark skin and black hair. The soul brothers extended arms upwards and sang.

You know you make me want to shout!
Jump-up and shout now!

As much as Zack enjoyed the show, he kept on task and moved soldier to soldier. "It's okay, okay. He'll be alright. Settle down." Zack's peculiarity never got in the way of what needed to be done.

At the rear of the ward Joker Berkowski used a bed like a trampoline, unknowingly jumping in rhythm with the Isley Brothers. He threw a pillow across the ward and pillows flew back at him giving him more soft ammunition to return fire.

Hey-hey-hey-hey-hey.
Hey-hey-hey-hey–hey.

Vasquez cursed in Spanish, picked up his nightstand, dumped its contents, and lifted the nightstand to his broad shoulders. He spun once around as if he were a track and field shot put contestant and flung the heavy brown metal into a corner of the room. Zack heard the crash. It sounded as if someone had tossed the Isley Brothers' drums and drummer off a stage.

A little-bit-louder now.

A little-bit-louder now.

Skinner clutched his bible and fell to his knees, "Dear Lord, save the major, save Sarge, save sergeants, save the soldiers in Charlie Company, save every soldier, JesusGod, save me . . ."

Sergeant Helms followed Sarge not to help but to threaten. "If you and your techs can't handle these crazies," short Sergeant Helms rose up on his toes, "the major will call the MPs and we'll lock this place down!" He came down.

"Are you ever going to get it, these are sick soldiers here?" Sarge said as he examined the mess Tabor had gotten his fist into.

"Sick hell." Helms did an about-face. He walked through Zack's apparition, the Isley Brothers, and off the ward.

Sarge spoke calmly to Tabor whose fist was still lodged between the window and the grid. "Unclench, go ahead, loosen your grip, slowly." Tabor, quite calm, listened and did as he was told. He was a good soldier.

Lawyer Lucas circled the table lecturing, his index finger pointed upwards. "We the People of the United States, in order to form a more perfect Union, establish justice, insure domestic tranquility, provide for the common defense, promote the general welfare . . ."

Obsessive Godwin, and the mumbling, not from Detroit, Grier, stayed out of the melee, as did Scarface Kelly who stretched out on his bed, hands behind his head, relaxing, waiting for the storm to pass. Slob Shumacher, reached into his back pocket, removed a half-eaten Clark bar, and bit into the warm and gooey chocolate. And as Berkowski catapulted upwards reaching the apex of his rise, the Joker placed his right hand to his temple in salute and loudly proclaimed: "Ward ready for inspection, sir!"

And the soldier Hardy, smiled like the Cheshire Cat.

The soldier jumped from the second story. (2014 photo)

Valley Forge General Hospital
Neuropsychiatric Unit

DAILY LOG - Ward 2A and 2B
October 27, 1967

DAY SHIFT

Another day - just like the other day.

EVENING SHIFT

The same.

NIGHT SHIFT

Same

The Prize

"One, and two, and three, and one, and two, and . . ." Obsessive Godwin counted methodically and watched his feet as Andy Williams' voice crooned from two large speakers on a corner table.

Moon River, wider than a mile,
I'm crossing you in style, some day.

The obsessive's partner, a young Red Cross worker, nametag Peggy, counted with the patient. "One, and two, and three, and one, and two, and three." Peggy's sky blue eyes matched the blue of her Red Cross outfit.

The Red Cross was sponsoring a dance for soldiers, the patients of the psychiatric unit. Earlier that week they had put out the call for volunteers who would more closely match the ages of the patients, and girls from the senior class of the local high school and some from a local college sorority had responded. The results of their enthusiasm were in full display. The walls of the psych building's activity room were decorated with orange balloons and black crepe paper and decorative leaves clustered around numerous paper pumpkins, several with jack-o-lantern faces, eyes cut out and mouths that highlighted a few large, crooked teeth. In keeping with the festive occasion, the girls wore brightly colored dresses, happy dresses, as if this were just another happy event.

For the soldiers, the evening began as a cheerful occasion except for the very depressed and for Major Vann. The base commander had volunteered the major to host an ecumenical committee of women from the local township's churches. The church women attending this special occasion were a proper-looking group. Most dressed in black as if a visit to the psych wards called for solemnity and mourning.

The women and Major Vann sat off to the far side of the room at a long table covered by a white tablecloth. The feminine touch of the volunteers included yellow, brown and red construction paper cut into leaves and strewn between the plates of cakes, cookies, and plastic containers of apple juice. Sergeant Helms stood behind the officer ready for any order from his superior.

While the major pontificated on his brilliant career in the service, the churchwomen sneaked glances at the psychiatric techs located strategically around the room. They were impressed with the young soldiers in their white smocks. The women loved that "doctor look." Playing host to the women was not what the major wanted. But the base commander had, once again, exerted his superiority of rank and there was nothing the major could do but follow orders and continue to count down his time till retirement. His nodding and smiling to the ladies had a bit of an edge.

On display for the visitors tonight were the soldiers, the patients of the psych wards. But while the women inspected the patients, the patients seldom looked to the major's table. As the night progressed, seeing the major and Sergeant Helms only reinforced their feelings of powerlessness. Their softball season had ended abruptly because of a patient's attempted escape and it had been over two weeks since the patients had any outside activity. Tonight, being put on display for the visitors only added to the patients' rising discontent. To them it was all the major's doing.

Oh, dream maker, you heart breaker.
Wherever you're goin', you're goin' my way.

An energetic White volunteer with bouncing breasts and an irresistible smile took to the dance floor with a Black patient from the upstairs ward 3A. And while Sergeant Helms fixed an unappreciative eye on the mixed-race couple, Major Vann couldn't help but notice how one church woman, oblivious of her over-the-top-of-the-scales-condition, munched on sugar cookies, one after another, her hand or mouth never without sustenance. He calculated the amount of calories she ingested and estimated the increase of her weight by the end of the evening. This was how he had become a numbers person in the first place. His mother had obsessively counted calories of every foodstuff or liquid she consumed or refused to consume. Despite her math, his mom never dropped below one hundred and eighty-five-pounds, not exactly proportional for a woman five-foot-three.

Chairs surrounded the dance floor where the patients sat. As young as most of the patients looked, this could have well been a high school event. The soldiers waited for the dozen or so girls to ask them to dance and hoped not to be asked by the half-a-dozen older-than-their-moms Red Cross women. An older, energetic Red Cross staffer, nametag Bea, moved from patient to patient with several young female volunteers in tow. "Let's not be shy now," Bea said to a ward 3A schizophrenic, "dance with this pretty volunteer." She left the two and moved on to others. Several soldiers hoped she would pass them by while still others wanted her encouragement to take to the dance floor.

Patients and volunteers soon crowded the floor. The catatonic Cart had been partnered with a wide-eyed and obviously nervous high school volunteer. She wore a brightly colored party dress for the occasion. She looked at him; he looked through her. Her lilting voice expressed her innocence and her anxiety.

"So where are you from? I'm from a town about twenty miles away. It's a nice place to live but I just know there must be more out there. Were you overseas? I've never been. I bet soldiers get to see the world. I'd love to travel. Someday I'll . . ." She hesitated, taking a breath to allow the catatonic to take the lead. He didn't, so she did. "I took a trip to Florida once with family to visit relatives. You ever been to Florida?" In answer, the patient raised his right foot slightly, and swayed to the left. He raised his left foot slightly and swayed to the right. In slow motion, the right, then the left. She took the soldier's hands and they stepped and swayed. Somewhere in there the catatonic Cart knew they were dancing.

An elf-sized, partially graying older woman selected the tallest soldier in the room. She took the hand of Cherry Pie Stover who was dressed in undersized patient blues that exposed his ankles and bony wrists. She led him out on the floor. He looked down at her, smiled warmly, and hid her hand in his. Stover missed his mom.

Soldier Skinner looked fragile tonight, breakable, a fine piece of china. And just as any traditional dancer his right hand took its place on the back of a volunteer; while her left hand went to his shoulder, his left hand untraditionally held his Bible; her right hand held his Bible with him. Not wanting to appear sacrilegious, she maintained a healthy distance from Skinner's body.

"Excuse me," Skinner said politely to the Open Ward patient, Rao, who, oblivious of others around him, steered his partner directly into Skinner causing him to drop his Bible. But Skinner did what he had to do to survive and reclaimed his security before anyone could step on it.

Tonight the booze free, back-on-the-wagon, patient Rao danced with a dark hair, dark eyes, olive-skinned young woman. Rao assumed that her ethnicity was like his, Italian heritage. And her nametag, "Maria," was further encouragement. He pressed his olive-skinned cheek to hers. She moved hers away slightly avoiding the scratchy growth of Rao's evening whiskers.

"Maria." Rao said softly. This was the kind of woman he could take home to Mama, if he ever returned home since being asked to leave by parents whose tolerance for his lack of respect and unruly behavior had been exhausted. Not having a home gave a young man a practical reason to join the Army. Rao at thirty-five was the oldest of the patients on the ward. He was a lifer, that's if the Army didn't discharge him first. He'd been twice a sergeant and demoted twice. His consumption of alcohol increased substantially during tours in Vietnam. This time he was sent to the psych ward to dry out; the Army needed experienced soldiers. The soldier Rao pulled the volunteer closer and moved his hand lower and lower. Maria returned his hand to her back.

Patient Vasquez was in love. That's what he told the blond volunteer in Spanish as he looked into what he called her Caribbean blue eyes. His translator, Perez, stood behind his buddy looking over his shoulder at the young woman. The attractive volunteer, a head taller than Vasquez, was amused by this her first bilingual experience of pickup lines.

"Te amo," Vasquez said looking up at her.

"I love you," Perez translated as he peered over Vazquez's shoulder.

"Siempre te amare," Vasquez said.

"I'll love you forever," Perez said with a whispery delivery.

"Quiero casarme contigo y que tu seas la madre de mis ninos," Vasquez said as if reciting a legal document that offered marriage and the desire for her to bear him sons.

"I will marry you." Perez edited the translation. It was clear to the volunteer Perez spoke for himself, as well as for Vasquez. The cheerful bilingual Perez wasn't the same soldier who arrived here from Vietnam. That Perez suffered from a what-do-I-have-to-live-for-now, a direct correlation between Perez's depression and being shot in the testicles by a Vietcong sniper. Maybe the sniper didn't want to kill him, just shoot him where it would do the most harm. Perez's depression was tied to that machismo thing and it took time for him to appreciate that he was even alive. Since being on the ward Perez's depression had lifted, but, unfortunately, not the rest of him. His romantic banter was a sign that Perez was regaining his confidence.

To the right of the visitor's table, a patient faced the wall and danced alone. He bowed at the waist, held his hands out front as if grasping someone's hands, danced for a few seconds, then stopped to apologize for stepping on his make-believe partner's toes. He again bowed at the waist and started again. The nearby committee of women whispered around the table and concluded he was dancing with an imaginary friend. This fit comfortably with what they'd learned about mental illness from Hollywood movies and TV talk shows. They would have been surprised to learn the solo dancer was extremely shy so before asking a young lady to dance he wanted to rehearse to get it just right. Besides, his imaginary friend had agreed it was okay for him to ask another girl to dance but just this once.

Smiling Hardy sat taking in all that he saw before him. He appeared, as usual, to be enjoying life. Mentally he constructed a poem that later he would transfer to pen and paper.

Dance

Poetic rhythm
You can love the words
But like a song
When it's wrong
You can't dance to it.

Private Hardy completed the poem while crooner Andy Williams sang the last line to his number one hit:

We're after that same rainbow's end,
waitin' round the bend.
My huckleberry friend, moon river, and me.

Song over, the DJ for the evening, a young volunteer, flipped through a box of albums to establish the order of the songs. One slow, one fast, one cha-cha, one slow, one fast, one cha-cha. The DJ, a shy unassuming girl was attracted to an album cover of famous Frank's daughter, Nancy Sinatra. The photo captured her wide smile, straight white teeth, long flowing blond locks, and an ever so short, short skirt and, of course, her knee length white boots. The DJ loved that sexy look, but she knew she would never dare, not with her parents, not in her hometown. She put the title song on the record player: "These Boots are Made for Walking."

You keep sayin' you got something for me,
Somethin' you call love, but confess.

Out on the center floor another young woman lived the DJ's fantasy. "Dare" should have been this volunteer's middle name. She wore a short skirt, white boots, and her light brown hair flowed to her shoulders. She attracted a number of patients who stumbled around her and continually cut in on each other as she gyrated to the latest steps picked up from watching TV's Bandstand.

Are you ready boots? Start walkin'!

Nancy Sinatra's last words were what many of the soldiers wished they could do: walk right out of there. Instead, it was the staffer Bea and a young volunteer that walked to the center of the room. Bea held a shoebox. "It's time for our door prize!" she proclaimed. "Door prize time! Get out your ticket. Who will be the lucky patient? Who will it be?" She nodded to the girl who giggled, reached in the box and removed a ticket.

"And the number is 5, 9, 6, 3," Bea announced. "Would 5, 9, 6, 3, please—"

"Yes! 5, 9, 6, 3, Send me home! I am a winner!"

From the circle gathered around the dance floor, a patient elbowed his way through and ran to the center of the room. Laughter broke out from the audience when the patient slid the last five yards as if on ice. He wore a mask of a jack-o-lantern with the eyes and mouth cut out. He had secured the pumpkin mask to his head with scotch tape, his smooth dome provided a compliant surface. From the crowd a patient yelled, "It's the Great Pumpkin, Charlie Brown!"

While the churchwomen smiled approvingly, the soldier removed the mask and bowed to the applause of the other soldiers. Major Vann whispered over his shoulder to Sergeant Helms, "Who is he?" Helms whispered back, "Berkowski. We have been warned. His intake report says 'a lack of impulse control.'"

•　　•　　•　　•　　•

Earlier that day Berkowski had already put on an over-the-top performance for fellow soldiers. That morning the techs, as usual, had distributed razors that would be collected once the patients had completed their cleanup rituals. The Army expected soldiers to shave their faces, not their scalps. But there wasn't a rule to stop him so every other day Berkowski would lather his head and with a few swipes shave it clean. This always drew a group of patients to comment on the Joker's actions. This morning the soldier capitalized on this attention to take shaving to another level, or, more accurately, a lower level. With an audience gathered, Berkowski completed the final razor swipe of lather on his unnatural bald dome. His next shaving objective brought the crowd alive.

"Shave it!" "Do it!" "No!" "Yes!" "Don't do it!" "Do it!"

Berkowski had covered his groin and the family jewels with a mound of Burma Shave cream. The Burma Shave was provided by the Army. The jewels, his own.

"Do it!" "Go ahead." "Shave it!"

The patients crowded closer, nudging each other, the ones in the back doing their best to see the action over the shoulders of others. He slowly lowered the razor to his foam-covered pubic region. Some patients' laughed, others cringed at the Freudian possibilities. Before Berkowski's right hand did the deed, his left hand moved to intercede. The left hand grabbed the wrist of the right hand that held the razor moving towards the white foamy mound. He struggled valiantly. The left hand "Good" fought the right hand "Evil" that clutched the razor. Berkowski grimaced as he arm wrestled with himself.

The patients took sides. "Don't stop!" "Do it!" Shave it!" "Go on!" "Do it!" "No!" "Yes!" "No!" "Yes!" "Do it!" "Noooo!"

It was as if they were watching Director Kubrick's film character, Dr. Strangelove, attempting to control his right hand, a hand that remained faithful to the Fuhrer. Suddenly "Good" overpowered "Evil" and Berkowski's left hand forced his right hand to release the razor dropping it into the sink. Exhausted from battle, he slumped forward. Suddenly, Berkowski turned, snapped his fingers, pointed to the audience, and like a raspy-voiced carnival barker said, "It's craaazzzyyy time." The show over, there was laughter and applause even from those who were disappointed the right hand was defeated.

•   •   •   •   •

"5! 9! 6! 3!" Berkowski held out his ticket and shouted the winning numbers. The Joker had won the door prize and a chance for another performance. He stood at the center of the floor and raised his hands over his head. He clasped them and gestured as if he had KO'd the heavyweight champion of the world. The patients laughed as he made a sweeping gesture and handed the winning ticket to the Red Cross matron.

"We have a winner!" Bea announced. "This soldier is the winner."

Berkowski turned to each side of the room and took a formal bow. The patients applauded loudly; the visitors politely; the major exhaled, relieved.

"And the prize, a pair of beautiful, black stretch socks. Fits all sizes," Bea said with smiling satisfaction. She held the socks high so the audience could see Berkowski's newly acquired footwear. The patients' applause fell dramatically, replaced with a few chuckles, laughter, and even disenchanted muttering, "Socks, who the hell needs socks?" Another concluded, "Socks suck."

But Berkowski saw it differently.

"Yes! Yes! What a surprise! Just what I needed! How lucky can this soldier be! Eat your heart out! I am a winner! I got 'em and you don't!"

Berkowski ripped open the stocking wrapper as if starved for the contents, all the while repeating, "Yes, yes I need these, I need these . . ." emphasizing 'need.' He held one of the black socks with both hands and stretched its opening. And stretched and stretched and stretched as wide as it agreed to stretch. He then fit the sock to his narrow marble-like head.

"Uhhhhhhh . . . Uhhhhhh." Berkowski grunted.

The audience stared, mesmerized. The major's face transformed to match the red leaves on the table. Quick gasps of air from the guests; mouths fell open but no one spoke. The matron Bea, with a life experience of 'time stood still' moments, was the first to react, "Oh my, young man, no, you mustn't, oh my, my . . ."

Berkowski secured the sock to the top of his head but wanted more. "I can do it. It will fit. Don't worry. I'll get it on." The objective, now clear to the patients, encouraged them to encourage him.

"Go! Go! Go! Go!" The patients' rallied to his support. They sensed something was taking place bigger than the moment. A few from the ward thought it might be Berkowski's way to protest not being able to play ball. They knew no soldier enjoyed those afternoons more than the Joker.

"Go! Go! Go! Go!"

What these soldiers didn't know was that Berkowski had years of practice. He'd spent childhood and teenage years playing baseball in every kind of league: little leagues, high school leagues, and in the summer, city leagues. Monday was for the YMCA; Tuesday, the Lion's Club League; Thursday, the Rotary Club League; and every Friday evening and Saturday morning, the East Side City League. On Sunday's, following services, he played for the Church League. Wednesday, his only day of rest, allowed the open scabs on his legs to partially heal until they again broke open when he slid into second, third or home on subsequent days.

"Go! Go! Go! Go!"

Berkowski's father seldom missed a game. His son's ball playing was the one thing that gave daddy bragging rights. The rest was an embarrassment. The father had made it clear to the boy that it wasn't enough to do your best; to run and dive for the ball; you had to catch the ball; you had to complete the play; you had to win the game. But his mother offered the opposite feedback. She was proud of almost any accomplishment, even the smallest task. "Ah, you're such a good boy," was her response to his shutting the refrigerator door.

"Go! Go! Go! Go!"

So at center stage tonight here on the dance floor an opportunity for Berkowski to complete the play, to finish what he started. Not for his dad, but for the team, the soldiers.

"Go! Go! Go! Go!"

But fitting the sock on his head was difficult. Berkowski tugged with both hands. The force of the struggle dropped him to his knees where he continued jerking and pulling and tugging the material.

"Go! Go! Go! Go!" The repetitive rhythm of the voices was not lost on the Obsessive Compulsive Godwin and he joined in sync with the others. "Go! Go! Go! Go!"

"They're stretch socks, they'll fit. I can do this!" Berkowski spoke through gritted teeth. His face flushed. "I . . . can . . . do . . . this!"

"Go! Go! Go! Go!" Patient Skinner thumped his Bible in time with the chant.

A photo of disbelief, Major Vann's eyes widened, eyebrows' rose, and his mouth fell open. Sergeant Helms responded. He motioned to two techs from 3A and the three of them ran to Berkowski. They grabbed the Joker's arms, but he refused to surrender his grip on the sock that was now anchored on his bald head almost to his ears. They dragged Berkowski on his knees from the center of the room and towards the door. He slid across the floor as if on wheels.

"Go! Go! Go! Go!" The soldiers chanted.

"Wait!" Berkowski implored. "I've got it. Wait! It'll fit!" He continued to tug. Berkowski's actions gave voice to those who wouldn't or couldn't act out. Patient Vasquez for the time being regained bilingual ability and shouted along with the others. For some soldiers: a way to thumb their noses at the visiting church women, especially to those who visited out of curiosity, who saw the soldiers as amusing, or who pitied those they watched. For others: a way to tell the major to "go to hell."

"Go! Go! Go! Go!" On-the-wagon Rao chanted and held a cup of apple juice aloft creating a chain reaction by others who lifted their cups in salute to Berkowski as he was dragged from the room. From the corridor the Joker's enthusiasm echoed back to his compatriots to reassure them. "They're stretch socks, socks-socks-socks. They'll fit-fit-fit. Soldiers don't quit-quit-quit. I can do this-do this-do this."

The techs, with Sergeant Helms leading the way, hustled Berkowski through the long corridor while chased by the sound of "Go! Go! Go!" Berkowski reveled in the enthusiastic applause the same way a Broadway performer relishes "bravos!" Sergeant Helms opened the ward seclusion and the techs deposited their cargo on the mat. Helms grabbed the sock with both hands, tried to pull it from Berkowski's head. It was stuck.

"If you get that sock off your head," Helms said as he gave up the battle, "hang yourself with it."

From the keys hanging off his belt, Sergeant Helms located the appropriate key and locked the door. He departed to rejoin the major. Berkowski took a deep bow to the tech who watched him through the door's small rectangular window, just large enough for the tech's eyes. The Joker then turned and bowed to the remaining three walls of the room before depositing himself on the mat, exhausted from the evening's performance.

Back at the Red Cross dance, Major Vann had already gathered the churchwomen and retreated out a side door. The DJ selected the boisterous New Orleans' group of Huey Smith and the Clowns who sang: "I've got a rockin' pneumonia and a boogie woogie flu."

That night the soldiers celebrated a victory and had a rockin' good time.

Valley Forge General Hospital
Neuropsychiatric Unit

DAILY LOG - Ward 2A and 2B
November 12, 1967

DAY SHIFT

Another day - just like the other day.

EVENING SHIFT

The same.

NIGHT SHIFT

Same

About Poetry
A Poem by Private Hardy

What do you know about poetry?

I know what I like.

Sonnets or Sestinas?

I know what I like.

Metaphors or Similes?

I know what I like.

Free Verse?

I know what I like.

Example please?

Roses are red–

Oh no, not violets are blue?

Fuck you.

So you like to rhyme?

I did this time . . . because I know what I like.

The Pool Game

"Four ball, side pocket." It was a simple matter of fact expressed without emotion. The soldier Schroeder stroked the pool cue softly. The stick was part of him, an extension of his long thin body. The four ball dropped into the frayed leather pocket. Then, still as a matter of fact but louder this time, as if announcing a train departure at the rural town's one room station, "Eight ball, corner pocket, corner pocket."

If you had to be a patient in the Army hospital's psychiatric unit, the Open Ward wasn't such a bad deal. Soldiers worked half a day on a detail assigned to them by a psych tech. The details, menial but necessary—cutting grass, painting, work in the laundry room, the motor pool, and waxing floors with a buffing machine—kept the soldiers occupied until they received their orders, back to duty or home. Following their daily assignments, the patients relaxed, congregated in the Open Ward's rec room where they watched TV and shot a little pool. While Closed Ward patients wore white wristbands, Open Ward patients wore blue wrist bands that signified to the MP's that they could come and go from the building. Sometimes the wristband was the only difference in a soldier's mental state on the Open or the Closed Ward.

This fall afternoon a Black patient, Tyrone Jones, or TJ as he wanted to be called, watched as a White patient, Schroeder, Side Pockets was what the boys back home called him, used a warped pool cue and pocketed ball after ball on the ancient Brunswick table. The pool table wore a green felt so worn that in spots the gray slate showed through. Both soldiers wore the uniform of patients: a dark blue cotton shirt and pants and black leather shoes. You wouldn't see white slippers on the Open Ward that was purely Closed Ward footwear. For the two soldiers, similarity ended there, not just in color but in size. TJ was average height but seemed shorter because he always stood, head slightly down, shoulders slumped, elbows tight to his sides, as if retreating into himself.

His opponent, Schroeder, when not leaning over the table pocketing balls, stood tall. He was once the aggressive sharp-elbowed rebounder for his high school basketball team. Not timid about his height; he enjoyed the attention. Side Pockets Schroeder never hesitated and seldom missed a pool shot, not so on the basketball court. Schroeder was heading back to duty; TJ was not.

For the Army, Private Jones was a short-term investment loss. The eighteen-year-old had made it through the eight weeks of basic training, mastering, at least the Army believed, the "fundamentals of combat soldiering." It was the first time TJ had mastered the fundamentals of almost anything. He had always been behind others his age. He was held back in elementary school and failing again in high school TJ dropped out.

Once out on the streets, even the drug crew in the neighborhood dropped him from their rolls because of his inability to carry out the simplest assignments. TJ then enrolled in but failed to complete several apprenticeship programs. When he turned eighteen, he enlisted.

When TJ made it through the first weeks of basic training, it gave him hope. *Just maybe this time,* he thought. He struggled to read his mother's letters, concise notes telling him "You'll make it, Tyrone." So he tried harder, making sure to watch the others, to do what they did. When they stood at attention and saluted, he did. When they ran or crawled, he did. When they cleaned their weapons, he watched and cleaned his. On the obstacle course, the final test of confidence and ability, when they climbed and jumped he followed their lead and made it through . . . but without the confidence. Then, standing at attention in his dress green uniform with hundreds of other recruits, his chest pushed out, he received his first ever diploma: he had graduated basic training.

Next stop, before more training for jungle warfare, TJ was back home on leave. His mother seeing her son wearing his dress green uniform with marksman medal pinned to his chest insisted they immediately walk to the nearby Greyhound bus station where they crowded into a booth, deposited coins, and through the dispenser received four black and white photos. Three of the photos were of them smiling. The last photo showed TJ with an embarrassed look on his face while his mom kissed him on the cheek.

Back home TJ's mom headed straight to the kitchen. "I'm putting them right up here for me and everyone to see." Before she could tape the four photos to the refrigerator, TJ cut off one photo and placed it into his wallet, the one with mom kissing his cheek.

It was when TJ was in the first week of advanced training, where not even letters of encouragement could help the quivering innards of his stomach, that TJ had a dream. There in his stomach a large butterfly had made a home. It's yellow, black striped wings, fluttered throughout the night. The second week was harder for TJ. Bunkmates couldn't see it, not from the outside, but he felt it; his stomach vibrated. And then the nightmare. The butterfly torn and ragged lay in the pit of his stomach while atop of the butterfly a bloated bumble bee buzzed in triumph and the sound grew louder and moved upwards through TJ's throat until TJ emitted a continuous Buzzzzzzzzzzzzz that brought the lights on in the barracks and had TJ sent for an immediate evaluation. And then off to the psych ward.

The soldier Schroeder, unlike TJ, easily made it through basic and advanced training and loved it. There was always something to do. Always on the run, and if not, he was too exhausted to complain about it. "Give him something to do." that was the mantra of his parents, and the same for those classroom teachers who tried, unsuccessfully, to get him to stay seated. The Army's active schedule was a solution for the inability to pay attention to mundane tasks. It wasn't that he couldn't focus, he could, so long as the activity had movement. Shooting pool had movement. He loved shooting ball after ball. He hated to miss and have to wait a turn, so he seldom missed. The money he hustled from locals, and now from fellow soldiers, disproved, at least he believed, the notion that he had a problem paying attention.

It wasn't until the Army assigned PFC Schroeder to quartermaster where every day for hours and hours he had to sit behind a desk and fill out forms that the problem resurfaced. Boredom got to him, the boredom of nothing happening. He became a sitting contradiction; he needed activity but couldn't get himself moving in the morning. He became listless, tired, and fell asleep at his desk. When not sleeping he felt ill. Headaches, backaches, shooting pains in his fingers. He checked himself into sick bay so many times they finally checked him into the psych wards. The meds and the change of routine helped dramatically so now he was waiting for orders to head back to duty. The doc had recommended Schroeder be reassigned to a different Military Occupation, one that provided stimulation and lots of activity. The Army complied. He'd soon be heading to a combat unit in Vietnam.

While Schroeder was pocketing balls on the Open Ward, two soldiers of contrasting size, a six-footer and the other barely reaching five-foot-six, turned the corner into the Closed Ward. The shorter one was the major's right-hand man, Sergeant Helms. Helms was accompanied by a Black second lieutenant, a combination of rank and color not usually found on an Army hospital base in 1967. The lieutenant was a cutout from a recruitment poster. He wore a starched beige shirt, black tie, shined gold buttons on a precisely creased, dress green uniform. The lieutenant's hair had been razor trimmed as if a sharp, pencil-thin line had been drawn outlining his temple and above the ears and then around the back of his neck. Not a hair crossed the line.

Watching the two approach was the Sarge and psych techs Zack and Turner. As usual, Sarge's wide smile offered a friendly welcome to every visitor even if accompanied by the soldier with Napoleonic tendencies, Sergeant Helms.

Helms began the formalities. "Sergeant McCabe, this is Lieutenant Sharpe. The Lieutenant is a psych-ologist," Sergeant Helms said cutting the word in two parts. "He's been assigned to the main hospital. He noticed our hidden outpost over the hill and wanted a brief tour."

"Welcome Lieutenant Sharpe, Sarge said and extended an enthusiastic handshake. But I do have a question. Why do those soldiers get your help and not us?"

"I'll be counseling men who have severe life adjustments ahead, soldiers who've lost an arm or use of their legs," the lieutenant said.

"We've got the wounded here," Sarge said, "in a different way, but still wounded."

Sergeant Helms interrupted. "Yeah, and we have other types too. You know, malingerers, some would say cowards," He said dismissively. Sergeant Helms crooked his thumb toward the Sarge. "Sarge could be a social worker. You two could set up shop in civilian life. You could treat all those—"

"Motha fucker!" A shrill shout from the Open Ward. "Motha fucker!"

A thud, a crash, more cursing. Sarge took off immediately for the Open Ward with Sergeant Helms. The lieutenant followed. Sarge yelled back to Zack. "Greek, you come with us. Turner, hold the fort."

In the recreation room, flat on his back and hanging over part of the pool table was the soldier Schroeder. TJ held the point of a knife to his pool opponent's throat, the same serrated knife missing from the mess hall's monthly inventory.

"Hey, yah can have the money back, it's yours, I don't want it," Side Pockets said, sounding more like "I donwonit."

"Hustle me. Call me names. Make jokes," TJ spat his grievances.

"Careful or you'll cut me. Hey—"

TJ nicked Schroeder's chin with the knife.

"Damn straight, I'll cut you. Bet on it. Make the bet. Three ball, corner pocket, four ball, side pocket, you never missed. Got my money—hustle me—play me for a fool—then call me names."

The three-man rescue squad came to an abrupt halt inside the room's entrance.

"You! Get off that man," Sergeant Helms ordered.

TJ went for Schroeder's ear and sliced the lobe. Schroeder grabbed the eight ball and hit TJ alongside the head. TJ rolled off the far side of the table. Both sergeants moved in, but TJ came up swinging a pool stick. He held tight to the skinny end and used the thick end as a weapon. The Army retreated, reconnoitered, and reconsidered its position.

Brandishing the pool cue, TJ worked his way around the room toward the exit to the corridor. The two sergeants refused to give ground. The patient changed direction and moved toward the main part of the Closed Ward. As he retreated, TJ took a hell of a swing at the TV screen. It exploded. No Bonanza tonight.

The battle shifted, the advantage momentarily going to the Army. TJ backed on to the main bedroom for the soldiers. The Army advanced cautiously, staying just out of range of the pool cue. The stick swished as it whipped through the air. TJ backed a few steps, swiiiish, back, bumped and then around a table, swiiiish, knocked over a chair, swiiiish. TJ moved to a corner on the ward and took a stand.

"Jones, you don't want trouble," Sarge said. "You're being discharged. Going home."

"Going home? I'm kicked out of the Army, won't be able to get a job." Tears welled up in TJ's eyes but he didn't stop swinging the pool cue.

"Hey, I'm bleedinere" The patient Schroeder had followed them on the ward. He held a bloodied handkerchief to his ear.

"I'm kicked out!" TJ yelled. Then much softer, "What do I tell my momma? My friends?"

A legitimate question from an eighteen-year-old who just a couple months back was so proud that he had made his mother proud. Sarge moved a few steps closer. TJ swung the cue harder. Sarge took a few steps back. TJ cried harder and swung harder. Sergeant Helms unlocked the Nurses Station door and picked up the phone. "This is Sergeant Helms. We've got a situation. Get the MP at the front door and send a couple of techs from upstairs to the Open Ward 2. Now! No, not the Closed. Damnit, the Open Ward. Now!"

Sarge gave it another try, "Jones, this problem can go away. You can put this behind you, just do what you're told and—"

"Jones, do this, Jones, do that. Majors, sergeants. All the time, do this; do that. TJ swung the cue at all the bosses in his life.

Sergeant Helms rejoined the group. "Listen boy, put down that damn pool—"

TJ stepped forward and took a wicked swing. Whoosh. It missed Helms by a nose.

"Don't give me that boy shit! Do I look like a boy? Damn, you ever going to learn? If I hit you alongside your head, you be learning. He calls me names—you call me names."

Lieutenant Sharpe, an observer, stepped forward. "Sergeants, let's see what I can do."

Sergeant Helms' tone suggested he was more than willing. "Yes sirrr, Lieutenant. Whatever you say, sirrr."

"Lieutenant," Sarge intervened, "you need to let us handle this. We've had experience with soldiers who—"

"Let me talk to him. There may be something else going on here," the Lieutenant said.

"Take my money, and laugh, and then call me names. I'll bust—"

"Brother Jones, I'm Brother Sharpe." The lieutenant moved closer. "Don't think of me as an officer. Let's talk like brothers."

TJ swung the cue with less ferocity.

"I know it's tough. Sometimes you believe things won't ever get better."

TJ stopped swinging the pool cue. He pointed it at the lieutenant who lowered his voice and moved still closer. "It's harder for a black man, in here, and out there. And I said, man, not boy. You are a man."

Sergeant Helms rolled his eyes. Lieutenant Sharpe moved deliberately, a step inside the swing zone. TJ stopped crying. He pushed the butt of the pool cue onto the lieutenant's chest. The two locked eyes and remained that way as an MP and several techs ran on to the ward.

"That hustler," TJ said, "dissed me, called me names." TJ spoke as if the Lieutenant and he were the only ones in the room.

"For you, for me, for all of us, it's about respect." Lieutenant Sharpe knew he had the patient's complete attention.

"He calls me names . . ."

"It happens, they call us names. You're a man and you deserve respect. Epithets, bigot slurs, no Black man should stand for that. You reacted. You had good reason." With his left hand the lieutenant slowly moved the pool cue to the side and moved another step closer to TJ.

"Call me a chump," TJ said, "He kept saying I was a chump. Chump. Hustled me and call me chump."

The "chump" part confused the lieutenant. "That's what he called you? Chump?"

"Take my money and call me chump." TJ repeated.

"You were going to stab that man for calling you chump?" The lieutenant wanted clarification. "That's what he called you, chump? That was it?" He turned away from TJ and looked at Sarge. The lieutenant's mouth opened, but he said nothing, his eyes narrowed, his forehead suggested confusion. He raised his palms upward as if wanting Sarge to give him something. The lieutenant spoke, "He . . . cut him. He . . . was going to hurt that man. Even kill him, just for—what is wrong with him?"

It was then TJ decided this was something he would finish. He swung the pool cue; swish and a crack of a jawbone, white specks of teeth flew from the lieutenant's mouth as he took a little hop to the left that raised him a few inches from the floor before he crumbled to his side.

"Shoot that crazy in the foot," Sergeant Helms told the MP.

The MP unsnapped his leather holster. He removed the weapon. TJ violently swung his own weapon, left and right. Sarge hoisted a mattress off a bed.

"Tech, grab hold of one side!"

Zack grabbed hold and the two held the mattress in front of them and rushed forward. TJ swung the cue. It struck harmlessly as the mattress pinned him into the corner. The other medics jumped in and held the patient as an MP snapped handcuffs on TJ's wrists.

"Major's orders, no second chances for these fuck-ups," Sergeant Helms said. "Lock him up."

Zack rushed to the barely conscious lieutenant and kneeled by his side. "Sir, you may have a broken jaw. We'll get you to emergency." And then Zack's peculiarity showed up, another oldie.

I couldn't sleep at all last.

Just thinking of you.

Everything was right,

Zack heard Bobby Lewis singing but didn't see where the singer was. He thought, *I'm too damn busy to even look for him. He's not here anyway.* This time just hearing the song, the saxophones, the drumming rhythm, the singing, it was enough for Zack.

But I was tossin' and turnin'

turnin' and tossin'

Sergeant Helms made an announcement. "Major Vann will back me up on this. You get those pool cues and balls off of the ward. Pool's too damn dangerous for crazy people. And don't be surprised if it takes a hell of a long time for me to fill out a requisition for a new TV." He then headed off the ward muttering, "Colored psy-cho-lo-gist. A dumb nigger."

• • • • • •

One week later the Open Ward was a racetrack. Slot cars of every color: red ones, blue ones, gold and black, flew around the speedway. The beds were hills, under the beds, tunnels. Pillows, books, shoes and chairs served as a foundation for the track's mountainous ascent to table tops. The track worked its way back to the floor that served as a desert speedway. A cadre of soldiers from the Open Wards 2B and 3B sat on the floor in the center ring manipulating the controls of their favorite cars that whizzed as they sped along. Fans sat on nightstands that now served as bleachers, while others found whatever open spaces were available. Every bunk but one was occupied. The patients had left a reserved seat for TJ who now took up space in the stockade.

"Whoa! Lookout, here comes one!"

"Here comes another!"

"Watch out! Watch out!"

When a car launched airborne hoots and hollers accompanied it as the model crashed into a nightstand or flew off to a corner of the room.

"There it goes!"

"Get it! Get it!"

Side Pockets Schroeder, with a bandaged ear, sat in the circle and served as ringmaster. It was his brainchild and money that had fronted this operation for the first Open Ward 500. The idea came to Side Pockets earlier that day as he walked anxiously aisle to aisle at the base PX searching for something. Something, something, what was he looking for? He would know it when he saw it. Whatever it was? He knew the "it" had to be a major distraction. The patient needed something to counter the sameness that the days on the ward had become. No pool games and no TV. And then there it was.

On a top shelf of the PX, boxes of the newest craze in boy toys: electric racing car sets, slot cars. He rushed to get access to a cart, returned and stacked one after another of the rectangular boxes with their photos of colorful race cars on the box top. Balanced precariously he wheeled the boxes to the front counter and returned to retrieve additional sets from the shelf. The clerk satisfied Schroeder's request and called to the stock room to deliver to the front all remaining boxes, giving Schroeder a monopoly on the slot car industry for the entire base.

Schroeder felt a deep satisfaction as he paid the clerk. This gift to the ward would serve as a celebration of sorts for his own survival at the hands of T.J. Although he bore no ill will to the man, after all TJ was being hustled. Schroeder transported the boxes past a bemused MP at the psych building's entrance, and to the Open Ward, returning several times to the PX before completing delivery.

It wasn't difficult for Schroeder to enlist volunteers to assist in setting up the racetrack. Side Pockets knew that the slot cars would also be an excellent diversion for the Open Ward patients especially since no TV. Schroeder and fellow soldiers worked for hours on the layout connecting track to track to track to track. Invitations for the evening's entertainment had gone out word of mouth to those patients on the upstairs Open Ward. They accepted and that evening it was standing room only.

Schroeder's rap sounded as if he were a veteran announcer of Wide World of Sports. "Corvette's in the lead with the Pontiac closing fast! The Thunderbird is fighting to close the gap! Hang on, you crazy bastards, it's one hell of a race!"

Just then, two middle-aged women, Red Cross volunteers, mothers to their own boys, entered the ward. They pushed a cart holding a metal urn surrounded by cupcakes and cookies. Like the patients, the cupcakes varied in color and the cookies in shape. The cold refreshment was donated on a regular evening basis by the local apple farmers. The ringmaster Schroeder directed the audience's attention to the nightly visitors. "The winner gets cookies and cake and all the apple juice he can drink!"

The patients, soldiers still, pumped their fists into the air and began a rhythmic chant of "Apple juice! Apple juice! Apple juice! Apple juice!"

Valley Forge General Hospital
Neuropsychiatric Unit

DAILY LOG - Ward 2A and 2B
November 20, 1967

DAY SHIFT

Another day - just like the other day.

EVENING SHIFT

The same.

NIGHT SHIFT

Same

Soldier Invisible

"Greek boy, the doc's ordered Huffman to the Open Ward," Sarge read from a memo and then dropped it on tech's desk. Zack sat at the corner table filling in the detail schedule for those same Open Ward patients.

"Huffman? Which one's Huffman?" Zack asked.

"He's putting his things together," Sarge said. "Take him over to 2B. Assign him a bed."

The tech wracked his brain playing word association to put a face to the soldier. *Obsessive Huffman, no; Paranoid Huffman, no; Smiling Huffman, no; Shaky; Angry; no, no.* "I can't take him if I don't remember who he is."

You couldn't blame the tech for not recalling Huffman. After all, he was invisible. At least that's what Zack told himself later to justify his own failure. Why couldn't Huffman have been more like him? Even back in grade school Zack made certain everyone in class could see him. And if they couldn't see their classmate, they surely recognized his voice. Like "Show and Tell." Five minutes to "Show and Tell" about something brought from home. Some kids would get up front, utter a few words about a toy or photo, and then return to their seats. You could barely hear what they said. They'd mumble through their time, not even looking out at the class.

Not Zack. It didn't matter what he would show. He'd announce it loud and clear. He'd stand on a chair at the head of the class and proclaim, "Here is my favorite pencil. It can perform all kinds of things!" He would be on stage for the full five minutes or even more depending on how long it took for the teacher to get him to return to his seat. And then he'd sit there in judgment of the other students who failed to use even a minute of their time. *What was wrong with them?* he thought. *I could have used the extra minutes.* And that's how Zack felt about Huffman. What was wrong with him?

"He's never trouble, and does what you ask," Sarge said.

"Yeah, quiet and follows orders; I didn't know that was a sign of mental stability."

"If the doc says so, then it's so. I'm a sergeant—"

"Yeah, and the doc's a captain."

Sarge shrugged. "For soldiers going back to duty or going home, first stop, Open Ward."

The tech rose and moved to the board that listed the patients and their Open or Closed Ward. There was Huffman's name, left column, thirteen down. The space next to the name read "Closed." The tech wiped off "Closed" with a dry cloth and wrote "Open."

"Ready or not," Zack said, "here he comes."

Huffman had been on the Closed Ward for almost two months. He rose in the morning, made his bed, dressed in his patient blues, took his meds, stood in line to the mess hall, sat at tables with the others, exercised in the activities room, and slept on the ward. He was there every day. And yet, during those softball games, when Huffman was in the field or would come to bat, techs and patients would get quiet as he took his practice swings. They'd watch him closely, trying to recall who he was and when had he become part of the team?

"Whoa, speak of the devil," Zack said. There at the doorway was a little guy with cheeks an aunt would want to pinch. Huffman's stubby fingers clutched a shaving kit and other personal items to his chest.

Patient Huffman followed a few steps behind Zack as they started up the hallway. Zack glanced over his shoulder. "Hey, congratulations on your transfer." Huffman nodded what Zack took to be a "thank you." The tech couldn't recall hearing Huffman speak in the months he'd been on the ward. Of course, Zack couldn't recall ever directly speaking to Huffman either.

"Huffman, are you heading home or back to duty?"

He shrugged. What that meant Zack had no idea.

"Do you have a preference?" This was Zack's own test of a soldier's sanity. If the patient wanted to return to Vietnam, Zack felt he hadn't been cured. Huffman shrugged again.

Zack exited the ward but behind him Huffman had stopped at the entrance to the Family Room. The patient's attention drawn to something inside.

.   .   .   .   .

The nine-year-old boy sat astride the chest of his mother as she writhed on the floor hitting herself in the face with her balled-up, arthritic hands. He was a child bronco rider and struggled to stay on top. His hands not large enough, nor was he strong enough, to hold her arms so he reached and grabbed hold of her vein-lined wrists. He couldn't stop the blows. Her fists, left and right, punched her face, her nose and lips bloodied, bulbous bumps rose from her forehead.

The young boy had never seen anyone act this way, never. He recalled a science fiction movie about robots that came closest. *That's it,* he thought. *My mother is a malfunctioning robot.* Her arms pumped with a piston-like rhythm striking her face and returning to her sides before rising to strike again. And with each punch, she hissed through bloodied lips, "Keep your mouth shut—don't talk—don't say a word—don't speak—don't talk—don't say a word—shut up—just shut up—don't talk." And another blow struck the face of the little boy's mother. And he cried, "Mom, Mommy, stop, please, Mommy. Help! Somebody! Help me! Help!"

She stopped. Her hands fell to her sides. Exhaustion had saved this day. The boy moved to his mother's side. He put his arms around her. He cradled her bruised and bloodied face to his small chest, and he rocked her as she had done for him when he had his nightmares.

.   .   .   .   .

"Hey Huffman, you coming?" Zack had crossed the main corridor to the Open Ward. "Get over here!"

Huffman caught up and they passed through the TV less rec room and entered a ward identical in layout to 2A. Beds with dark blue blankets lined both walls separated by brown nightstands. Light streamed from windows lining one side of the room. The Open Ward seldom had more than half a dozen patients because they moved through far more quickly than the Closed Ward patients. The Open Ward Nurses Station was always locked protecting an empty desk and a medicine cabinet with no meds.

Because it was still morning, the ward was empty. The patients were at or should have been at the base details to which Zack had assigned them. He walked to the rear of the ward with Huffman trailing behind. He selected an empty bed and nightstand.

"Is this bed okay?"

Huffman nodded. He began putting away his belongings.

"Everyone's out on work detail. I'll give you an assignment tomorrow. On this ward, you can come and go, but don't forget to pick up your meds. And don't violate curfew."

Huffman nodded.

"Best of luck."

Huffman nodded.

"You don't talk much do you, Huffman?"

Zack's question went unanswered. The tech considered whether he should try harder to engage Huffman in conversation. But if he talked, or if he didn't talk, Zack couldn't see how that could possibly change the most important thing for the soldier . . . his orders. Huffman was going home or back to play war games.

·   ·   ·   ·   ·

Had Huffman talked he could have told Zack how much he respected medics for helping sick people. How he had to be a medic to his own mother. How when he was just seven years old he had watched his mom's sister, his Aunt Flo, place a paper bag over his mother's mouth, hold it tightly as mom lay on the floor struggling for breath. How his aunt reassured him it was for her own good, it would stop his mom from hyperventilating. His mom's gasps for air slowed and returned to a familiar rhythm of inhale, exhale, inhale, exhale.

Huffman could have told about the day when he held the bag. How afterwards, he phoned his Aunt Flo to tell her. "Dad told mom to shut up and then he left and Mom started hyper ventling. I used the bag. She's okay now." And how he needed to know so he asked, "What's hyper ventling?" And from then on he made sure paper bags were hidden in every room of the house, just in case.

But the boy never talked about what went on. Not to anyone. And the more the boy's mother acted out, the more the boy retreated into himself.

* * *

Less than a week later in the clerk's office of the psych building two MPs, one White and one Black, stood, like mismatched bookends on each side of a very dark, Black man. His skin color matched the holsters at the sides of the MPs. The thrust of his chin and sharp glare of eyes gave him an angry bearing. The clerk opened a folder and perused the papers. The patient Huffman entered the room carrying a bucket and cleaning supplies. He proceeded past the MPs and their human delivery and into the major's office.

The clerk scribbled a name and date of entry on a sheet that sat on the corner of the desk. He rose and tucked the new patient's folder under his arm. "Okay, let's take the patient Hood to—"

"My name's not Hood," the patient said.

"Damn, here we go again." The white MP shook his head.

"Not Corporal Hood?" Confused, the clerk returned to the folder to recheck the name.

In the adjoining office the patient Huffman sprayed clear liquid cleaner on a dented, gray file cabinet. He wiped it carefully. He took extra care with the front drawers where the handles had accumulated a week of smudges.

The clerk looked from the folder to the new admittance and back again. "I refuse my slave name," the soldier said. "I'm Corporal X." He said this with authority.

"Who? X? X? What?" The clerk closed the folder and looked to the MPs for an explanation. The white MP rolled his eyes while the Black MP's look said, "Don't ask me."

"We brought him to the right place." The white MP said.

The clerk shrugged. "Let's take what's-his-name to—"

"Corporal X," X interjected.

"Riiiight," the clerk said. "Let's take Patient X to 2A. First, let's store the weapons. No weapons on the wards, only for emergencies or on major's orders."

The MPs followed the clerk into the major's office where he opened the bottom desk drawer, and the MPs deposited their weapons. With a small key, the clerk locked the drawer. The four left the office to deliver Patient X to his new assignment.

Huffman finished wiping the dust from the shelves of the metal bookcase filled with Army manuals. He then moved to the desk. He moved folders and an inbox from the right side to the left side. He wiped the side clean, moved things back and wiped the other side. Satisfied that everything was in proper order, he sat.

Huffman opened the top drawer. He took out a letter opener in the shape of a cavalry soldier's sword, Major Vann's wish for a more meaningful military past. Huffman slid the opener into a slot above the bottom drawer. The lock snapped. He removed a firearm. It was heavier than he expected. He located the safety and released it. He carried the weapon with two hands as if the weapon were fragile and walked to the front of the desk. He recalled something he learned in basic training: *This is my weapon, this is my gun, one is for shooting, one is for fun. This is my weapon, this is my gun, one is for shooting*—His mother's voice interrupted, *Michael, get a move on, you'll be late for school. Michael, Michael.*

In the corner of the room was the nation's Flag. Huffman faced the Flag. He put the barrel of the weapon in his mouth and pulled the trigger.

"I gave him the detail then forgot him . . . Sarge, did you hear me? I forgot him."

Sarge looked up from his paperwork. "Who could've known?"

"The doctor could have known," Zack said, "he—"

"You're looking for someone to blame but—"

"I blame him, blame me, I blame the Army."

"Pass the blame around, it won't change things," Sarge said.

"I, I didn't know Huffman." Zack looked up to the board filled with soldiers' names. "If I'd have taken time to listen . . ."

Sarge looked at the young tech and seemed to recognize something. Maybe he recognized himself. He then turned his attention out the office window to the ward. The soldiers knew what happened, that's why it was especially quiet today. Did they speak of the suicide? No, too threatening. The table of regulars played cards, Crazy 8's. Others wrote letters; a couple worked a jigsaw puzzle; one read a comic book; another soldier read the Bible. The Sarge spoke, not to the tech but to them out there, the patients, soldiers still.

"I used to listen. I've listened and still not seen it. Gotten to know them, the part the soldiers are willing to tell, about mothers and fathers, a wife or girlfriend, sometimes kids, and then one of them will go ahead and do it; kill himself."

A quick shudder, Sarge cleared his throat and turned to Zack. "Trust Sarge on this, it's better not to know. Cause you can't stop the most important thing . . . when they die."

Sarge left the office. The tech picked up the phone and dialed home.

"Mom?"

"Son? Is that you?"

"I wanted to call and . . . see how you're doing."

"Zack, Is everything all right?"

"Everything's . . . okay. How are you? How's dad?"

"Son, are you sure everything—"

"Mom, is dad there?"

"He had a late night, son. Now's not the right time to—"

"Okay, I didn't get a chance to say goodbye when my leave was up."

The chance had been there but the young man's own stubbornness of denying he even wanted his father's attention kept him from seeking it. All he had to do was walk to the corner bar where dad spent most of his time consuming the beer made by a local brewery. His father no longer drank hard liquor; his stomach had gone on strike and now only permitted the foamy suds. Zack believed that for his dad saying goodbye wasn't as pressing as his desire to drink.

"Is there something you wanted to tell me? Has something happened?" Mom asked in that tone of hers that expected only the worst news.

"Everything's fine," He said.

Then she gave him some advice, every mother's hope. "Be happy, son," she said. And then with a somber tone, "I just want you to be happy."

His mother had suggested that "happy" be his objective in life ever since he had gone off to first grade and every grade thereafter. The most recent "be happy" counsel was a year ago when he departed for basic training. A smile never accompanied her "be happy" advice. And she repeated it so often her son knew she was wishing it for herself as much as for him.

She needed to hear him say it, so he did. "I'm happy, Mom." Zack hung up the phone. He thought, *"I wonder if Huffman's mother wished him the same?"*

Zack erased Huffman's name from the board.

Valley Forge General Hospital
Neuropsychiatric Unit

DAILY LOG - Ward 2A and 2B
December 4, 1967

DAY SHIFT

Another day - just like the other day.

EVENING SHIFT

The same.

NIGHT SHIFT

Same

Signs of a Nervous Breakdown

A Poem by Private Hardy

Around the building in which I live,
a forest introduces the farmland and terrain beyond,
but my property is marked by nightstands and beds.
My view is slashed by a thick-wired grid,
I can open a window,
I cannot go out a window.

The calendar tells me it's autumn,
when green leaves turn yellow, gold, and brown,
with an intermittent splash of fiery red.

Overhead a formation of geese,
a chorus of Canadian visitors,
sing songs of freedom.

But something is wrong with my eyes.

Color's faded,
Green to gray–
Gold to rust–
Mountains hills–
Rivers streams–

And something is wrong with my ears.
Guitar's not tuned,
Singing off key–
Rhythm's lost the . . . beat–
Poetry doesn't rhyme–
Music's noise–

The voice in my head seeks to destroy . . . me.

The Riddle

The psychiatrist, Captain Lane, sat staring at his own fingers that he drummed on the desk. The patient Grier sat across from the psychiatrist. He looked everywhere but at Dr. Lane. The soldier thought about what the psychiatrist had said. *If he wanted to go home, a discharge, home, home for good, if . . . if.*

The army captain's dress green jacket hung haphazardly on the doctor's chair. A black tie draped across the chair nearly touched the floor. The top button of the psychiatrist's brown shirt was unbuttoned. The shirt collar was damp from sweat that formed in drops on his forehead and seemed to perpetually trickle from the back and sides of his thick head of hair, a cut above his ears, an army requirement. The sweat gave sheen to his almost pinkish skin.

Dr. Lane was overweight by any standard, not just the military. It seemed the army didn't force the issue of fitness on drafted psychiatrists, perhaps feeling guilty for delaying what should be a financially rewarding occupation. As a boy he had always been soft, pudgy. It was a body type, exaggerated because he never participated in strenuous activity. Even in school a medical excuse kept him from gym class, a time his mother believed was "a daily wasteful hour of physical education." His mother had arranged for the doctor's note. It informed the school nurse that the boy had palpitations when he exercised. The family physician who wrote it was a member of the same country club as his parents.

But it wasn't the boy's physical appearance that kept him from having friends. It was an attitude, the way he looked at classmates when they were called on and failed to answer the teacher's question. He knew the answers. His hand would go up and he would look around the room to catch the other students' eyes so they would see his slight smirk of triumph.

Triumph when the young student would come forward to place an assignment on the teacher's desk, with his double chin thrust forward and carrying his report as a sacred document, he would move to the side of the desk so classmates could see him stack his work on top of the others, his report being at least two inches thicker, with a colorful protective cover and yellow tabs delineating the various chapters on the establishment of our nation's first colonies. Another "A" to show mother, who expected nothing less and received nothing less.

"Oh, I do hope I can get a passing grade on this report." He would announce it so even those who sat in the back rows could hear. It was especially galling to those who had submitted a report of a few pages believing it was good enough for a passing grade of at least a "C."

"Why don't they do assignments as well as I do?" he asked his mother.

"The other boys and girls are less intelligent. They don't have a superb family background as we do. It's in our genes. And," she added almost mouthing the words, "you'll learn later as for those people of darker color," she patted her rouge colored, pinched white cheek. "God made us smarter."

If you could call her a friend, the boy did have one, his mother. She was his support and his constant companion. His father, seldom home, "traveled the world" she said, "making business deals in far-off lands and making money for us so we can enjoy the wonderful life we deserve." And enjoy they did: regular visits to art galleries and museums, evenings at the theatre and opera, spring breaks in Paris, and when not taking vacations, the boy partnered with his mother in the neighborhood bridge club. His only sport, private golf lessons. The few times he played a round, he played alone and he road in a cart. "Walking" he told mother for her amusement "seemed something much too pedestrian." She appreciated her son's sharp sense of humor.

When her son went on to the university and completed medical school he continued in the field of psychiatry, believing that field would be a bit more challenging. And it was during this specialization that he noted that his mother's admonition about not mixing with colored people was validated. There were only white faces in his classrooms, testimony to the inferiority of all colored people.

The timing of his entering the profession was fortunate. It coincided with the new development and appreciation of drugs. He was relieved that most professors extolled the efficacy and superiority of pharmaceuticals. He would have found it demeaning to have to listen to the whining and the excuses and the rationalizations of a client for whatever had prompted them to seek treatment in the first place. He was unwilling to spend more than a minimal amount of his time listening to their trials and tribulations before prescribing pills. Here on the psych wards, in keeping with his beliefs, he eliminated group sessions. Why, he felt, should he encourage a patient to broadcast weaknesses to others, who in turn were waiting to confess their own, resulting in a spiraling dumbing-down of the entire group.

• • • • •

"You do understand what I'm telling you, don't you?" It seemed to the psychiatrist that he had been waiting a lifetime for the patient Grier to respond. He waited and thought of his own situation. *What a terrible time in my life to have to serve in the Army and deal with the likes of those with but a rudimentary knowledge of how the mind works. How had it come to this? I'm a doctor, drafted as if he were a high school dropout. How could my mother with all her contacts not get me out of this?*

Dr. Lane ruminated. He still hadn't gotten over this past month's ECT incident. As the soldier Grier hemmed and hawed, saying absolutely nothing, the psychiatrist held a mental conversation with himself. *How dare those presumptuous techs. I was handling the glitz in the procedure. They hadn't given me time to respond. Those techs, one looked Italian, a Dago, and his partner the Negro, emotions rule their actions. The remaining procedures that morning completed without any difficulty. I should have reported them to the major. But who knows what lies they would tell to protect each other. Those types were always jealous and resentful of me; my success is an announcement of their failures. And now sitting across from me is another Negro, who unless he takes my advice could let emotions interfere with the intelligent action he should take.*

"I will say this one last time as clearly as I can." Dr. Lane slid his chair closer to the patient. "If you want to go home, you must say nothing. No one, and I mean of any authority, will believe you."

The soldier Grier stared down at his hands. He seemed to be checking each digit multiple times to ensure all his fingers were there. His voice so low Dr. Lane strained to hear him.

"What do I do." Which came out in Grier's mumbled style as "*Whaldo.*"

"Do? You do nothing. Do nothing and you can be going home."

As Mumbling Grier exited the room the doctor repeated, "Nothing, you hear. Do nothing."

Grier closed the door, and before he moved any farther, he heard noises from across the hall. Grier walked closer to the Family Room. From inside there was an orange glow.

·　　·　　·　　·　　·

Shots, shouts, high-pitched screams while red and yellow sparks and embers rose like giant fireflies into the night sky from the dry roof of the hooch. They ran from their home like startled sheep, the very old and the very young. A White soldier, as if he were a cowboy, swung a crude torch above the family. "Yahoo! Get-a-long little doggies!"

A second soldier put fire to another hootch. The cowboy soldier turned and held out the torch. "Grier, don't stand there! Take the torch!" the cowboy said. The fire behind him made the cowboy's head and face appear to jump along with the flames. A brown hand and arm emerged from the darkness and took hold of the torch.

The Vietnamese village transformed to a dark night and a small house in the woods. Four white-hooded men held a Black man to the ground. Another man held a torch to the low-hanging roof that crackled and burst hot and bright casting a circle of light and dancing shadows on the surrounding bushes. A child hid there, eyes wide, with both hands clasped tightly over his mouth.

"Come on Grier," the cowboy soldier shouted, "Burn these Gook shacks!" The brown hand that held the torch didn't move. Suddenly, more yelling, more soldiers, a platoon led by a White lieutenant entered the circle. In the excitement the cowboy and his sidekick moved quickly to lose themselves. The lieutenant looked from the village directly at Private First Class Grier standing at the Family Room door in the hallway. The officer approached as close to PFC Grier as the room would allow.

"Soldier, put down the torch! You hear me? That's an order. What's wrong with you? Can you move? Medic! What's wrong with this man? Medic!"

The patient Grier lunged away from the doorway to escape the heat from the torch, the last thing he remembered of the burning village. He quick stepped to the ward. He found an empty table, sat, took out a cigarette, struck a match, or tried to. The flame caused him to flinch, the match went out. Grier struck a second match and held it out in front of his face, mesmerized by the flame. The match went out. Grier lit another match and watched again as it burned out. Tech Turner joined him at the table, took the matches and lit the cigarette for Grier.

"I didn't do anything," Grier said. And with the ping and pong sound from the back porch in the background, Mumbling Grier surprised Turner by speaking quietly but clearly. "They burned the huts. They said the 'Cong were the lowest form of life, so they burned them out. They called them gooks, slopes and slant-eyes."

"What are you talking about?" The tech leaned forward to hear it all.

"So maybe someone was lower than me," Grier said, looking somewhere beyond Turner's shoulder.

"I'm not getting this," Turner said, and he wasn't. It wasn't in Turner's body, Grier's feeling of worthlessness.

"That we, you, me, Negroes, we're not the lowest." For the briefest moment Grier tried to swallow a sour taste in his throat. It came back up in a whisper, "My buddies believed the gooks were."

"Buddies?" Turner said. "But you didn't go along with–"

"I didn't stop them, I . . . I . . ." Grier looked directly at Turner who saw a deep sadness in the patient's eyes. Grier spoke a bit louder and deliberately, "I watched it happen."

Turner responded quickly. "It's hard to stop others from doing wrong, from doing terrible things." Turner said, "But you stopped yourself." The tech, ever the caretaker, true to his training had reframed a negative.

Their moment was interrupted when Sergeant McCabe came out of the office carrying a clipboard. "Vasquez and Perez," Sarge announced, "Amigos, pack up your stuff. You're going to the Open Ward." He had everyone's attention. "When the paperwork clears, you're going home. Vasquez, back to Puerto Rico. Perez, say hello to New York."

Some smiles and laughter, and even a couple of patients applauded their roommates' good fortune. Perez excitedly translated the message to Vasquez who grabbed Perez in a bear hug and lifted him off the floor in exhilaration.

Sergeant McCabe approached Tech Turner who was lighting another cigarette for Grier.

"Okay, Dr. Freud," Sarge said, "get beds for those twins on the Open Ward. But first stop at Dr. Lane's office. He never met with Vasquez and needs to get that done before he can be discharged. You stay with the doc and keep Perez there to translate."

Tech Turner whispered to Grier, "We'll talk later," and went to help the Spanish speakers.

•   •   •   •   •

Tech Turner knocked on Dr. Lane's door.

"Enter-now-now, quickly, quickly."

Perez and Vasquez with their belongings in their arms waited as Tech Turner entered the room leaving the door partially open.

Dr. Lane, glanced up from a notebook, "Who have we here?" He asked and then answered his own question. "A medic that likes to play doctor. I haven't forgotten what your buddy and–"

"Yes sir." Turner said quickly. "I've been told you need to–"

"Meet with Senior Vasquez." Dr. Lane said with a sigh of resignation. He closed the notebook and turned and faced Turner. "Do you want to hear my theory?" Dr. Lane paused to stare at the tech's nametag and then a sharp short exhale on "Turner."

"Theory, sir?"

"You do know what a theory is?"

Turner didn't respond. Doctor Lane leaned back in his chair. He interlocked his fingers with the knuckles on top and raised his index fingers bringing them together. For a moment, Turner was reminded of "This is the church, this is the steeple." The psychiatrist brought his index fingers to his chin.

"It's a theory I've developed thanks to the Army throwing together every race of people on this godforsaken ward." Dr. Lane waited for Turner to respond.

"And that theory, sir?" Turner said flatly as he counted the craters on the doctor's cheeks and forehead.

"This is the nation's first war, the first," Dr. Lane said, "where races other than the White race have fought in large numbers. It's my theory that Puerto Ricans, Mexicans and so-called Hispanics, and, of course, you Negroes, are prolonging this war." The doctor waited for questions.

Turner by now had counted fourteen craters on Doctor Lane's face and the only question he wanted to ask: *Had it been acne or smallpox that had marked the man?* He decided to remain silent. Dr. Lane then followed his own question with another.

"You may ask why you people are the reason for how terrible this war's going?" The psychiatrist waited again for Turner to participate. He waited.

Finally, "And the reason, sir?" Turner felt he had to move this along.

"Because you Negroes and Senior Vasquez out there are of much lower intelligence, lower on the socioeconomic ladder, lower on every measure to White Americans."

"That's your theory, sir?" Turner responded without emotion but wished he hadn't responded at all. It might encourage the doctor to continue. And he did.

"Mine and a lot of other educated people," Dr. Lane shot back, frustrated that Turner didn't seem upset, impressed or even interested. He vowed to go after Turner another time. The psychiatrist looked down at a chart. Turner understood the Racism 101 lecture was over.

Outside of the slightly opened door, Perez had translated for Vasquez the crux of the psychiatrist's theory. "The doctor says the war goes badly because we Puerto Ricans are poor and stupid."

Tech Turner stepped to the door and motioned for the patients to enter. Seeing two patients enter Dr. Lane said sharply, "I need Vasquez, only Vasquez."

"Vasquez doesn't speak English, sir," Turner said, "Perez serves as his translator."

"I certainly do not need a translator. I speak three foreign languages. Spanish is the simplest of the three," the psychiatrist said in his proficient superior tone.

"Sir, it's not just for language, these two are always together and—"

"Playing doctor again? Leave. You and his security blanket." Dr. Lane motioned to Perez as if shooing a fly, "Out, out."

"Sir, the sergeant ordered me to—"

"You see these bars?" Dr. Lane pointed behind him to the captain's bars on the coat hung on his chair. "If you don't know what the bars stand for, read this sign." With his pudgy hand he held up the nameplate on his desk: Captain Lane M.D.

"You tell your sergeant, that the caaaa-ptain said that you two were not needed. Now out of here."

Tech Turner and Perez departed the room and headed to the main ward. Sergeant McCabe, Sergeant McCabe, standing at the watchtower, was surprised to see them.

"Why are you here? Where's Vasquez?"

"I told the doc I was to stay," Turner said, "but he said something about him being a captain and he ordered us to leave."

Sarge shook his head. "Perez, is the doc safe with your buddy?"

"Are you familiar with the Puerto Rican saying?" Perez asked in return. His attention to back down the hallway signaled a serious concern.

The sarge took a deep breath. "Guess I'll hear it now."

"Never," Perez raised his index finger in emphasis, "leave a crazy Puerto Rican in a room with a racist doctor."

The shriek came precisely at the end of Perez's Puerto Rican cultural lesson. From the opened door of the psychiatrist's office the cry reverberated down the hallway. Dr. Lane was launched through the air out of his office. He landed on the floor like a tossed duffel bag of dirty laundry. The chubby doctor tried scrambling to his feet. A green trashcan flew from the room, hit him in the chest, and knocked him back down.

The doctor sat stunned in the dregs of his own pipe tobacco that a few minutes ago he had emptied into the trash. Folders, papers and books flew from the office and landed on and around the bewildered man. Something heavy hit the wall above his left shoulder. Dr. Lane saw it was his bible, the Diagnostic and Statistical Manual of Mental Disorders. He looked left off the ward and considered whether he should try to run from the building. A framed medical diploma arrived in time to knock sense into his head. He wouldn't have made it. The prestigious diploma glanced off the side of the doctor's skull and the frame shattered against the wall behind him.

The captain, ear bleeding, saw Sergeant McCabe and scrambled toward the main ward. His movements resembled a jumbo crab doing the low crawl escaping the boiling pot. Behind him Vasquez entered the hallway. The soldier reached for the heavy large metal ashtray outside the door and lifted it with one hand. A trail of sand and cigarette butts poured to the floor as Vasquez stalked his therapist.

Sergeant McCabe, Turner and Perez ran to the doctor crawling towards them on all fours. Dr. Lane focused his terror-filled eyes on Vasquez's Puerto Rican partner. He reached translator Perez and grasped him around the legs. The doctor whimpered.

"Salvame-salvame-Save me-Por favor-Por favor-Save me-Salvame."

Perez yelled at Vasquez who was closing fast. "Parate! Nada mas! Nada mas!"

Vasquez heard his compatriot's call to stop. He stopped. Perez continued but now calmly, "Ya pronto nos vamos para nuestra casa." Reassured by Perez that they would be going home soon, Vasquez put down the metal weapon. Perez turned to Sergeant McCabe. "Vasquez is okay now. He's back with me."

"And he'll stay with you," Sarge said, "until you get on that train for home,"

"Thank you-Thank you-You saved me-Saved me . . ." Captain Lane went on and on. And he was saved, at least, from more physically harm. But mentally perhaps he never recovered. That day the psychiatrist informed Major Vann that he had been traumatized and could no longer perform his duties. He insisted on a leave of absence. The major rather than granting Dr. Lane his request had him transferred immediately to a psychiatric unit for officers somewhere in Texas. Rumor had it, not as a doctor but as a patient.

What wasn't rumor were the last words that the soldier Perez said to Dr. Lane as the psychiatrist clutched the soldier's legs begging to be saved. Perez responded in what this time may have been a Puerto Rican riddle: "So who is more valuable in the Army, the poor and uneducated, or you?"

Valley Forge General Hospital
Neuropsychiatric Unit

DAILY LOG - Ward 2A and 2B
December 10, 1967

DAY SHIFT

Another day - just like the other day.

EVENING SHIFT

The same.

NIGHT SHIFT

Same

Lost

A Poem by Private Hardy

There's verse that meanders on city streets for miles and miles,

then turns sharply into an alley,

Losing its way zigzagging through poverty looking for an escape,

then pulled over by the police,

the obsessive-compulsive driver hits his head on the windshield

and screams,

"Non-metrical verse is a curse!"

The Beer Truck Hijacking

Drip ... Drip ... Drip. Four soaked MPs stood at the rear of the major's office their hats tucked tightly under their arms. The ranking MP stepped forward taking his place next to Sergeant Helms. Drip ... Drip. Major Vann leaned forward in his chair, elbows on desk, chin supported on clenched hands. The major focused on the hat tucked under the MP's arm. He watched a drop of water release its precarious hold on the brim and fall out of his sight to the MP's feet. No military rank could have stopped that drop.

"Major, best you hear the facts as MP White told them to me," Sergeant Helms said.

The major stood, turned his back on the men, and stared through the window to the main hospital across the narrow blacktop road. A moment passed. He sighed, one of regret. Still no medical officer to replace him and coasting through the remaining month of December until retirement wasn't going to happen.

Outside, the torrential rain told only part of the story. MP White removed a damp notebook from his wet shirt pocket. He cleared his throat. "Sir, today, at approximately 1100 hours, a civilian delivery truck was stolen from the front of the NCO Club."

•   •   •   •   •

The white Budweiser truck made its way slowly through the downpour and parked at the NCO Club. You could barely make out the red of the Budweiser logo through the deluge. Everything else that morning was the color of rain, no color at all. The driver, a man in what may have been a white uniform, exited the truck and blindly stacked several cases of beer on a dolly. Trying not to slip and slide, he rolled the cases up a ramp.

At the sound of the truck's motor revving and gears grinding, the delivery man let go of the dolly, changed direction and ran back down the ramp, slipped and fell on his ass. The Budweiser logo drove off through the driving rain. The truck sped along the base's narrow back road then veered across a soggy fairway of the base golf course.

• • • • •

"The delivery person," the MP said, "contacted us from the NCO Club and reported the hijacking. But" the MP paused, cleared his throat again and continued, "our MPs at the gates never saw a beer truck leave the base."

"Sergeant," the major turned back from the window, "did he say beer truck?"

"Yes sir, a beer truck." Sergeant Helms's eyes raised and his head slanted as if to indicate unbelievable but true.

The major stiffened. He turned back to the window.

MP White continued, "A few minutes after the truck was stolen, we're not exact about the time, four golfers—"

"Sergeant," the major interrupted and quickly turned back to Sergeant Helms, "did he say golfers?"

"Yes sir, golfers."

• • • • •

This wasn't the first time the patient Rao had hijacked beer. He had a history of teenage petty crime including stealing beer in the wintertime from neighbors' back porches. His parents were honest people, but their son somehow came to admire the crooks and hoodlums he saw in the old black-and-white films on late night television. His favorite show was "The Untouchables," a popular series that lauded the work of Eliot Ness and his crime fighters during prohibition. But Rao only watched the first half-an-hour because that was when the gangsters were winning. And today, while speeding the beer truck around the base road, Rao pictured himself back in prohibition days, working for the mob and delivering illegal brew to a speakeasy.

The beer truck stopped alongside a soggy, manicured green. A wet flag was stuck to its pole hiding the hole's identification. The truck door opened and Rao, wearing patient blues and an Army camouflage hat, jumped from the cab and ran on to the green where he unfurled the flag to reveal the number "Six." He returned to the truck, reached into the cab and removed a collapsible army shovel. Rushing to a nearby mud trap, a sand trap on any other day, he jammed the shovel into the ground. He paused every four or five shovels-full to wipe rain from his eyes. When he had removed almost

4

enough dirt for a foxhole, he returned to the truck and rolled open the cargo area. He removed a case of beer, carried it to the beer hole, and lowered it carefully as if the contents shouldn't be shaken. He returned to the truck, removed another case, and made another delivery.

* * *

"Ahemm." The MP, not appreciating Sergeant Helms's interruption, continued reading from his notebook. "Four golfers were standing at the sixth tee when they saw a beer truck pull up to the green and a patient exit."

"How did they knowooooo...?" The major seemed to hold on to the "o."

Interrupted again, MP White looked up from his notes to ad lib, "It's reasonable to infer that he was a patient because ... and major let me quote what the golfers said here," the MP returned to his notes, "even in the pouring rain we agreed the man was dressed in patient blues. We watched him dig a hole and bury a couple cases of beer."

"Sir," Sergeant Helms stepped in, "the story gets a little weird here, but even the men who would chase a little white ball around especially in the rain have got to be a little—" He stopped himself realizing his slip as the major nodded toward the bookcase where the puniest golf trophy ever awarded an officer was on display.

The MP absorbed in checking the notes started again. "The golfers wanted to continue so they yelled to the patient to let them play through." The MP looked at the major. "Sir, playing through is a golf expression meaning—"

"I know what the hell it means," snapped the major who played to a twenty-five handicap.

* * *

Patient Rao waved an arm motioning for the golfers to play through. The other golfers had already teed-off so the last took his turn. He wiped the rain from his eyes and swung at the ball. The golfers lost sight of the Titlest as it soared skyward. The tee shot descended, still unseen, and struck the side of the Bud truck with a clang. The ball rolled within five feet of the flag. The golfers slapped hands and hustled to the green where Rao stood chugging a can of beer.

"The golfers," the MP said, again referring to his notes, "approached the green and saw that the patient was inebriated. They believed it would have been risky to interfere with this patient because he could've had a weapon. And they were of the opinion–" The MP stopped reading the notes to interject "and I am quoting here," then back to his notes, "a person out there doing what he was doing had to be crazy, and therefore, potentially dangerous."

The MP looked up again. "Sir, I believe this was the appropriate response from the soldiers. We try to tell everyone to let the MPs handle potential problems because you just never know when–"

"Could we speed this up?" The major's left eye began to twitch, his patience at an end. This was a bit surprising since the major was a golfer, and golf certainly takes patience. Wait. Hit. Walk. Wait. Hit. Walk. Wait. Putt. Wait. Putt again. Wait. Walk. Wait . . .

Rao handed each golfer a beer. They stood on the green in their soaked hats, pants and muddied tasseled golf shoes and popped the tops, wiped rain from their eyes, and toasted Rao for his willingness to share. While the golfers putted, Rao finished burying the beer and returned to the truck. As he prepared to drive off, the golfers came to attention and saluted him with beer cans, rain dripping off their faces. They didn't know it but the patient Rao deserved the salute. The soldier Rao had served our country in peace times and now through war. In Vietnam, Rao was a platoon leader, a leader of young recruits. And Rao was a binge drinker. The amount of beer he would drink would multiply after each trip back from the field and after the loss of still another young man. Rao expected to be sent back to war again.

The misadventure that led to his being shipped stateside had happened just over a month ago. The then, Sergeant Rao, in an NCO club near Da Nang, waited until closing time and hid under a pool table until lights-out and the doors were locked. Rao went behind the bar turned on the plastic ornamental Bourbon Whiskey sign with Jim Beam providing a pinkish glow to the surroundings. He sat at the bar, rising only for a bathroom break or to get more Lucky Lager beer from the cooler, beer was his preference.

Because it was 2:00 AM Sunday morning and the club didn't open again until that evening, Rao sat, drank, and talked to ghosts throughout the night about how it had happened; how fast it all went down; how one decision could have changed things. How. How. How.

At sunrise, for breakfast he chewed on beef jerky, drank more beer and continued drinking until that afternoon when the barroom became his bedroom. Drunk as he was, he still took time to remove the balls from the pool table and drop them in the pockets before he climbed on the table, stretched-out, and got some Z's. That's how and where the proprietor found him Sunday evening. But it wasn't entirely bad for Rao. His squad paid the bar bill. It was the least they could do for their sergeant who had helped most of their young inexperienced asses stay alive in the field . . . most of them.

•   •   •   •   •

"Unfortunately," the MP said, and shook his head in resignation, "the golfers didn't report the incident until they had completed eighteen holes. However, they did direct us to beer buried in sand traps on," he returned to his notes, "the twelfth, fourteenth, and sixteenth holes."

"Major," Sergeant Helms raised up on his toes and interjected, "the truck was next sighted where it was abandoned at the fence of our ballfield."

•   •   •   •   •

The middle-aged couple arrived at the base after a long day's drive from their home in North Carolina. The man had a difficult time seeing through the car's rain-streaked windshield. He had meant to replace the wipers before the trip but he just didn't seem to care about the day-to-day things, not since news that his son had been seriously wounded. His wife nudged him as they drove past a parked Budweiser truck where at a fence a man was digging a hole.

•   •   •   •   •

"Thanks to citizen involvement," the MP said with satisfaction, "visitors reported to an MP that they witnessed a man in the pouring rain, and in their words, 'frantically digging a hole under a fence.'"

•   •   •   •   •

Rao pushed a case of beer under the fence, and low-crawled through the grass and mud as he sang in a heavily labored monotone, "Ninety nine bottles of beer on the wall, ninety nine bottles of beer, if one of those bottles happens to fall . . .," where he joined the brew on the inside.

•   •   •

"We MP's confirmed . . . ah . . ." He flipped to the end of the notebook, "that a hole was dug under the psych unit's ballfield fence. We believe—"

"That a crazy has come home." The major completed the MP's report.

"It's only been a few hours, sir." Sergeant Helms said, "If we move now—"

"Lock down the building. Find him." The major got louder. "Find him. Find him!"

"Yes sir." Sergeant Helms stepped to the phone and dialed. "This is Sergeant Helms." He went up on his toes. "Major Vann has ordered a lockdown. Have every patient at his bunk in five minutes. Same thing goes for the Open Ward. No one leaves the building."

In the Nurses Station, Tech Turner answered Sergeant Helms's second call. "Ward 2A, Turner here . . . No, Sarge is at the main hospital. I'm in charge. No, it's just Tech Tonakis and me. I was left in charge." Turner didn't believe it was his young age that had Sergeant Helms questioning the tech's leadership. He had been warned by other Black soldiers that the color of his skin was what the sergeant really questioned. "Inspection? Yes sergeant. Got it."

Turner alerted his partner for the day shift. "Zack, Sergeant Helms is on the way, a surprise inspection. I'll get them going here and you get the Open Ward." Tech Turner quickly issued instructions, "Everyone to your bunks! Inspection! Let's go people! Please clean up your area."

Zack hustled across the corridor to the Open Ward where a soldier's psychological treatment program had ended, successful or not. On the Open Ward a group of patients stood at the foot of Rao's bed. Recent Open Ward transfers: Vasquez, heading back to Puerto Rico, Perez to his home in New York, Slob Shumacher, home to Pittsburgh, and the recent convert of Elijah Mohammed, the Black Muslim, Patient X., birth name James Wyatt was heading back to Atlanta, Georgia. Also part of the crowd, still waiting for their orders to a combat unit, were Side Pockets Schroeder, Push-ups Tabor and Model Maker Leaverton.

The soldier Rao who had sneaked in from the ballfield entrance was now passed-out in his bed. He still wore a wet camouflage hat that covered his dark head of hair. His shirt and pants were damp and dirty, his boots muddy. A dozen empty beer cans lay on his bed and on the floor. In the opened nightstand, beer cans crowded his personal belongings.

Zack rushed in. "Listen up! In five minutes, there's going to be an inspection. It sounds serious so . . ." Zack arrived to the group and to Rao's bed. "What the? Oh, man, Rao, not now."

"Rao is fucked up," Leaverton said. This from the model maker with serious anger issues.

"Everyone," Zack said, "let's go. Get those boots off, and the dirty blues." He picked the beer cans off Rao's bed. The patients watched.

"Are you soldiers getting this?" Zack looked at the group almost fiercely. "If Rao's caught, they will lock him up. The stockade!"

Schroeder and Patient X began removing Rao's boots and clothes.

"Cover his clothes in the hamper," Zack said. Perez motioned to Vasquez who seemed to understand perfectly what the tech had requested and grabbed the boots while Perez carried and buried the wet clothes.

Patient Shumacher, a candy bar stuffed in his mouth, pulled-up his pants, grabbed a pillowcase and began filling it with beer cans from the nightstand. Zack used a sheet to wipe mud from the floor. The patient Leaverton did nothing.

Rao was down to his skivvies and bare feet. The tech knelt at the bed and hoisted Rao onto his back. "You," Zack said to Leaverton, "Strip the bed and put the sheets in the hamper."

"Ah, I don't even like the guy, why should I have—"

"You don't even like yourself," Shumacher said, as he dragged the pillowcase now filled with beer to the center of the room.

Leaverton responded. "Fuck you and the horse you rode in on."

Zack mediated. "Hey, let's just say it's God's test. Sometimes you've got to help people you don't like." Zack couldn't believe those words came from his mouth, but they did.

Leaverton considered the tech's words. He shook his head, as if clearing confusion. "That makes no fucking sense at all." The soldier Leaverton, an atheist, stripped the bed anyway.

"Shumacher," Zack said, "On the Closed Ward Dr. Lane's gone for good and his office is empty. There's a file cabinet and desk, find space to hide the beer." Shumacher hesitated. "Go," Zack said. "Go," Zack said again. And the soldier did. Zack turned to the others. "The rest of you, wipe the area; then stand by your beds."

Shumacher, pants hanging onto his buttocks, dragged the loaded pillowcase off the ward. The tech followed with Rao on his back. Zack arrived at the main corridor, looked left to check the status of the MP who manned the building's front entrance. He was there, but he was holding the front door open, mesmerized by the torrential downpour. Shumacher had already entered the empty psychiatrist's office and closed the door behind him. Zack completed his reconnaissance at almost the same time Sergeant Helms, with four MPs behind him, pushed open the door from the office hallway and entered the corridor. They turned in the direction of 2A.

Too late, Zack with his human backpack had already crossed. Out one door while in the other, couldn't have been closer if the Marx Brothers had performed it. Zack continued down the hallway of the Closed Ward and entered the first of the two seclusion rooms. He deposited the unconscious Rao on the mat.

On the Closed Ward a witness to the transfer was Shaky Metz. Metz had exited the latrine in time to see Zack, resembling Quasimodo, enter the seclusion room and then exit without the hump on his back. Metz with facial tics in full operation watched as Zack locked the door.

Shumacher left the doctor's office after loading the last of the beer cans into the top drawer of the desk. He turned to cross to the Open Ward and collided with Sergeant Helms and his deputies.

"You . . ." Sergeant Helms growled, "Are . . ." He gritted his teeth and went up on his toes, "to be . . ." his voice higher "at your bunk." Then even higher, as if he were a submarine's dive alarm, "Now! Now! Now!"

MP White instructed two of the MPs. "You two follow that sad example of a soldier and check his ward."

MP White looked in the first room on the Closed Ward, the empty family room. Chairs, a couch, and a TV, no one hiding there. The other MP opened the room that had been visited by Slob Shumacher. A desk, a chair, a file cabinet, a couch, no one hiding there. Sergeant Helms approached Zack at the door of the seclusion room.

"Patients ready for inspection." Zack stood at attention.

Sergeant Helms motioned the tech aside and looked through the room's window. The patient Rao in his skivvies lay on a bare mat.

"Who's that character?"

"Sergeant, that's Patient Rao. He woke up last night agitated and shouting. Night crew gave him a shot. The daily log has the report if you want to read it?"

"Stuff the log," Sergeant Helms said, and moved to the next seclusion room's window. The room was empty. Helms and the MPs hustled to the main area.

Across on the Open Ward the patients stood by their beds as the two MPs, more to harass than any other reason, checked nightstands, lifted mattresses and even went to the floor and looked under several beds. Rao's area was clean; the bed was stripped, no sign that anyone lived there. An MP ventured to the clothes hamper. He glanced in at the dirty towels, crinkled is nose, and decided against any further probing in case insanity was contagious.

On the Closed Ward Tech Turner accompanied the MPs as they moved bed to bed raising mattresses and opening nightstands. Zack stood next to Sergeant Helms at the head of the ward.

"What are they looking for?" Zack asked.

"A truck was stolen at the NCO Club," Sergeant Helms said, as he watched the MPs complete the search.

"Let me get this straight, the MPs are looking for a truck . . . in a nightstand," Zack said.

"No, smart ass, we're looking for the patient who stole the truck," Sergeant Helms responded.

"Okay, now it's clear," Zack said and pointed to the nearest nightstand. "You're looking for a patient in a nightstand."

"When we catch him, smart ass, it'll be court martial and dishonorable discharge." Tech Turner joined them in time to have heard Sergeant Helms's edict.

"Shouldn't it matter if the soldier's sick?" Turner said.

Sergeant Helms looked in disbelief at Turner. "He's a thief."

Shaky Metz shuffled up to Sergeant Helms. The tattletale pointed a shaking finger toward the seclusion rooms. "Se-Se-Se-Seclusion, Se-Se-Seclusion Room."

"That's right, that's right," Sergeant Helms said. He spoke slowly as if to a child, "there's an empty room just for you." Just for a moment it appeared the sergeant was going to pat Metz on the head. He didn't. He hated to touch the patients. The search completed, Sergeant Helms and his posse headed off bound for the upstairs ward.

A day later after the Budweiser deliveryman retrieved the beer buried in the sand traps and had conducted an inventory of the truck's contents, he found that several cases of beer were still unaccounted for. Military history will record that the soldier Rao was responsible for drinking one of those cases but wherever he hid the remainder would remain a military secret. The binge drinker on awakening a day and half later in the seclusion room could not recall the previous thirty-six hours at all. Experienced from previous blackouts, Rao knew before his adventure that he'd have that problem so back when he was burying his treasure he took time to sketch a map. He didn't count on the map being left in his blues and sent to the base laundry where the "X marks the spot" was washed clean.

Rao didn't recall nor did he ask what happened that rainy day, and neither the techs nor the patients spoke of it. Two weeks later, the lifer soldier, Rao received his marching orders: Back to the Mekong Delta, back to where he was needed most; back to lead the inexperienced into the jungle. Maybe he would complete the next detail without the death of another young man.

Maybe then he wouldn't need to lose himself in drink. Maybe.

What once was the base golf course. (2014 photo.)

Once was the golf course caddy shack. (2014 photo.)

Valley Forge General Hospital
Neuropsychiatric Unit

DAILY LOG - Ward 2A and 2B
December 12, 1967

DAY SHIFT

Another day - just like the other day.

EVENING SHIFT

The same.

NIGHT SHIFT

Same

The Scream

A Poem by Private Hardy

AAAAAIIIIIIIIIIIEEEEEE!
Birth
AAAAAAAAAAAAAAAA!
Anger
AAAAAUUUUUUUUU!
Anguish
EEEEEEEEEEEEEEEEEE!
Fear
OOOOOOOOOOHHHHH!
Terror
AAAAARRRRRRHHHH!
Madness
NOOOOOOOOOOOOOOO!
Death

The SCREAM of self:
the tormented; trapped; defeated.
The SCREAM for others:
the chaos; horror; war.
The SCREAM
AAAAAIIIIIIIIIIIEEEEEE! AAAAAAAAAAAAAAAA! AAAAAUUUUUUUUU!
EEEEEEEEEEEEEEEEEE! OOOOOOOOOOHHHHH! AAAAARRRRRRHHHH!
NOOOOOOOOOOOOOOO!
of the writer.

Into the Night

The psych ward's midnight peacefulness was sporadically interrupted by the burst of angry mutterings of patients who argued with themselves as they slept. The patients who were awake adjusted to the sounds by realigning their sheets and blankets and altering their position, one side to the other and back again. For those awake, it was the moaning and whimpering that disturbed them the most. Perhaps crying would have been easier to bear because it seldom happened and when it did happen, it was by so few and for such a short time. Out there and done with. But the whimpering was continual and hinted at actions and events and fear too dark to share.

Patient Kelly, his scarred face hidden by the pillow, slept a deep technicolor sleep. Kelly's most telling feature wasn't his size or deep voice it was the left side of his face and neck. It was as if a volcano had erupted at Kelly's temple and a trail of lava had flowed down his cheek to his neck and disappeared under his blue collar. How much farther did it flow? How low can you go? Scarface Kelly was a gentle bear until he got one of his migraines. And with the headache Kelly could hear the rumbling of engines and see flashes of light.

Kelly looked upwards, searching. He saw it over the hill the chemist in the sky splashing liquid from a silver beaker igniting the green skyline. The tops of trees and all the green below turned white and red, fiery red. The trees, bushes, brush, and grass, burned. Kelly ran and the fire ran with him. Not until he was safe from the flame, not until he touched his face and his skin came away on his hand, did he scream.

The scream woke Kelly but no one else, it was in his dream. For the napalm and who delivered it, he held no animosity, no unanswered questions as to how the mistake was made, or why it happened to him. He had enlisted and it was war. But the headaches, when they came, they took him to another place. A place later he couldn't recall. His squad described how he had "exploded," "blown his top," "gone ballistic." He broke tables, threw chairs and destroyed inanimate objects. No soldiers got hurt because they got out of his way until the rage passed.

Tonight, Kelly rose from his bed at the rear of the ward. Outside the office, at Watchtower, Kelly stopped next to Tech Grey asleep and slouched in a chair. Balanced on a chair in front of Grey was a small television powered by a long extension cord from the office. The TV was allowed but only for the night shift to get them through the quiet time. The light from the black-and-white screen flickered off of the tech's face.

Kelly stared down at Grey. Kelly's lips stretched wide framing clenched teeth. His body tensed and then stretched upwards. He was even bigger now. Kelly raised his hands to his temples and pressed. If he could just squeeze harder, he could force out the infection and drain the abscess.

Kelly sucked air deep into his lungs and held it. Holding, holding, holding, holding, holding, until his lungs demanded relief and he exhaled, little by little by little by little. His eyes tightly closed, seconds passed and reached the minute mark, his arms dropped to his sides. He opened his eyes, moist from the fatigue of the battle. He went into the latrine.

At a table at the far end of the ward under the golden glow of the overhead nightlight, Smiling Hardy had been struggling for an ending to a poem . . . until now. And so he finished writing "Into the Night."

The book cart entered the ward
pushed by pretty volunteers,
young, like me,
but as I used to be,
I feel old now.

Dressed in compassionate blue outfits
they offered dog-eared paperbacks,
and with the kindest of looks,
creased comic books,
I feel young now.

I perused the literary donations
discovering a collection of words,
poems I've read,
by the famous and dead,
I'm inspired now.

Nighttime with notebook at a table

dimmed ceiling lights cast an orange glow,
over the soldiers in beds,
tranquilized by meds,
I must write now.

"Do not go gentle into that good night"
Thomas wrote it, I read it, but they live it,
they toss, turn, sit up, lie down,
sleep in deep water and drown,
I watch them now.

Not to go gentle into the night, a soldier rises
and walks, back and forth, whispering to self,
suddenly gesturing to the ward,
right arm slashing like a sword,
I hold my breath now.

Stationed between office and latrine
A medic sits watching TV, night shift's company,
no one passes the watchtower,
on guard for the bogeyman's hour,
I am grateful now.

But no, our sentry sleeps, a victim of time
the soldier stands over him with face contorted,
a clenched fist his weapon,
held only for a second,
I close my eyes now.

I can't stop him, can't move, can't yell
Words on paper are all I know,
I was the class oddball,
I wrote through it all,

And while others here continue to fight,
I'll escape gently into this night.
I'll go inside me now.

A Leader of Men

The young boy's mother cooked for him, cleaned his room, ironed his clothes, fixed his lunches, packed his favorite peanut butter and jelly sandwiches, made certain he brushed his teeth every night, and before he went to bed, kissed him on the cheek, and then, in the middle of night, checked to make certain his covers hadn't fallen off, or that he wasn't having bad dreams.

The young boy's father worked ten and twelve hours at the mill, overtime paid for the extras, the boy's bicycle, the baseball glove and bat; the vacation at the beach; and his parents reminded him, to study hard, always tell the truth, be respectful of others, and he would grow up to be a leader of men.

●　　　●　　　●　　　●　　　●

Gray clouds passed over the Pennsylvania hills and descended on the valley and the hospital. The ward darkened as if shades were drawn over the opened windows that lined the ward. On ward 2A the techs and patients moved to close off the approaching storm. Zack headed to the Open Ward to do the same there since the patients were elsewhere at their daily details.

●　　　●　　　●　　　●　　　●

The neighbors and the minister said he was such a cute young boy. A mop of sandy hair over his ears and forehead, leaving only earlobes visible; a square jaw with straight white teeth that could have served as an ad for top and bottom dentures; his chest pushed out as if he were a grown man and a self-important one; clenched fists at his waist and his arms bent outward at the elbows he stood mimicking a testosterone-laden professional wrestler. When he walked, he rocked his body forward as if to propel himself. This resulted in a half-stride because of his bowlegs, and his refusal to sufficiently

169

bend his knees not wanting to appear even shorter than he was. His gait an abbreviated stomp as if angry at the grass or pavement on which he walked.

●　　●　　●　　●　　●

The soldier Leaverton returned early from his assignment of painting crosswalks and rounded the corner from the corridor and entered the Open Ward ahead of the tech. Zack noted the manner in which the patient walked, methodical, as if he were stalking someone or something. Zack didn't have a good take on the patient since Leaverton had been transferred from the upstairs ward over a month ago and had stayed out of trouble. Word was he had alienated a number of the Open Ward patients upstairs and those in charge thought it best to give him a fresh start on 2B. Zack recalled how he had made a harmless comment to the soldier and Leaverton had responded "go fuck himself." Zack understood the decision to transfer the soldier since transferring a person from one place where someone wasn't wanted to another place where eventually they won't be wanted originated in the Army.

●　　●　　●　　●　　●

And the young boy, with neighborhood boys in tow, carried a burlap bag containing a stray cat meowing in cat language, trooped into the woods, to a tree in a clearing, climbed to a low-hanging limb, and with a clothes line tied the sack, removed from his pocket lighter fluid, then doused, and slowly lowered the sack, while the cat's nails slashed through the bag, painting the burlap crimson, adding to the anticipation of the boys, and the frenzy of the growling, snapping, howling pack of dogs, attracted by the wailing cat, and the dogs ferociously sunk their teeth into the sack, and the boy snapped the lighter, and the flames engulfed the bag, the dogs, and the cat inside.

●　　●　　●　　●　　●

Zack was several steps behind Leaverton as they crossed through the rec room with its pool table with no pool balls or cues; and the TV stand with no television. Both activities were still on hold until Major Vann determined that the patients had been punished enough for the explosive behavior of just one of them. Leaverton entered the ward and moved to the first bed on the left. Zack continued past and headed to the rear of the ward to check the windows.

•   •   •   •   •

And the boy, a teenager now, on a summer job painted the town's water tower, captured a pigeon, and while others watched, smacked the bird against the railing, broke its neck, and then tossed the bird off the tower, and laughed as the disoriented bird winged left, right, left, smashing into the tower, then plunging down, down, down to the ground.

Zack's walk to the back of the ward was interrupted by Leaverton's outburst. "What the hell happened here? What's going on? What?"

Zack noted that Leaverton who he had seldom heard speak other than the "fuck you" had a raspy, harsh, voice as if he had gravel in his throat.

"What the fuck! What . . ." Each question louder until it was a demand: "WHAT THE HELL WENT ON HERE!"

Zack moved quickly to the front to see who was being questioned. The interrogator was Leaverton. He was alone.

And the teenager, now a soldier, fired his weapon and the scraggly, barking mongrel was catapulted past the mother through the opened door of the hooch and landed a bloody mass at the foot of her three children who screamed and screamed and screamed and screamed and screamed and screamed and . . .

Cluttered on the buffed floor next to and beneath Leaverton's bed were parts of plastic plane models. The wings from various models had been detached from the fuselage. The cockpit of one plane appeared to have ejected itself from the body. Plane parts were scattered. The only gray plastic planes that appeared to have kept their wings and bodies intact were planes that had successfully landed on his bed. The soldier knelt next to the wounded models on the floor and retrieved the pieces. What surprised Zack was the soldier's ability to curse for vengeance yet retrieve the parts and place them in his palm as gently as if he were holding a butterfly. Leaverton continued questioning the nonexistent culprit, "What the hell happened here? What's going on? I'm not believing this. Damn! Damn!"

$\bullet$ $\quad$ $\bullet$ $\quad$ $\bullet$ $\quad$ $\bullet$ $\quad$ $\bullet$

And when the soldier on weekend pass from the jungle saw through slit-opened eyes the prostitute reach to the chair where his pants were hung and before her piano-like fingers could remove the wallet, he grabbed her hand and one by one snapped the fingers as she pleaded in Vietnamese that she was sorry, so sorry, before she passed out.

And why the boy, who became a teenager, who became a soldier, did those terrible things was something no one would ever know.

$\bullet$ $\quad$ $\bullet$ $\quad$ $\bullet$ $\quad$ $\bullet$ $\quad$ $\bullet$

Zack watched as Leaverton placed the dismantled wings carefully on his bed that now served as an airport hangar hospital. As he carried out his search and rescue operation for the planes' shattered bodies, the soldier vowed to retaliate, to avenge this sneak attack on his homeland.

"Son-of-a-bitch, Son-of-a-bitch! I'll break his fucking neck. When I find out, he will pay. If I get my hands—"

"Whoa, easy there, Hoss, cool off." The tech took a chance to intervene. Zack called the patient Hoss because he couldn't recall his name.

"Cool-off hell, I'll hurt the guy that did this. I don't bother nobody. I go to my piss-ass job, and on my own time I build my models. He will pay!"

Leaverton continued to transport pieces to the hangar. The window next to his bed was wide open and the curtains billowed from a strong gust of wind. Mother Nature attacked the last upright model plane on the patient's nightstand. The wind scored a direct hit. But the plane's pilot managed to keep the plane under control. The plane spun around once, stopped and waited for the next attack.

Zack witnessed the attack. Leaverton didn't. He was busy planning how he would torture the alleged perpetrator of the airfield bombing. Zack felt that this was a time to put his own preference for non-engagement on hold to increase his own chances of getting off the ward without a physical confrontation. Or possibly save another patient from this mad model maker.

"Time out, think for a second," Zack said, even though he didn't believe thinking was a priority for this patient. "Soldier, look at the window. The wind is blowing." Zack's pulse raced but when he spoke his words were deliberate but restrained, "Wind, the wind blew your models to the floor."

Leaverton stopped retrieving pieces of plane from the floor. He turned his attention to the tech. His eyes narrowed; he scowled. Zack stood still. He waited. Leaverton looked to the window. Just then Mother Nature taunted the soldier. A sharp gust of a wind and the curtains billowed. The fighter jet on the nightstand spun around and toppled to the floor. Leaverton advanced to the window. The soldier leaned forward his face almost touching the thick wired screen.

Zack could tell that Leaverton was considering all that had transpired and, perhaps, all that he had sworn to avenge. Leaverton waited. Zack watched. The wind struck again. The curtains blew inward. Leaverton's face contorted, teeth clenched. The tech recognized the hate, he'd seen hate before. Leaverton raised his hands. He balled his fists and squeezed, tighter, the color drained, tighter, the nails bit into his own flesh, tighter. He growled, "You, you fucking wind." The soldier held his grip until he had strangled the wind and the wind was dead.

Leaverton's retaliatory act completed, Zack decided it was safe to leave. The tech had only one question for the patient, "Soldier, you going back to duty or back home?"

"Back to duty. I'm ready."

Leaving Leaverton to his models, Zack retreated through the recreation room and headed back toward the Closed Ward. Behind him the rock n' roller, Little Richard, let go with:

Ready, set, go man go,
I've got a gal that I love so, I'm ready.

Zack glanced back expecting to see the flamboyant entertainer banging on a piano.

Ready, ready, Teddy, I'm ready.

But Mr. Penniman, Little Richard, was nowhere in sight. *I don't see him*, Zack thought, *but I hear him.* And Zack was out of there.

Ready, ready, Teddy, I'm ready, ready, ready, Teddy.
I'm a ready, ready, ready to rock n' roll.

Laughter Heals

A Poem by Private Hardy

There once were some folk from St. Ives

Who broke out in a bad case of hives

They scratched where they itched

And had to be stitched

To their limericks for laughs to save lives

The Bowling Alley

The softball season was never completed and fall soccer was a no show. It was almost the middle of December and the major still hadn't lifted his ban on outdoor activities. His philosophy for dealing with the soldier's escape from the ballfield was to punish all for one, not one for all. The major's wishful thinking was to make it to his retirement day right before Christmas. No escapes; no suicides; no riots on the wards. What he hadn't counted on was how edgy the patients, soldiers still, were reacting for being sequestered indoors. The soldiers in white served more as referees trying to keep the peace. Fire fights started with morning meds call.

"I don't want any fucking pills." Firenza said as he stood in line at the opened half of the office door. Nurse Hill glared back at the paranoid's glare. She held out the paper cup with pills and glared him quiet.

"You are crowding . . . ME." Scarface Kelly's rumbling baritone didn't have to announce it again. Bible Skinner backed a step into a no-longer-enthusiastic-glad-to-be-here Cherry Pie Stover. Stover picked up Skinner and threw him and his Bible to the rear.

"Hey, hey, hey!" Sarge moved in. "Get your pills, get back to your bunks and police your area. This ward's a mess."

"How long are we going to be punished? How long?" Obsessive Godwin sat at a table and asked the question to no soldier in particular.

Lawyer Lucas zeroed-in on the word "punished" and rose from a table and strutted back and forth as if addressing members of a jury. "I ask you. Isn't this another example of cruel and unusual punishment? I claim it is. It is."

Even Joker Berkowski's antics crossed the line.

"AAAEEEEEIII!"

The scream came from inside the ward latrine. The door opened and from inside a thud and a loud OHHHH! The bald-headed Berkowski exited and quickstepped past Zack and out to the ward. The Joker had the look of a child caught with his hand in the cookie jar. Zack hustled inside the latrine and found a nude wet patient writhing on the floor.

"He locked me in—I couldn't get out—Not my fault—Not my fault!"

The patient's white body had taken on a pink glow, his elbows and knees scraped raw from his fall to the tiled floor. His upper torso tangled in the shower curtain that had been ripped from the shower stall bar. Hot water sprayed out of the shower and the mirrors above the sinks had steamed over.

"Hot water—I had to get out—Not my fault. Not my fault—not my fault!"

"It's okay, it's okay," Zack spoke calmly to the newly arrived patient Spencer who, as of yet, had not earned a nickname from the techs.

Nurse Hill entered and knelt over Spencer to assess the damage. She responded to the soldier on the floor as if disgusted. "For God's sake, you're not dying."

Zack turned off the shower faucets while Nurse Hill directed "Take this guy to his bed." Zack removed a towel from a hook and handed it to the patient. The nude soldier covered his not-so-private parts and nodded in appreciation to the tech's act of kindness. Zack led the patient to his bed as other patients gawked and gathered around. Nurse Hill joined him there and began to clean and dress the patient's superficial wounds.

Out of this crowd of voyeurs, Shaky Metz stepped forward. His head vibrated along with his hands. His shoulders twitched. With a shaking finger, he pointed across the ward to Berkowski who now stood at attention by his bed.

"Ber . . . Ber . . . Berkowski did, did it . . . did it." Metz spoke with a whining lilt to his voice, a voice meant to annoy. Then having done his civic duty Metz shuffled away in his white slippers.

Joker Berkowski, as if it were inspection time, stood at his bunk, knees locked, shoulders back, and hands tight to his sides. Tech Krupp moved quickly to Berkowski and stared coldly at the Joker. He took a tight grasp of the soldier's elbow and hustled him to the front of the ward. As they walked by the wounded patient, Berkowski expressed his remorse: "It was a joke, a joke, Spence, are you okay?"

Spencer raised his head slightly, peered over Nurse Hill's shoulder and nodded in the affirmative.

"Gotcha," Berkowski said with a grin.

"But I got you now, Berkowski," Tech Krupp said and jerked the patient's arms to move him faster. Berkowski yanked his arm away. His eyes narrowed and he bit his lip. He contemplated how far he wanted to take this.

The tension of the moment seeped through the audience. Soldiers pushed back from tables, letter writing stopped, puzzles left unfinished, and the Crazy 8's card game folded. A couple patients stubbed-out cigarettes while a couple others hastily lit them. Some looked to the potential confrontation while others looked away. Some walked quickly to their beds to sit, hands tucked between knees and waited.

The patient Lucas paced and lectured about rights, his rights, others' rights, everyone's rights, building to "All God's children got rights!" His rant encouraged voluntary and involuntary responses while a number of patients mumbled to themselves. The louder Lucas got, the louder they got. The patient Skinner sat a table and rocked. He turned the pages of his small Bible searching for a passage to fit the situation. His glasses slipped from the bridge of his nose. He pushed them back into position and continued the search.

Joker Berkowski exhaled his anger and walked on his own volition toward the seclusion room. Tech Krupp followed him while practically on the patient's back. The speed with which Berkowski entered the seclusion room took the fire from Lucas's legal presentation. The Joker took a seat on the mat.

"Okay, asshole, off with your shoes," Tech Krupp ordered.

Nurse Hill entered holding a syringe filled with pink fluid.

"I don't need a shot. Give me a break." Berkowski said it as if he knew no breaks were coming.

I'll give you a break. I'll break your arm." Tech Krupp said.

Nurse Hill interjected. "Boys, boys, no violence, drugs work just fine."

Berkowski rolled into a fetal position. Tech Krupp, the aggressor, and the timid Tech Grey grabbed the Joker's legs and worked to get his posterior in position to take his medicine and punishment, a two-for-one.

Berkowski played "Let's Make A Deal." He started, "I promise no more jokes. No shot, for no more jokes. A deal? Deal?"

Techs Krupp and Grey weren't having any success in keeping Berkowski in the proper position. No sooner had they straightened his legs and moved to flip him over, he sprung back like a slinky toy. An impatient Nurse Hill said, "Anytime you guys are ready."

Berkowski recognized the futility of constantly returning to the womb and accepted his fate. Tech Krupp yanked down the soldier's pants. Nurse Hill held the syringe upward and released a bit of pink fluid. She then smacked Berkowski's ass so hard he could have pledged a fraternity. She stuck the needle into the only fleshy part the wiry soldier had back there.

"Pull up your pants, stud." She chuckled as if she knew that no man could be a stud with his pants to his knees and a needle in his ass.

Having medicated Berkowski, the techs and Nurse Hill cleared the room. Berkowski was quiet, his eyes closed, slowly his head fell forward. Suddenly, Berkowski jerked his head up, eyes and mouth opened, "Deal?" he muttered, and closed his eyes, lowered his head, and fell asleep. Thorazine could slow down Seabiscuit.

Tech Krupp locked the door. He peered back through the window. The tech imitating the drawn-out nasal delivery of early film star W.C. Fields cracked a joke that only Krupp would appreciate since no one else was listening: "Ah, peace and tranquility, Thorazine, Thorazine."

Because of the major's off limits to the outdoors, other than the indoor morning calisthenics, the soldiers had no other physical outlets. The Sarge felt bad for the soldiers. He also could feel the pressure. So Sarge improvised. He reserved time at the base gym for the Closed Wards to play a little volleyball.

●   ●   ●   ●   ●

Closed Ward 2A set up a net on one half of the gym while 3A set their own net on the other half. This was a first for the patients, and the techs were a little anxious. Zack and Tech Turner directed patients Scarface Kelly and Cherry Pie Stover, the two tallest players, to opposite sides of the net. Everyone else filled in where they wanted; in the catatonic's case where he was placed.

Volleyball may not be a contact sport but when the giant, Scarface Kelly, spiked the sphere downward into Smiling Hardy's face blood spurted from his nose and painted Hardy's white slippers. Zack quickly moved Hardy, still smiling, off the court and had him tilt his head back to slow the flow while the game continued.

On the court, Cherry Pie Stover, size-wise made for volleyball, soared high above the net, slammed the ball and knocked out Shaky Metz. It was one of the few times Metz was ever completely still. Two serious injuries in two minutes forced the techs to call the game. A few patients grumbled, but the techs agreed it was better to err on the side of life than death by volleyball. The patients returned to the ward and the results of the outing were reported to Sergeant McCabe. The sarge searched for a less dangerous indoor activity and found one: bowling.

Ward 2A boarded an Army bus at the rear of the psych building and rode to the other side of the base where a nondescript, one-story brick building housed the bowling alley. The alley was off limits to enlisted personnel, and seldom used except by a few officers and their families. Taxpayer dollars had satisfied the previous base commander's favorite recreational activity.

Tech Krupp at the head of the line led the patients in. The smell of fresh popcorn permeated the six lane establishment. Two soldiers in fatigues sat behind a counter, leaning back in chairs, eating popcorn. On the counter was a glass-enclosed popcorn maker with a handwritten sign taped to the glass. "No food or drink while bowling."

These bowling lane sentries had been forewarned they would be hosting an unusual group of soldiers this afternoon. "Damn, here come the crazies," one soldier said. Tech Krupp heard him and nodded back in agreement.

The patients walked straight to the counter where the popcorn-eating soldiers provided bowling shoes and directed the group to adjoining lanes. Surprisingly, the dispensing of sizes eights, nines and tens went smoothly, even the extra large sizes to Kelly and Stover. Tech Krupp took a seat at a scorer's table and filled out lineups.

"Okay, it's the Sickies vs. Psychos," Krupp declared. He scribbled names on a lined pad.

"Make no mistake," Zack said as he leaned closer to Krupp and whispered, "you're the sick one."

"Yeah, yeah, play the game. You take Berkowski and that catatonic."

"Berkowski's our captain," Zack said, knowing that would irritate Krupp even more.

Berkowski took to his new assignment, reached over Krupp's shoulder, grabbed a pencil and scratched out Psychos. "Name change. I'm captain of the Avengers!" Berkowski pumped his fist upward.

"You, and you," Krupp pointed to members of his team, "start on the left lane."

Berkowski hustled to the right lane, stuck his fingers in several balls before making a selection. He took his position. In a smooth and effortless movement Berkowski swung his arm back in a pendulum motion and then the ball forward increasing his speed and then released. The ball sped down the alley. Crash! The pins jumped and flew into each other, a kaleidoscope of red and white. Sight wasn't necessary, the sound itself registered the result. Strike! Berkowski spun around to the group, snapped his fingers and pointed to Krupp. "Streeeek! Score one for the Avengers!"

Krupp, ever the good sport, flashed his middle finger at Berkowski.

"He's going on tour. I'll represent him," Lawyer Lucas said as if it were a done deal.

Zack took the seat next to Obsessive Godwin. The patient, now with his physical abilities restored, not the mind but the body, was one with whom Zack felt he had a personal stake in the soldier's journey to sanity. They both had arrived that same day to the hospital and they both needed mending. Godwin was an excellent example of how the passage of time with no drugs had healed at least his drug-induced stupor. Zack couldn't imagine giving credit to Dr. Lane other than he had taken Godwin off the meds when he arrived and had forgotten to prescribe anything new.

Crash! Pins flew. Another strike for Berkowski. Cheers, applause, and backslapping from the Avengers. Even Krupp's team joined in the congratulations, their way of showing Tech Krupp they couldn't care less for his sick humor, or being on his team.

Reseated after joining in the applause Zack took the initiative. "Godwin, you have a brother, right?" Zack asked.

"Brother and sister. Both younger."

"Where's your family?"

"Philly."

"Philadelphia's really close, do they visit?"

"I've told them not to."

"It's not that far, why would you not—"

"They're ashamed of me," Godwin said.

"How do you know that?"

"Cause I'm ashamed of me." Godwin said.

Godwin rose to help Catatonic Cart who stood at the head of the lane. Obsessive Godwin went to the rack, examined the bowling balls very closely, and chose one. He took a small white towel that hung on the rack and carefully wiped the ball and handed it to Cart.

"Hey, no help from the peanut gallery." Krupp interjected his rules.

Both teams yelled for one of their own, another soldier. "Knock 'em down!" "You can do it!" "Come on, soldier!" "Knock 'em down! Knock 'em down!" Cart took a step forward. "You can do it!" He took another step. "Go buddy!" Another step. The encouragement got louder. "Do it!" "Come on soldier!" He brought the ball up into position. "Let it fly!" someone yelled. Cart released the ball. It dropped to the floor and missed his foot by a toe. The patients quieted, disappointed, not just in him but for themselves.

"That sucked. That's a big fat zero," Krupp chuckled as he marked the score sheet.

"Peanut brain and a zero." Berkowski responded. "Hey Krupp, who does that describe?"

"Keep it up, Berkowski, you jerk off," Krupp said.

"Jerk off around here? We're not like you, we need privacy." Berkowski closed his fist and moved it in an up and down motion. The patients laughed. A few made "whooo! whooo! whooo" sounds. Others copied the motion.

Scarface Kelly jammed the tips of his thick black fingers into the holes of the black sphere as if the ball were part of him. He swung the cannon ball forward, a medieval catapult. He released the ball airborn. No roll, one bounce and into the head pin. The pins exploded. The floor vibrated shaking the scorer table. The explosion brought one of the bowling alley sentries to monitor the action. The palace guard crossed his arms and projected a stern look that told everyone that this place had rules.

Joker Berkowski, always the idea man, approached Zack.

"How about getting popcorn to take to the guys on the ward?" As he spoke, he nodded his head "yes" as if that would influence Zack's response.

Patient Stover followed Kelly to the lane and did him one better by one foot. He lobbed the ball a thousand miles, no bounce, right into the center pin. The boom! played catch-up to the scattered pins that flew across several lanes.

"No lofting balls! No lofting! I'm not telling you again." The sentry duty soldier ran down the lane to retrieve pins that had escaped the rickety clickety-clack device resetting for the next bowler.

Zack approached the other sentry who had arrived to back up his partner. "Hey soldier, where can I get a container? I want to take popcorn back for the ward."

"In the supply room," the sentry mumbled not thrilled with sharing their booty.

The supply room entrance was between two soda machines each with an "Off Limits" sign taped to the front. The signs had been placed there when the sentries were notified that the psych patients were to be their guests. It was a sad example by some of their own who failed to respect fellow soldiers on the psych wards. Inside the room Zack found that the two soldiers had stored away every bag of chips and piece of candy in the building. Boxes of hot dog buns sat next to a hot dog rotisserie still warm from recent use. Obviously, not to be shared with the psych patients.

Zack spotted a pile of empty, white, plastic containers. He returned to the lane with the largest container he could find. Berkowski took the bucket and headed off to impound the remaining popcorn.

On the lane Shaky Metz was making a sports comeback since being knocked out the previous week by the volleyball. He approached the lane, ball in shaky hand. Metz's fellow soldiers believed any encouragement would only add to his nervous condition, so they got quiet. Metz sensed what they hoped. He didn't hesitate; he quickstepped forward. He swung the ball back and then forward as fast as his skinny arm allowed and released. The ball flew at an angle, not due north where the pins waited but off to the northeast where just a few feet away was a wooden post. The wooden column had been there for years, from the very beginning, untouched other than a yearly paint job. When Metz released the ball, all eyes saw the direction it traveled. They expected the impact. They could see it coming. But when it hit, a solid **"CRACK!"** and with that sound a splintering of wood, the column had been sliced. A couple patients dropped to the floor and covered their heads.

"What the fuck?" The soldier sentry responded.

Aftershock, tremors, the floor shook. Overhead, hanging light fixtures swayed. On the lanes, pins fell. Berkowski holding the oversized container of popcorn yelled, "Score that!"

"Holy shit! That's it—Fun's over!" The sentries took turns closing things down. One yelled in an escalating tone "Damage is done, out of here," Then higher," "Out of here!" and higher, "You're out of here!" The other sentry joined in, "Lane's closed. Now. Shoes off." The first repeated the last, "Shoes off! Get the shoes off!" The other said, "It's over!" They never stepped on each other's lines, not once. "Now!" both sentries said.

The patients removed their shoes and lined up, another hasty departure. Unnoticed was the black-stamped FTA on the soles of several pairs of shoes.

The bus with the bowling teams arrived back at the psych building's back gate just as the sun hid behind a curtain of steely gray sky. The MP, usually stationed at the building's front entrance, was there at the rear to greet the bus and to unlock the gate. A bowling alley sentry had already placed a call to Sergeant Helms to voice complaints about, as the sentry soldier put it, "destruction of property by the crazies."

The patients filed out of the bus following Tech Krupp into the back entrance of the building. The early evening darkness captured the mood of the returning bowlers. Even Berkowski looked downcast as he exited the bus and munched on popcorn that he carried in the large bucket.

Once back on the ward Scarface Kelly asked, "Where's the popcorn?"

"Where's Berkowski?" Tech Krupp asked.

"Wherever the popcorn is." Zack answered.

And then they heard Berkowski. "Hey Creep! Krupp! Creep!" It sounded as if Berkowski was using a bullhorn the way his voice bounced off the walls and entered the ward from the main corridor.

"Hey Creep, Krupp! Creep!" Berkowski's original words were hard to distinguish given their echo through the corridor into the ward.

Krupp responded to Berkowski's original words with, "That son of a bitch." And then again to Berkowski's echo with, "That son of a bitch." Krupp then sprinted to the corridor.

At the far end of the dimly lit corridor the MP had not yet returned to his post but Berkowski had. He held the white plastic bucket with one arm while he ate a handful of popcorn. Berkowski greeted Krupp's presence with an offer, "You want some popcorn, Creep? I mean, Krupp."

"What I want is my fist on your face." Krupp marched menacingly up the corridor. He hunched his shoulders. He clenched and unclenched his fists.

Berkowski placed the container of popcorn on the floor. He reached deep inside the bucket. Popcorn spilled and salted the waxed floor as he removed a bowling ball. He assumed the correct bowling position. Feet together, ball out front, eyes on Krupp, the head pin.

Krupp stopped. His sneer replaced by an incredulous stare. He thought, *"What the hell is he doing?"*

Berkowski, once a member of the "The Pinboys," the local Canton, Ohio league champions of 1965, began to imitate the voice of television sports announcer Howard Cosell. He clipped each word and phrase separately as if each one was of equal importance, separate sentences: "Here. On center lane. Bowling. For Ward 2A. Wearing. Blue pants." Berkowski finished with a flourish, "It's Captain Avenger!"

Joker Berkowski stepped forward with a smooth approach. Tech Krupp turned and began a retreat. He looked back over his shoulder. Berkowski mouthed his bowling mantra, "Follow through and finish high." Krupp started to run. Berkowski the Avenger released the ball. Krupp's cry announced, "score a strike!"

Berkowski trotted past Krupp as the tech writhed on the floor. The look on the Joker's face was one of disbelief that he had hurt the tech. As if he were saying "Oh Geez, what have I done now." The sarge and Zack hustled out to the corridor to see the damage. Berkowski hustled by them into the ward and headed directly into a seclusion room. Zack followed to confront the Joker.

"Aaaww, don't give me a shot. I'm not dangerous, I'm just dumb," Berkowski said to Zack who now too had a look of disbelief on his face.

"Dumb and dangerous. And lucky," Zack said, "Nurse Thorazine is off duty. I'm going to let you slide. Now give me your shoes. What were you thinking?"

"I didn't want to hurt him."

"What are you saying? You threw a bowling ball at him."

"I just wanted to hit him, not hurt him. It was an April Fool's joke."

"It's December," Zack pointed out, "not April."

Berkowski shrugged his shoulders. "Yeah, well, that's why it's so funny."

Zack took Berkowski's shoes and left him seated on the rubber mat. Just then, Sergeant McCabe returned to the ward having transported Tech Krupp to the rear of the building to await the ambulance. The Sarge looked in the seclusion room at Berkowski and then nodded his head in resignation.

"How's Krupp?" Zack asked.

"A broken leg," Sarge said. "Ambulance arrived out back to take him to Emergency, Tech Grey's with him."

"So bad ones come, and bad ones go." Zack said. Sarge smiled at the tech's words of wisdom.

From outside the ambulance's piercing siren pervaded the ward. The soldiers on the ward looked out the windows to the ballfield. They were animated, excited at what had taken place inside, and now, excited by something outside. Just then, Tech Grey ran onto the ward. He opened his mouth to speak but instead bent over and gasped for air. He'd run a marathon to report news of a battle.

"SSSarge." Grey stopped and took in more air.

Zack thought, *Could that siren get any louder? Was it ever going to stop?*

"That'sss." Grey's breathing slowed, "One of ours running that siren."

The news delivered, Sarge, Zack, and Tech Grey moved to join the crowd at the windows. As Zack walked by a table, just for brief moment he recognized the voice of Bob Dylan, the troubadour. No visual sighting of the baby-faced musician just his nasal-toned singing and playing his harmonica:

Something is happening
and you don't know what it is,
do you, Mr. Jones.

The crowd at the windows watched as the ambulance's light flashed and headlights lit up the outfield before returning it to darkness as the vehicle spun around and headed toward the infield racing over second base. The horn couldn't possibly compete with the wailing siren, but it tried. Siren wailing, horn honking, the driver hit the brakes at second base. The ambulance that served patients as both a lifeline and a hearse spun again and headed again to the outfield. The headlights came on, then off, then on. Honk the horn, hit the lights, honk the horn, hit the lights, the driver played a syncopated rhythm.

Sergeant Helms and an MP raced on the field. The MP had his weapon drawn. Helms pointed emphatically, once, twice, again, as if instructing the MP the number of shots to fire and where. The MP raised his weapon. He aimed at the tires of the ambulance. Bang! joined the cacophony. Bang! Siren! Horn! Siren! Horn! Bang! Clang! The rear hubcaps flew off and rolled, rolled and rolled to the fence. The MP fired again. Bang! Siren! Horn! Goodyear exploded and a front tire unraveled.

The ambulance stopped, door opened, and Cherry Pie Stover sprung out. He saw the MP and Sergeant Helms racing towards him. He raised his hands as if to demonstrate that he held no weapon. He looked to the building. Faces were crowded to the windows on both floors. These were the faces of those who soldiers fought the battle for, the guys next to you, your buddies. Stover grinned. He extended his arms upward and began to jump.

"Sto-ver!" "Sto-ver!" "Sto-ver!" "Sto-ver!" The patients on 2A jumped with him.

It happened so fast, the MP grabbed him, spun him around and forced him over the hood of the ambulance. Sergeant Helm's pushed Stover's head onto the heated metal while the MP wrenched Stover's arms behind his back and cuffed him. Helms' pressed harder flattening the smile on Stover's face. The sergeant looked to the building's windows seeking out someone to blame. He settled on blaming everyone.

The patients lost their celebratory mood. But Shaky Metz raised an interesting question, "Is, is, is KKKKKrupp in the ambulance?"

The soldiers could only hope so.

The following afternoon Sarge and Zack were in the office doing busy work when word came that Stover wasn't going to stay in the stockade. And he wasn't coming back to the ward. Stover's stint in the Army was over, he was going home.

"He lied about his age, he's sixteen. It took the jailers to find that out?" Zack said.

"Now he can apply for a driver's license," Sarge said.

"I do believe you made a joke."

"This memo's no joke. Major Vann just made the Bowling Alley off limits."

Zack erased Stover's name from the board.

What once was the base gymnasium. (2014 photo)

Valley Forge General Hospital
Neuropsychiatric Unit

DAILY LOG - Ward 2A and 2B
December 15, 1967

DAY SHIFT

Another day - just like the other day.

EVENING SHIFT

The same.

NIGHT SHIFT

Same

Are We It?

A Poem by Private Hardy

A monometer consists of one foot

Fortunately that rarely occurs

But when we see

It

We have a hard time averting our eyes

As the word passes us by

A Private Matter

The base chapel was something out of a religious recruitment film, white on white with a steeple and a bell that tolled Sunday morning services. Inside the double doors the harmonic organ pumped traditional sounds to soothe. The pews were an egalitarian mishmash of soldiers in patient blues or Army khaki seated alongside officers in dress uniforms, something only seen on Sundays. Patients in wheelchairs crowded the middle aisle. Families were there, the mothers and fathers, wives and sweethearts who had traveled on their day of rest to sit at the side of the wounded.

Some patients saw religion as salvation, to others, religion was just an escape. When the call had gone out at the psych wards that Sunday morning Closed Ward patients lined up. On 2A the patient Skinner joined the rear of the line carrying his Bible still wrapped in cellophane that had protected The Word during his morning shower. The Bible had crossed the ocean with Skinner from Vietnam and even after two months on the ward he still carried it with him everywhere.

Several patients who hadn't heard the call moved quickly to catch up, and not content with being last in line elbowed their way forward clipping Skinner who spun like a white and blue top and fell to the floor. He scrambled and frantically reached for his Bible but only managed to push the Good Book farther from his grasp. The medics and patients continued on without him. Skinner pulled the Bible to his chest at the entrance of the Family Room. He stood, too quickly. Lightheaded, he watched as the curtains, couch, chairs and coffee table of the visiting room transformed.

• • • • • • •

The stench of rotten fruit so pungent that PFC Skinner thought he would vomit. Weapons fired and flashed, and an explosion lit the sky equal to a night ballgame at Yankee stadium. Skinner curled his body and burrowed into the mud, his eyes tightly closed, his hands covered his ears as he pushed deeper into the earth. And then, more explosions, closer and louder. Dirt, branches, limbs, fell on and around him. And there in the jungle, in the dirt, a sudden calmness . . . he was walking behind his father who clutched a Bible tightly to his chest and who seemed to the boy to be as high as the stalks of corn that surrounded the simple white church that they entered for the Sunday service. And in the darkness, in the dirt, the soldier Skinner began a mantra to return him to a safe place: "JesusGod-JesusGod-JesusGod-JesusGod-JesusGod . . ."

    •   •   •   •   •

From the hallway, Skinner stared at his other self. His head throbbed louder and louder like a bass drum. The sound joined the Boom! of explosions in the Family Room and he shut his eyes and whispered, "JesusGod-JesusGod-JesusGod-JesusGod-JesusGod."

The jungle faded, the bushes to couch, tangled brush to chairs, trees disappeared, and the morning sun's rays reflected from the black-and-white TV. Patient Skinner clutching his Bible moved to the main corridor to catch the other patients before they exited the building.

The brown Army bus that departed the back gate of the psych building was crowded. It seemed that every patient on the Closed Wards 2A and 3A rode the "bus to salvation." The Joker Berkowski recognized he had a captive audience. He began clapping his hands rhythmically, first on the knees and then hands together, then knees, then hands, and burst forth with "Give me that old-time religion, give me that old-time religion." Throughout the ride to the base chapel, he was a choir of one, rocking left and right, clapping hands and singing, "It's good enough for me."

Bible Skinner, eyes closed, listening intently, was taken by how Berkowski's uptempo and joyous singing was the antithesis of his own experience. He vividly recalled as a child walking with his father who clutched a Bible that was practically invisible with the black of the man's suitcoat as they ascended the wooden steps to the white church at the top of the hill. He could still see the church's narrow steeple that served as a sentry to acres of cornfields. He could hear the bell that tolled a melancholic rhythm as sternly as his father had treated him.

"Give me that old-time religion" ended at the base chapel. The patients entered in a single line and took their places in the two pews at the rear of the chapel reserved for the soldiers from the psych wards. They crowded shoulder to shoulder when they stood and knee to knee when they sat. The psych techs served as monitors seated at each end of the pew. Their white smocks framed the patients' blues resembling a Norman Rockwell magazine cover of the Saturday Evening Post. God may have trusted the patients' behavior but no one else did. Zack and Turner's 2A group sat in the back row while immediately in front of them sat the 3A patients and their caretakers.

At the altar, two Army chaplains, one balding and the other with a military haircut, were impressed at how filled the little church was on this Sunday morning. They congratulated each other on how their Catholic and Protestant interfaith services had grown in acceptance. Neither chaplain considered that the hospital now housed more wounded soldiers.

"All those wishing to partake in communion, please come forward," said the balding chaplain. "For those in wheelchairs, the communion will be brought to you," said the chaplain with hair.

Worshippers in khaki and those in blue moved out from the pews to the center aisle. Bible Skinner, who wanted to cover all religious bases, joined several other patients from upstairs 3A and proceeded through the maze of wheelchairs to the altar. Paranoid Firenza took up the rear stopping to scrutinize each row of pews before moving forward.

"Body of Christ," the balding chaplain said, and placed a wafer into the hands of a patient.

"Amen, and peace be with you," said the chaplain with hair.

"Body of Christ."

"Amen, and peace be with you." The chaplain with hair added the 'peace' line praying it would make a difference.

"Body of Christ."

"Amen, and peace be with you."

The crowded line moved forward, and one after another a patient took communion and returned to a seat.

A seated psych ward patient from 3A whispered to his neighbor, "I didn't know that Levin was Catholic."

The patient who had received the message commented loudly to the neighbor to his left, "I didn't know that Levin was Catholic."

"I didn't know that either," a third patient said even more loudly.

The psych tech from 3A, pew monitor for this outing, joined the information trail. "Didn't know what?" the tech asked.

"That he was Catholic," responded the nearest patient getting the attention of everyone in the last four rows.

"Who's Catholic?" The tech asked while trying to lower the sound level considerably.

"Levin, the Jewish guy." The patient almost yelled it.

In front of the altar, Patient Levin, the Jewish guy, accepted the host from the bald chaplain.

"Body of Christ," The bald chaplain said.

"And peace be with you," said the chaplain with hair.

"And peace be with you," Levin said. "And shalom."

Psych patient Levin, a soldier still, placed the wafer on his tongue and closed his mouth. He did a military about-face and looked back to his fellow soldiers in the last rows. They looked at him. He stuck out his tongue, on the end of it sat the wafer. Levin turned and bolted past the chaplains, knocking the balding one aside. The chaplain's shoulder struck the podium, which toppled into a sandfilled, candlelit holder that collapsed onto the first row of worshippers. Hot wax on flesh brought shouts of "Jesus Christ! God Damn!" as Levin ran out the altar side door.

The patient Levin's escape, although short-lived, brought on the last punitive action that would be ordered by the temporarily-in-charge of the psych unit, the non-medical, Major Vann. Sergeant Helms carried out what was to be his last act as the right hand of the major.

Date: 12/17 /67
To: Sergeant Helms
From: Major Vann
Neuropsychiatric Unit
Subject: Base chapel is off limits for the Closed Wards
Until further notice, prayer is to be a
private matter.

And so religion came to the wards.

• • • • •

Dr. Shaw entered 2A's main ward moving comfortably among the mentally wounded. Unlike the nurse and techs who were dressed in traditional white, the psychiatrist wore a khaki uniform. The psychiatrist performed double duty providing therapy for 2A as well as the upstairs 3A. Regardless of being on call most nights and weekends, the doc's positive approach to healing was demonstrated during his daily rounds.

"How are you doing today? What's that you're reading? That's a book I've wanted to read." And on to another patient, "What's that, a photo of your girlfriend? Ohhh, she's very pretty. You're a lucky man." And another,

"Do you have a minute to talk with me? Is this a good time?" And another, "You're from Cleveland, a football fan? Great football town." After another, "You've got a few questions? Well, certainly, ask away." If positive remarks could cure, these patients would all get well. "You will get better," Dr. Shaw would declare, or, "You are getting better." And better was what most felt after the doc spoke with them.

This afternoon's entrance was Dr. Shaw's second of the day, having completed his regular rounds earlier that morning. This time, along with Zack, a patient accompanied the doc. The patient was slender with sinewy arms, ruddy complexion and, unlike the other patients, he had a substantial amount of hair. There was a serene air about him. The prayerful positioning of his hands held below his pointed chin conveyed a sense of peacefulness. The patient was from the upstairs ward where he was known by the techs and other soldiers as 3A Jesus. With 3A Jesus at his side, Dr. Shaw stopped at the table of regulars playing Crazy 8's.

"Who's winning?" Doctor Shaw asked.

"No one yet, doc," Scarface Kelly responded. "First one out in the game gets to go home, right guys?"

"Right. Right. R-r-r-ight." Not quite in unison but the response was the same from Paranoid Firenza, Mumbling Grier, and Shaky Metz.

"I wish it were that simple," the doc said.

"Did you bring us another card player?" Patient Kelly asked, nodding towards the doc's companion.

"No, no, he's just visiting." Dr. Shaw glanced at Jesus From 3A. "He's from ... upstairs."

"Ha!" Kelly guffawed, a burst of his operatic baritone. He pointed to the ceiling. "They're even crazier than us up on 3A."

"Time to move on," doc said smiling. The doc took 3A Jesus by the elbow and followed Zack.

"Aaachoo!" Patient Skinner sneezed just as Dr. Shaw and 3A Jesus passed by.

"Bless you," 3A Jesus said.

"Thank you," Bible Skinner said.

"It's what I do," said 3A Jesus. He noticed the Bible in Skinner's hand and nodded approvingly. Then He bowed his head, made the sign of the cross to Skinner, and moved on with Dr. Shaw. They arrived at the bed of a soldier who had been admitted just that morning and who earlier Dr. Shaw had spent over an hour with conducting an intake interview. An interview in which the patient revealed that he wasn't who the Army thought he was. He could never condone war: He was the Son of God.

"Here's someone I want you to meet," Dr. Shaw said to the newly arrived soldier and motioned to 3A Jesus.

Before the new patient could respond 3A Jesus took the initiative. "Hello, I am Jesus of Nazareth."

"It's nice to meet—it's nice to—" interrupting himself and with a confused look the new patient, Jesus on 2A, asked, "Who are you?"

"Please, tell him again." Dr. Shaw respectfully asked the soldier from upstairs.

"I am Jesus of Nazareth," 3A Jesus said softly. His eyes conveyed sincerity.

"But . . . but . . . I'm Jes . . . Jes . . . ah . . ." the new patient hesitated, perplexed. He looked to Dr. Shaw. "Ah . . . if . . . ah . . . if . . . he's ah . . . Jesus . . . ah . . . who . . . who am I?"

"When you told me this morning who you were, you didn't seem that certain." Dr. Shaw reached out and ran his index finger across the nametag pinned on the patient's shirt. "But I know who you are." The patient tucked in his chin and looked down trying to read his own nametag, a nametag that read "Scott."

"And we both know," Dr. Shaw said nodding towards the visitor from 3A whose hands had now returned to a prayerful position beneath his chin, "if he is . . ." Dr. Shaw paused, "then you can't be. Right?"

The soldier Scott looked to Jesus from 3A and then to the doctor. His mouth opened. He seemed to want to speak but didn't.

"You," Dr. Shaw said simply, "are Joseph Scott. Go ahead now, repeat after me, I am Joseph Scott."

"I . . . I am . . ." The patient was absorbed in thought as if searching inside for a way out.

"Say," Dr. Shaw repeated slowly, "I am Joseph Scott."

"I . . . I . . . am Joe . . . Joseph Scott . . . Joseph Scott." He shuffled his feet, the white slippers made a scraping sound on the polished floor.

"A bright individual," Dr. Shaw said quietly.

"A . . . bright . . . A bright . . . in-di-vid-u-al," the last part came out as a gasp.

"A patriot," Dr. Shaw said.

"A . . . patriot," another exhale from Scott, and a bit more from inside the soldier escaped.

"A good son of a loving family," Dr. Shaw said.

"A good son," tears ran down Scott's face, "of a loving family." His eyes became another exit for whatever was inside the young man.

"And," Dr. Shaw continued, "I'm confused, but I will get well."

"I am . . . confused but . . . will get well" Scott said. He wiped his damp face with his sleeve.

"Okay, Scott," Dr. Shaw said, "that's a fine start for the both of us."

"Okay, Scott, that's a—" Scott stopped, recognizing his mistake he gave the slightest of smiles.

Dr. Shaw squeezed Scott's shoulder reassuringly. 3A Jesus made the sign of the cross to Scott, bowed his head, and murmured something about his being "a child of God."

Dr. Shaw turned his attention to 3A Jesus. He placed his hand gently on the patient's back. "Let's go back upstairs." Dr. Shaw said. As they passed by the soldiers, there was a flash before Skinner's eyes, a snapshot just for the briefest moment in which he saw that Shaky Metz wasn't shaking; Paranoid Firenza wasn't looking over his shoulder; Scarface Kelly had no scar; and Mumbling Grier was talking like a DJ on the radio.

As Doctor Shaw and the patient from upstairs left the ward, Skinner had an overwhelming feeling of calmness and confidence that he was no longer sick. The soldier had been healed. He would go home again.

Therapy can take years and years of hard work . . . miracles, not so much.

What once was the base chapel. (2014 photo.)

195

The Right Way
A Poem by Private Hardy

This has been a problem
since I was young
people telling me
what I should have done
the right way

Tie your shoes
the right way
eat your food
the right way
brush your teeth
the right way

Hello and please
always thanks
seen not heard
watch your mouth
bow and pray
the right way

Stand in line
sit up straight
salute the Flag
pay attention
take direction
the right way

Throw the ball
swing the bat
play the game

run the track
give high-fives
the right way

Start the car
give it gas
not too fast
not too slow
press and brake
the right way

Shine your shoes
make your bunk
clean latrine
march in step
fire your weapon
the right way

Talk to girl
kiss the girl
touch the girl
walk the aisle
and get divorced
the right way

Dance and sing
the right way
work and play
the right way
spend and save
the right way

Been a hell of a problem
since I was young
to do all the things
I shoulda done
the right way

A Crazy 8's Christmas – Soldiers Still

December on the wards was a time for holidays, the forgotten Chanukah, and the remembered Christmas, a time for the rebirth of sanity. On Ward 2A everything was in its proper place; beds were made with blue blankets tightly tucked, the tops of the brown metal nightstands in acceptable order with a book or two or a pack of stationary or some with family photos.

The sun hid somewhere behind a gray blanketed sky. Temperatures had dropped reminding the soldiers what the cold could bring. Snow was in the forecast. The windows they could not go out of were to remain closed. A holiday wreath of green fern with red ribbon hung from the opened half of the Nurses Station door. An area was reserved at the rear of the ward for the late night visitor expected on Christmas Eve. A cardboard cutout of Santa in his sleigh pulled by reindeer covered the back wall. In front of Santa was a freshly cut Christmas tree with its scent of pine. Several boxes of ornaments were left on a table for those so inclined to feel joyous. Meanwhile the tree stood at attention, alone.

It had been over two months since Major Vann had punished all the soldiers for the escape of one soldier from the ball field. It had been three days, seven hours and thirty-three-minutes since Major Vann's retirement and his official medical replacement arrived. The vindictive Major Vann was gone, replaced by a doctor. A compassionate soldier, Major Rogers took his vows seriously, "to do no harm." The new officer brought in his own right-hand man, a Sergeant Clancy, who mirrored the major's practical and caring philosophy towards the psychologically wounded.

The hard-nosed Sergeant Helms got immediate marching orders to join the ranks of drill instructors at Fort Jackson, S.C. He could now berate trainees and be rewarded for it. The Christmas tree was a gift from Major Rogers, one of his first official acts for the wards upon his arrival.

On return from mess hall this morning, being a Saturday and much less structured, most of the patients along with Tech Turner retired to the TV room. They were watching a comedy filmed before most of these soldiers were born. Abbott and Costello were making a mess of things in the outside world. Inside, Ward 2A soldiers were laughing and Joker Berkowski was laughing the loudest.

Those not in the TV room were seated at tables reading and writing letters, working puzzles, chain-smoking cigarettes, watching the smoke rise. As usual, four longtime ward veterans Mumbling Grier, Shaky Metz, Paranoid Firenza and Scarface Kelly were playing another marathon series of Crazy 8's. The game's objective hadn't changed: go out before the others; a goal they all shared from the day they arrived on the ward. Obsessive Godwin was the only patient who had ventured to the rear of the ward to decorate the tree. Zack stood at the watchtower. It was a lazy Saturday morning. Things were quiet, another normal day.

Scarface Kelly bellowed in baritone "I call hearts! Yeeeohhh!" He slapped the eight to the center hard enough to test the strength of the table's construction.

Shaky Metz threw his cards in the air and dropped to the floor. It hadn't happened recently but it should have been no surprise that the sudden clap of Kelly's hand on the table had elicited a reasonable response from any soldier who had spent time in a war zone. The clap was an explosion and just for a moment Private Metz was back in the jungle.

"I'm watchin', I'm watchin'. I know, I know. Trip wires, trip wires, watch every step, I hear you. How many times you gonna say it? Watch it, watch it. How about not worrying 'bout me, Worry about—"

On the floor Metz whispered to himself: "Oh no, Sargeant. Where'd you go? Where'd you go?" Metz returned from the past to the regrets of the present. He picked up his cards and rejoined the game. His hands shook so much he practically fanned himself with the cards.

"So sorry. Soooo sorry." Kelly was sincerely sorry.

It was Firenza's turn to play a card. The paranoid soldier held his cards close to his chest. His eyes darted left and right making certain no one was looking at what he held. It had been almost three months since he was sent to the ward and Firenza still felt he had cause to be suspicious. It was, after all, when he had less than thirty-five days left on his duty tour in 'Nam when he was convinced that others were trying to get him killed, and that was in addition to the enemy.

• • • • •

"You get into that tunnel," the Second Louie ordered.

"No one goes down in a fucking tunnel," Corporal Firenza responded.

"That's an order. You get in the tunnel and check it out."

"I've got 35 days to go. There ain't no fucking way. You're trying to kill me."

"Are you refusing an—"

"I'm not letting the Cong; the snakes; the fucking poison food; no cherry Lieutenant; or anyone, keep me from going home. You're trying to kill me."

• • • • •

Firenza didn't go into the hole. He came to 2A where he finally played a heart.

It was Grier's turn to play a card. The patient mumbled something that no one at the table could decipher and played a heart on top of the previous one. Mumbling Grier was tired today. It was at approximately three in the morning when he awoke with night sweats. He rose and changed his PJs then fell back to sleep mumbling over and over, "Shoulda done somethin, shoulda done somethin' . . ."

While the card players continued their marathon, Obsessive Godwin was in high spirits as was the location he was about to place the last ornament on the tree, very high. He had another reason to be in a positive mood today, he expected to be discharged soon after Christmas. But for now he had to complete this holiday project. He considered the color of the ball and from each and every angle the space where it would hang. It was an approximation but given that he had no ruler he trusted his instincts. He jumped down from the chair, moved it to the side, and stepped back to evaluate the project undertaken over two hours ago.

Mistake. Godwin noted an imbalance, too many balls in one area. He made the necessary adjustments, inspected the tree again, back and forth, as if he were a soldier on honor guard duty. Another mistake, too many green and blue ornaments in close proximity, not enough reds. He dispersed colors to other locations on the tree. To get the full perspective, he backed several steps away, then several more, he moved left, then right, and then, as the creator of what was before him, the obsessive concluded that this was a beginning and it was good.

"You guys mind if I watch you play cards?" Patient Hobbs asked politely as he approached the table of soldiers. Admitted several days ago Hobbs was a muscular little guy with a wide neck and broad shoulders. He had already earned his nickname from the techs. He had a friendly smile and was forever saying "please" and "thank you" or "excuse me" to everyone whether it be appropriate or not. After a few minutes of watching over the players' shoulders, Polite Hobbs said, "Thank you" and ventured to the back of the ward where Obsessive Godwin prepared to anoint the tree with tinsel.

The obsessive opened several boxes of tinsel on a table, selected a few choice strands and carefully draped them across his left palm. He selected a branch and, one by one, placed the tinsel making certain each glittery strand hung evenly to its fullest length. Finishing one grouping of four, he moved to another branch. Again, he placed four strands to the center of a gold ornament and then moved on to adorn another ball.

Having watched for a few minutes, Hobbs asked, "Excuse me, may I help?" Hobbs waited for an answer but none came. He asked again, "Please, may I help?" Godwin continued to methodically place tinsel. Hobbs shrugged and moved to the table and grabbed a handful of tinsel.

"I'll help. I like to trim Christmas trees," Hobbs said.

Polite Hobbs began to move about the tree placing clumps of tinsel indiscriminately. He quickly completed the distribution of one handful, and then hustled to the table for more tinsel and returned to the tree to place more clumps.

Obsessive Godwin followed after Hobbs working frantically to remove and straighten the tinsel, trying to save a world that seemed out of control, of chaos and madness. "Stop! Stop! You can't do it that way!" Godwin's eyes rolled, he swayed, dizzy, "You can't. You can't–"

"Huh?" Hobbs looked at him, confused.

"You have to stop. You're not helping. You don't know what you're doing." Godwin's voice rose higher, tinny. He didn't wait for a response from Hobbs and turned to the front of the ward. "Hey Tech. Hey Zack, Tech Tonakis!" He shouted. He almost pleaded, "Someone, tell him to stop. He's ruining the tree. It's a disaster!"

Before any response from others Polite Hobbs stopped what he was doing. "I'm sorry, I apologize," Hobbs said. He returned the unused tinsel to the table and then took a seat close by. The soldier Hobbs folded his arms and watched with detachment.

Back in control, Obsessive Godwin turned to Hobbs to make nice. "I apologize that I got upset, it's not personal" Godwin said as he removed several clusters of tinsel from the tree. "No offense but there is a right way to do this, a right way." He continued repeating "A right way" as he hung tinsel in the right amount, four strands, never five, and in the right places, never more at the bottom than the top. Instead of whistling, Godwin whispered as he worked, "There's a right way, a right way, right way."

While the obsessive whispered his mantra, the Lawyer Lucas may just as well have used a megaphone. "Constitution!" "Constitution!" Lucas ranted as if he were paid by the minute. He stopped at the card players. He pointed at each one as if they were the jury. He gave his final summation, his favorite close to all arguments: "All God's children got rights." He spun around and headed in the other direction pointing his finger upward "Constitution! Constitution! Constitution!" The patients adapted to his freedom of speech the same as house cats adjust to humans who repetitively intrude on their naptime. They paid Lucas no mind.

Validating that patience is a virtue, after another hour of attention to detail, Obsessive Godwin announced, "Finished!" He turned to the ward. "Hey everybody! Hey look, it's done." He stepped to the side of the tree and waving his arm with a theatrical gesture said, "Ta da!" Supremely proud of his accomplishment, he gave himself kudos, "Beautiful! Perfect! Perfecto!" He did everything but sing, "Oh Christmas tree, my Christmas tree."

Polite Hobbs watched as Godwin bowed repeatedly. He clapped politely, almost silently. He rose and stretched his wide frame to relieve the stiffness from having sat for an hour. He walked past Godwin and stood at the tree. His eyes searched for a moment, he picked a spot, reached in with both hands, grabbed a firm hold of the trunk and began to shake the tree in broad sweeping motions. Left and right, left and right, ornaments flew, left and right. The tinsel danced in one direction and back again, adding a silvery blur to the green tree and colored ornaments. A red ball flew and crashed against the wall. A blue one hit a table. A gold one fell to the floor and cracked and a part of the shiny, round ornament went missing. The shard had entered the inside of the sphere while the outside now reflected the psych patients themselves, damaged, broken, missing a necessary part they were created with.

Throughout the sudden violent storm, the tenacious tinsel on the tree stayed the course while ornaments deserted their post. Some ornaments, the same as soldiers, were braver than others and hung on for dear life.

"Aaaaaawwwww." Obsessive Godwin let out a loud guttural sound and pounced on the source of the storm. Hobbs clutched the tree tightly and the two patients fell to the floor. They rolled over and under and over the tree that emitted snapping, popping and crunching sounds.

Patients close by made it to the pair before Zack from the watchtower or Turner from the TV room. Surprisingly, the two combatants separated without difficulty. Polite Hobbs rose calmly, located an empty table and took a seat. Tech Turner pulled up a chair next to him and prepared to listen in case Hobbs wanted to talk.

The ward quiet again the patients returned to what they were doing. Those who had come out from the TV room to watch the melee headed back to their movie. Sarge entered from the main corridor carrying today's mail. He couldn't help but see the mess at the back of the ward but decided since the ward was quiet an explanation could wait until later. He moved patient to patient not wanting to upset those soldiers who hadn't received any mail. The remembered ones returned to tables to read and respond to letters. "Please get well and come home soon. Dad loves you and I love you. Always, Mom."

A puzzle maker interlocked a corner piece and the perimeter was complete. Now if only the patient could put together the inside of the puzzle. At the front table, the card game continued. It was back to Crazy 8's.

Obsessive Godwin was alone again. He looked down to his pants that had been assaulted by splinters of pine needles. He methodically removed one after another as if oblivious of the broken branches, ornaments and disarray at his feet. Finally, having cleared his blues of needles, he moved to the fallen tree. Compassionately, as if raising a fallen comrade, he lifted the tree and placed it back in the stand. As he did so, more ornaments fell and broke on the floor. He flinched at each death rattle, he shuddered, he cried softly.

Standing by his bed Catatonic Cart, almost in slow motion, began to move towards the tree. Left foot shuffle, right foot shuffle. Left foot shuffle, right foot shuffle. He arrived at the tree and in a deliberate manner reached to the floor and picked up a bright red ornament. The catatonic then shuffled over to Obsessive Godwin and held out the ball. Godwin wiped his eyes with a handkerchief and carefully folded the hankie before returning it to his shirt pocket. He accepted Cart's offering. The catatonic, like a slow moving robot, picked up another ornament, but this time he shuffled to the tree. He selected a bare branch and tried to attach the ball. He struggled, his hands failed to cooperate, or was it Cart's mind? He maneuvered the hook on the ball, and failed again, and failed again.

At the card table, Scarface Kelly spoke just loud enough for the other players to hear, "Let's go." Mumbling Grier responded, "Okay." Shaky Metz placed his cards firmly on the table and rose with the others. And Paranoid Firenza, without hesitation, trusting it was the thing to do, joined them as they headed for the tree.

Lawyer Lucas interrupted his ranting to pick up a far-flung star-shaped ornament. He went to the tree and returned the star to a naked branch. "And that's what I have to say about that," he said to himself, with no compulsion to share that information aloud. The puzzle maker, the letter writers, and the book readers joined the rescue squad. Even those addicted to nicotine stubbed out cigarettes to join the mission. They policed the area for unbroken ornaments and returned them to the tree while the catatonic continued his struggle.

Bible Skinner stuck his head out from the TV room to find out why things were so quiet. He returned to the room, set his Bible on a chair, and told the others, "Come on guys, we're needed out there."

Smiling Hardy hesitated as did a number of the others. For these patients the TV room was a safe place, a memory of being back home, a young boy on Saturday morning, everyone else asleep, and you had your bowl of Cheerios, and you had the TV to yourself, and everything felt just right. But when Berkowski saw what was happening on the ward any hesitation was gone especially with how seriously he said, "Come on, a soldier needs us."

Then the snow began to fall. Thick substantial snowflakes, the kind these soldiers loved when they were kids. They'd stick out their tongues and snowflakes would settle and melt in their mouths. There would be no school tomorrow. There would be sledding and snowball fights. And here now, the snowfall quickly covered the psych ward ballfield.

"Hey, it's, it's sno-sno-snowing," said Shaky Metz. "It's snowing, it's really snowing."

The squad at the tree continued what they set out to do, to decorate the tree and to make things right for a fellow soldier and for themselves. Others moved to the windows where they watched, almost reverently, as the snow, not yet blemished, not yet corrupted, laid a white down comforter over the ballfield. The white canvas was interrupted by the slash mark of the high fence that served as a demarcation between the psych building and the main hospital, those scarred on the outside and those in here.

Zack watched the soldiers come together to support each other. He thought about his father, about reaching out to him, to try harder to make things right. Zack moved to the window and joined the other soldiers. *Would he be here in the spring watching soldiers play ball on this field? Would the war be over? Would it even matter for them?* Just then a patient, a soldier still, turned on the radio that sat on the windowsill. The catatonic hung the ornament in the perfect place, and the Drifter's sang:

> I, I, I am dreaming of a white Christmas,
> with every Christmas card I write.
> May your days, may your days, may your days
> be merry and bright.
> And may all your Christmases be white.

Zack didn't see the singers. He no longer needed to. But he heard the music. Zack didn't want to give that up.

And "our Flag was still there." (2014 photo.)

Valley Forge General Hospital
Neuropsychiatric Unit

DAILY LOG - Ward 2A and 2B
December 25, 1967

DAY SHIFT

Another day - just like the other day.

EVENING SHIFT

The same.

NIGHT SHIFT

Same

ABOUT THE AUTHOR

James Karantonis is a writer and performer appearing numerous times on the successful Stoop Storytelling series out of Baltimore MD. His true stories have been broadcast on Baltimore's public radio station WYPR.

James served as a psychiatric specialist during the Vietnam War. After the war he went on to a civil rights career. He directed the Washington Office for the first Martin Luther King, Jr. Holiday working closely with Coretta Scott King.

He founded Human Relations and Communications, Inc. and as a presenter James delivered "Entertainment with a message." Jim has published numerous short stories. His first short story: "A Crazy 8's Christmas" won the Spotlight Award from New York's *Slice Magazine.*

NOTE FROM THE AUTHOR

Word-of-mouth is crucial for any author to succeed. If you enjoyed
Crazy 8's: Soldiers Still, please leave a review online—anywhere you are
able. Even if it's just a sentence or two. It would make all the difference and
would be very much appreciated.

Thanks!
James

Thank you so much for reading one of our **Military Fiction** novels,
If you enjoyed the experience, please check out our recommended
title for your next great read!

Augie's War by John H. Brown

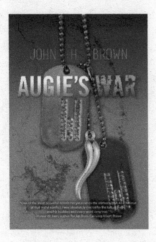

"One of the most powerful novels I've yet read on the Vietnam
War. As a veteran of that awful conflict, I was absolutely
riveted by the tale of Augie and his buddies
and every word rang true."
- Homer Hickam, author *Rocket Boys, Carrying Albert Home*

CPSIA information can be obtained
at www.ICGtesting.com
Printed in the USA
BVHW071911161021
618804BV00005B/167

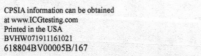

9 781684 335534